No Life But This

A Novel of Emily Warren Roebling

by Diane Vogel Ferri

Diane Vogel Ferri

No Life But This
A Novel of Emily Warren Roebling

by Diane Vogel Ferri

Cover art: *Sulking*, Edgar Degas, 1874
Author photo by Lou Ferri

ISBN - 9781626133006
LCCN - 2020938279

Copyright 2020

Publisher's note: This is a work of biographical fiction. All encounters and dialogue are from the author's imagination and are not to be construed as real. In all other respects any resemblance to persons living or dead is coincidental.

Published by ATBOSH Media ltd.

Cleveland, Ohio, USA
http://www.ATBOSH.com

Also by Diane Vogel Ferri

The Desire Path (novel)
The Volume of Our Incongruity (poetry)
Liquid Rubies (poetry)

For Connor, Ethan,
Lydia, and Violet

May the world build new bridges
to all of your dreams.

I have no life but this,
To lead it here;
Nor any death, but lest
Dispelled from there;

No tie to earths to come,
No action new,
Except through this extent,
The realm of you.

Emily Dickinson

Prologue

The Brooklyn Bridge took its first life when John A. Roebling, its chief engineer, died. My father-in-law was a formidable, brilliant man, and we shared a mutual fondness and respect for each other. The construction had not yet commenced, but were it not for his vision and design, the great bridge would not exist.

My husband, Colonel Washington Roebling, inherited the task of bringing his father's dream to fruition on that fateful day. My life changed its expected course as I, too, was called to dedicate myself to the completion of the bridge. I applied myself to the study of engineering and assumed the role of chief engineer when Washington could not—something many men found inconceivable.

Oh, the glorious day when I held a white rooster while crossing that magnificent structure! The Brooklyn Bridge is one of the greatest architectural feats of the 19th century and the world's longest suspension bridge. It is the Eighth Wonder of the World!

I have been called a woman of strong character, a woman with an almost masculine intellect. My husband calls me a woman of infinite tact and wise council.

Yet, the Brooklyn Bridge was just one of my endeavors....

Book 1
At the Bridge

Cross from shore to shore, countless crowds of passengers!
Stand up, tall masts of Mannahata! stand up! beautiful hills of
Brooklyn!

Walt Whitman
from *Crossing Brooklyn Ferry*

Chapter 1

Hicks Street, Brooklyn, New York 1869

Moments after the peach of dawn slipped over the horizon, the firmament abruptly blackened. My son and I gazed at the transformation as we sat nestled by the bay window. The clouds were like spilled ink in the sky; propelling themselves lower and lower as if to suffocate the earth. Thunderous moans reverberated in the distance. Leaves turned inside out in silver waves as birds swooped into trees; the scarlet streak of a cardinal flew past our window.

I pointed to the flags snapping furiously at half-staff for my dear father-in-law. I tried to explain to John, his namesake, how important his grandfather had been. But my son was not yet three years old, and could not conceive of what had happened to our family or how our lives would change now that his father was the chief engineer of the Brooklyn Bridge project.

"Bird!" John exclaimed, pointing his plump finger, interrupting my tears.

"Yes, a cormorant!" I said.

"Go ousside?"

"Oh, no, there is a storm coming, Dear." He looked up at me with clear sapphire eyes, "A very big storm."

"Mama is sad," John said, with the empathy of one much older. He placed his hand on my dampened face.

"Yes, we are sad today because Grandpapa has gone to heaven." I pulled his round, pillowy body close.

"Heaven! In the sky!" He pointed upward as the cormorant flew into the tempest. My son's innocent elation at his grandfather's transition reminded me of my childhood faith.

"Yes, where there is no pain."

My father-in-law, John A. Roebling, suffered greatly in his last days. On Monday, June 28, 1869, he and my husband, Washington, were working at the foot of Fulton Street, where the first tower was to be built. I was writing letters in my study and young John was playing with blocks on the floor at my side. Suddenly, there was a commotion downstairs. I could not imagine who had entered the house at that hour of the morning. My husband had taken to spending long hours at the work site and rarely came home before seven o' clock at night.

I took my son in my arms and rushed down the stairs to see my father-in-law on a stretcher, struggling for breath, his skin gray and deathlike. At his feet there were bloody bandages which caused me to gasp and pull my son's head onto my shoulder. Just then the maid came and took little John away from the sight of his grandfather's agony.

"Lord, what has happened?" I went to my husband's side as he directed the men carrying the stretcher into a downstairs guest bedroom.

"It was as if his toes were cut off by a large pair of shears," Washington said, wincing. "We had gone down after breakfast to inspect the site of the Brooklyn tower in the spare ferry slip. In order to see better, my father climbed on a heap of cord wood. Seeing a boat coming, and fearing that the heavy blow would knock him off, I shouted to him to get down. He was standing on the ferry slip, and as he stepped back, his right foot became trapped between two beams. He could not move and the boat could not stop. It ground against the wall, crushing his boot and toes."

"How awful for him," I said, looping my arm through my husband's trembling one. He looked as if the blood had been siphoned from his body, his stone gray eyes darkened.

"Do you know what he did then?"

"I think I can guess."

"My father attempted to go right on working as if nothing had happened. After a time, he was undeniably overcome with pain. I took him to the doctor, where it was decided that his toes must be amputated. He would accept no anesthesia, but was determined to use the power of his mind to overcome the physical wounds of his body. His screams were vociferous, and caused me to retch."

"Oh dear, how horrible." I then took him in my arms. "He will need all the care we can give him. I will secure nurses immediately."

"After the surgery, he insisted on binding his own wounds!" My husband continued. "His pride and stubbornness know no bounds!"

"That does not surprise me in the least. He is the most stoic of men."

In the coming days, nurses attended my father-in-law around the clock, and I checked on him hourly as well. All he would speak of was the bridge, as if nothing else had happened.

On July 8, the Brooklyn *Eagle* reported that he was busily engaged on his plans and drawings for the bridge. *"The distinguished engineer has his notions about survival treatment, and seems to be very brave in regard to physical pain."* The article claimed that in ten days he would be out surveying again. This seemed absurd to me.

A week after that report my father-in-law took a turn for the worse. His pain eventually became unbearable to witness. His body wracked with such rigidity that it would arch until his heels almost met the back of his head in a horrific contortion. His face was drawn into hideous expressions, and he could not swallow or speak. The muscles around his jaw and neck were as stone.

"I have seen carnage on many a bloody battlefield," said my husband, "but these horrors overcome me."

Any words I could conjure seemed useless, even cruel in the face of such agony. When a loved one has a heavy heart, you cannot attenuate their grief with mere words. My only recourse was to attend to all the matters at hand and hover near my husband in the hopes that my presence would be of comfort. Wash could not be convinced to leave his father's bedside.

My father-in-law was dying of tetanus, and we were helpless to relieve his suffering. The seizures and excruciating spasms resulted in respiratory distress and then, on July 22, he had a massive convulsion, and he was gone. We watched, stunned, as his face returned to its handsome form and became peaceful. Our pastor, Henry Ward Beecher, arrived shortly after the death to find Wash sitting at the bedside, holding his father's hand. His prayer was of comfort to us all.

"Heavenly Father, You know our anguish at the loss of our beloved. Take your servant John to the Church Triumphant, where there is no suffering. Bring him gently into Your perpetual and eternal light, and bring peace like a river flowing into this family. Amen."

Washington was devastated over his father's abrupt departure, as was everyone who had known him. I mourned with my husband as if John Roebling had been my own father.

The *Eagle* wrote this tribute:

He who loses his life from injuries received in the pursuit of science or of duty, in acquiring engineering details, is as truly and useful a martyr as he who sacrificed his life for a theological opinion, and no less honor should be paid to his memory. Henceforth, we look on the great project of the Brooklyn Bridge as being baptized and hallowed by the life blood of its distinguished and lamented author.

So great was my admiration for this man that Washington and I had named our son after him. I wrote to him when the baby was born: *The name of John A. Roebling must ever be identified with you and your works, but with a mother's pride and fond hope for her firstborn, I trust my boy may not prove unworthy of the name.*

I could detect in my husband some hesitancy about his unexpected position as chief engineer. He was certainly well trained in civil engineering at the Rensselaer Polytechnic Institute. He assisted his father on the Allegheny Bridge project, and when that was completed, worked in his father's wire mill business. I saw no reason that he should not be capable of doing everything his father had planned.

"Now that the funeral is over, I will need to travel to Trenton to settle my father's estate and handle other affairs until my brothers can take over the family wire business." My husband stood near the window, the sun glistening on the river behind him.

"I understand, dear. John and I will be busy while you are away. I will write to you every day."

"As I will write to you, sweet Emily," he said as he took me in his robust arms. As we stood motionless, his grasp on me suddenly tightened, and I realized he was weeping.

"I will miss him, too, Wash. He was a wonderful man, and I know he would be so proud of all you will do to make his wishes come true."

"Although my father's bold ambitions often supplanted his family responsibilities, I still loved him deeply. We moved so many times to satisfy his need to achieve more than other men in his position, but his achievements were, indeed, greater than most. The bridge he built in Cincinnati is my lodestar. It is my job now to carry the responsibility, and one cannot desert one's job. You can't slink out of life, or out of the work life lays on you."

I took out my linen handkerchief and wiped my husband's tears away.

"He was not only a genius, but a kind and generous man," I said, "My goodness, the number of people who came to the funeral! Hundreds of workers who respected and loved him. His sympathies for the working man were large, and he lost no opportunity to promote harmony and good feelings between the employer and the employee."

"Yes, I intend to follow his example in that." Wash's hands covered his face.

"What is it, dear?"

"He could also be a stern man, a hard character, a tyrant, even. My mother did not have a happy life. His work was his love," Wash turned to me. "I did not witness the love between a husband and wife in my childhood." He took my face in his hands, "I will never treat you that way, Emily. My mother died at 45, after an unhappy, unfulfilled life. She was a martyr to engineering. This bridge will never replace our happiness, I promise you."

"I do not doubt that," I said. "I regret never knowing your mother. But you are the best of your father."

My husband looked at me beseechingly, as if waiting for comfort.

I continued, "His benevolence, his charity, all he left in his will to schools, orphans…"

"Yes, if only he could have been as charitable to his family." Wash broke in. "I loved him in spite of all and will learn from his ways. He was a brilliant, but flawed man, just as I am, as we all are."

"You have no flaws that I can detect," I smiled at Wash and saw a hint of a brightening on his handsome face. We embraced and left the rest unsaid.

All I could do for my grieving husband was to hold him gently and let him weep and reminisce. Washington was unafraid of crying, one of the rare and beautiful things I loved about him. He was a dignified, quiet man with a low, sonorous voice that always drew me into his words. My husband had great integrity and honesty in all that he did. I could walk into his study at any given moment and see him there, deep in thought, his shirt sleeves rolled up, the hair sticking up on the crest of his head as it was wont to do. He checked his pocket watch repeatedly and faithfully, always on schedule, always precise in his every move. It was only when I heard his deep humming of some unknown tune that I knew he was frustrated or discontented.

But I wondered whether the work and responsibility before him; the tremendous effort of the bridge, the daunting task of replacing the enormous character of his father, were embedded in his grief and tears.

Chapter 2

The glory of each generation is to make its own precedents.
                                        Belva Ann Lockwood

After the Civil War, Brooklyn was a burgeoning, vibrant community. As the third-largest city in America, we had our own schools, fire, and police departments and nearly 400,000 residents. New York and Brooklyn changed rapidly with the growing numbers of businesses such as blacksmiths, boot and shoe makers, dressmakers, merchants, lawyers and piano makers, all in demand as a result of the growing population.

There was terrible crowding in the tenements of New York. The lack of clean water and sanitation led to rampant diseases; smallpox, cholera, typhus, measles. Part of the solution was to build hundreds of cottages for the working class in Brooklyn. The Fulton Ferry was the only way to get back and forth, so transportation between the cities was desperately needed. In the winter months, the river clogged with ice and made the commute impossible for days or weeks at a time. A young boy was killed when two ferries crashed in a pile of ice, and this seemed to sway public opinion toward building the bridge.

When I was young, I had no notion of the importance waterways would have in my life from Cold Spring to Brooklyn. The waters of the Hudson made their way over 50 miles from my childhood home to New York Harbor, just as I did.

Never far from the enchantment of a river, I grew up playing on the banks of the Hudson River, where you could hear turtles plop into the water, the gulp of jumping fish, and bullfrogs opening their throats to belch. The banks were lined with magnificent weeping willows and fragile white birches. In autumn, the rolling banks of the river became enflamed with color, and in winter, we sledded on the cold cotton mattress of snow. The whistles of the side-wheelers blowing in the night brought me comfort.

Being an adventurous child I loved exploring nature on the sparse, languid days of summer; ladling cold spring water from the stream near our home or lying on a blanket of delicious pine needles and looking for God in the clouds. My brothers and I captured lightning bugs and dragonflies, although Mother thought it unladylike of me to do so. Warty toads would hop into the palms of our hands, somehow trusting us to place them back into the dusty leaves. We chased furtive butterflies and searched for the elusive fox. We picked blueberries and blackberries and traipsed the forest like gypsies. My childhood was a lovely intermezzo before the tragedies and turmoil of life arrived.

One spring day, I decided to go off on my own. I was bored playing the same tiresome games my sisters enjoyed. They were content to sit on the floor with marbles, dominos, and jackstraws. I yearned for the adventures my mother read to me in books. I couldn't have been more than six years old, but I wanted to know what it felt like to be untethered from my family. In the woods I came across a doe and two fawns settled into the leaves and I announced to them, "I am a free girl!" The doe stood up and snorted at me. Frightened, I ran through the woods as far as my little legs could carry me. I soon realized I was lost, but did not despair. I rather enjoyed the feeling of being unencumbered by rules and boundaries. Eventually, my brother, G.K.'s voice could be heard echoing through the forest, and I was rescued, although I was loath to go home. I had not finished my explorations. I excitedly told my brother of my adventures, and from then on G.K. called me "Emmy, my free girl."

Upon arriving home, my father's disappointed look was enough punishment for me. He would always tell me to "be a lady, Emily, dear." My mother, I could plainly see, had been amused with my antics but did not defend them to my father. It was out of her respect for him, not fear. Of that, I was quite certain.

Cold Spring sits at the deepest point of the river, directly across from West Point. It was named for the crystalline waters of a local spring, a feature much enjoyed in my youth. We'd picnic near the springs and play in the waterfalls as children.

As an adult, G.K. established the West Point Foundry near our home to produce artillery pieces for the government. Of the twelve Warren siblings, I was closest to my brother, Gouverneur Kemble, named by my father after his friend of the same name, a local congressman and diplomat. Although he was much older, we held a special bond. He was a playful, generous brother who paid me much attention. We were sewn from the same independent fabric, unlike my other siblings. Because my father had died when I was young, Wash had to ask G.K. for my hand in marriage; a terrifying experience for him because G.K. had been his commanding officer during the Civil War. But, as always, my brother placed my happiness above all.

Grief for a parent never leaves you. They are the only people you have known every day of your life, the only ones who truly loved you unconditionally. It is unnatural for them to be gone, especially so unexpectedly. You can understand that someday it will happen, but that does not make the wound any kinder. My mother died when I was a girl of fifteen, and my father, a year later. Their spirits and memory are never far from my heart.

    I often dreamed of sitting at my mother's knee, talking the afternoon away as we did when I was young, or hearing her lilting voice at the piano, playing her favorite hymns or a Chopin melody. Sometimes the fragrance of lemon verbena or a certain face powder brought her presence close. It was a great loss to not have a mother to advise me as I grew into a woman. There were so many things I didn't have the time to ask her. Being the second youngest in the family, I was away at school when my sisters married and left home, so I had no bond with older women.

    My father had a boisterous laugh and a hearty sense of humor. If one of his children was unhappy, he would make funny faces or sing a silly tune, and soon everyone would be smiling once again. After my mother died, we witnessed the joy drain from his spirit and the laughter was silenced.

It was through my dear brother, the great General Gouverneur K. Warren, that Wash and I met. My husband was not just a chief engineer, but also a courageous veteran of the Civil War. He served in the Union army and was made a colonel in 1864 for his gallant service in such battles as Gettysburg and Little Round Top. I had the good privilege of being raised in a family that valued education for girls, and I attended Georgetown Visitation Academy in Washington, DC.

On February 22, 1864, I attended the Second Corps Officer's Ball with G.K. Approximately 150 fine ladies graced the assemblage from all quarters of the Union. I was not searching for a husband, but had donned my best silk dress with as many petticoats and flounces possible. I wore a new bonnet with velvet ribbons.

Three hundred gentlemen attended, one of them being my Wash. He had crystal gray eyes, heavy brows, and a shock of mahogany hair tinged with copper. His nose and ears were perfectly shaped, and his warm and friendly smile drew me to him. We were charmed by each other upon our first encounter. His letter following the ball expressed his enchantment with me:

> *It gives me the greatest pleasure to say that I have succumbed to your charms. My love for you, I find, is, after all, paramount to every other feeling, and the lapse of time only deepens it. There is no woman living for whom I would be willing to give you up.*

I have never considered myself a beautiful woman; I am a bit over average in height and weight, my nose is a pug shape, my eyes are hazel, my teeth and complexion, adequate. My chestnut hair, although lustrous and abundant, was difficult to contain in the upward style of the times. But Washington Roebling, in addition to complimenting my appearance, was the first man to consider my thoughts on many matters. Our conversations became a lifeblood to me, uplifting in the unity they brought to us, and flattering in the intensity of his attentions to all my opinions.

After expressing concerns over my appearance in a photograph he had requested, Wash wrote back:

> *Some people's beauty lies not in the features, but in the varied expressions and the countenance it will assume under various emotions. Your appeal cannot be captured in stillness.*

But to my consternation he signed the letter; *Good night, my broad-hipped beauty - Your adoring Washy.* I knew his heart was pure, even if his words were not.

When in each other's presence or in the letters we exchanged, he took a sincere interest in my mental aptitude and convictions, of which I had many. Our immediate, intense physical attraction to each other enhanced our anticipation of a carnal union as well. We wrote to each other every day after our first meeting, and the next year, we were joyfully married in my home town, Cold Spring, New York, with my brother by my side.

Chapter 3

I hate to hear you talk about all women as if they were fine ladies instead of rational creatures. None of us want to be in calm waters all our lives.

Jane Austen

The day after Mr. Roebling's grand funeral, men gathered in our parlor to discuss how to proceed with the bridge. Washington was now the chief engineer, and clearly in charge of the meeting. I tried to keep John entertained while I strained to listen to their animated conversation through closed doors.

"The caissons are of vital concern, Colonel. Are you sure the massive size of your caissons is even possible? Some of our engineers here have never heard of caissons in the first place," General Horatio Wright, one of the consultants, said indignantly.

"My extensive study of them in Europe allows me to be confident that this is the only way to build a bridge of this magnitude," Wash replied confidently. "They are, in essence, a huge diving bell built of wood and iron, with sturdy sides and roof, but no floor. They will be sent to the bottom of the river, filled with compressed air for the workers to breathe. As they progress downward, stones will be piled on top to press them further into the river bed so men can excavate to the bedrock. Once they have dug to the greatest stable depth, the box will be filled with concrete, and that, gentlemen, is the foundation for the bridge tower."

I pushed my ear against the closed parlor door, proud in the certainty with which my husband worked to convince the skeptical men of his father's plan. The discussion went on for some time, and although I am not the type of woman to rush to wait on men, I took some fresh lemonade into the parlor so I could hear more.

"This seems dangerous for those willing to experiment with this unheard-of plan!" John Newton practically yelled in my presence.

"It is not experimental," Washington replied calmly. "It has been used successfully in Europe for more than a generation, as early as 1831 by Lord Thomas Cochrane. The pneumatic caisson was used for a bridge foundation in Rochester, England, in 1851. I will admit, these caissons will be much larger than the ones in Europe, and will have to be sunk much deeper for us to achieve the strength we'll need for this bridge, though."

"Gentlemen, let me assure you that my husband knows what he is talking about. I was with him in Europe during the two years...."

"I believe, Mrs. Roebling, that that was when you were giving birth to your son, was it not?" Mr. McLaughlin interrupted me.

"Yes, but I am well aware of the efforts of my husband to learn all he could about the caissons, childbirth notwithstanding. What exactly does that have to do with it?" I was incensed, but, as usual, Washington tempered the discussion by confirming my words and my worth.

"My wife did, indeed, follow all I learned with great interest, and I never sensed that she was unable to understand the engineering involved. She has a keen mathematical mind. We were there for two years—childbirth took but a day." He smiled at me.

That shut Mr. McLaughlin's mouth for a while.

"I apologize, Mrs. Roebling. No insult was intended."

"I'll leave you all to your work. I do have a child to care for, after all," I added, somewhat unnecessarily. I left the room, closed the door, and kept listening. Mr. McLaughlin and General Wright continued to challenge Wash, and after a time, I had to stop listening for fear of bursting back into the room and embarrassing myself and my husband.

I settled John down for his nap, and returned to the doorway.

"My brother is a doctor," I heard Mr. Martin say, "In discussing this project, he brought up the danger of this type of work. It's called "the bends," when someone is not able to withstand the air pressure or coming up from the depths in the compressed air. Men have experienced a mysterious sickness, with pain and sometimes paralysis."

"Yes, I'm aware of that, Charles," Wash responded, "It is sometimes called compression disease, but I have been told it is a very rare reaction. I'm sure we can proceed slowly and carefully to ensure that no man will suffer in the building of this bridge. You have my word."

"Well, Colonel, I hope the workers we hire will have as much faith in you as you do in yourself."

I could not help myself. I opened the door quietly and stepped back into the room with the men. I could see that they were dismayed to see me once again.

"Mrs. Roebling," Mr. McLaughlin nodded demurely to me as if to repair the earlier insult.

"Mr. McLaughlin," I nodded back. "It may not be to your liking, but I have participated in this project from its inception. My edification concerning the caissons continued for the entire two years that we lived in Germany while my husband was studying. I am an educated woman, and I have extensive knowledge of math and the sciences."

The men stood speechless. Wash put his arm through mine as if to validate my statement. He patted my arm, too, signaling for me to remain calm.

"What other questions do you all have about the caisson?"

"Well, Mrs. Roebling, uh," Mr. Martin stammered, "I am having some difficulty picturing in my mind what these caissons will look like." He looked over at Mr. McLaughlin and shrugged his shoulders. I suppressed my smile.

"I recall that their size will be enormous. One-hundred, sixty-eight feet by one-hundred-two feet. Isn't that correct, Washington?" I turned to my smiling husband.

"That's correct."

"That would be comparable to a half of a city block, I believe."

"Yes, yes, I believe you are right about that," Wash continued to pat my arm. "I was about to show our visitors the drawings my father made."

"What I am looking forward to is the launching of the first caisson," I continued, "Once it is built at the Webb & Bell yards—the shipyard my father-in-law determined was the only one who could handle such an order—it will be transported down the river to the location of the first tower on the Brooklyn side like a great wooden ship! Can you imagine the sight, gentlemen?"

Several of the men looked at each other instead of me, but said nothing.

"Each caisson will contain 110,000 cubic feet of timber and 230 tons of iron. The seams will be made airtight with an oakum caulk to a depth of six inches on the inside and outside of the box. They're to be made of yellow pine brought in from Georgia and Florida."

"We've discussed the needed supplies already, dear, but thank you for the clarification," Wash said, still smiling at me. I did not return his smile.

"Senator Murphy and William Tweed are not present with us tonight. Do we have any reports from them?" Wash asked.

"Mr. Tweed has been invaluable in winning the backing of New York aldermen in the bond issue so we can move forward. As a stockholder in the bridge I will contact him for a financial report about the $1.6 million bond issue," General Slocum said.

"Mr. Kinsella, I'm so happy to see you here tonight." I reached out my hand to him. "As editor of the Brooklyn *Eagle*, we desperately need your support and your great influence on the public."

"I am honored to be a part of this undertaking," Thomas Kinsella replied. "The great boast of this land is twofold: the political works of the Founding Fathers and the material triumphs of science, of which Mr. John A. Roebling was, with scarcely any exception, the greatest hero. One such life such as his was worth more than those of a whole convention full of jabbering and wrangling politicians."

We all laughed.

"Mr. Kinsella, we are assured that you know well of which you speak," I said, "I'm sure your influence will be of the utmost importance to reaching our goals."

"I think we will be concluding this meeting for the night," Wash spoke up.

"Well, I will continue to be interested in every aspect of the project and willing to help in any way possible. Gentlemen, can I get you anything else?" I asked.

Later that evening, when we got into bed together, I apologized to my husband for interrupting the meeting.

"There is no need to apologize," he reassured me, "You have a better understanding of the caissons than many of the men in that room, Em. Before I met you, I would have doubted a woman's ability to comprehend such things, but you have shown me differently. I welcome your involvement from this point forward whenever you wish."

"Truly?" I was surprised. "I don't think your father would have approved. Remember when he instructed you not to take your wife around with you?" I set my head in the hollow of my husband's shoulder and curled my body around his, feeling his strength. "I am grateful for your confidence in me."

"It no longer matters whether my father would have approved or not. This bridge will be the focus of our lives for several years to come. I will need all the strength and encouragement I can get from my wife and partner." Wash pulled me close to him under the covers of our bed and kissed me deeply. His love draped over me like a heavy cloak.

"Our son keeps me busy, but I promise to be here every night to hear about the progress of the bridge."

He kissed me again, and there was no more discussion of an engineering project that night, although questions were bubbling in my mind.

When I was a girl, my mother said I was too curious. Seeing bats around the street lanterns, I would leave my bed and walk out into the dark in my nightgown to investigate. My mother would find me there, and punish me for leaving the house. From the time I could read, I sought out books about science and nature, wanting little to do with fantasies and fairy tales. I would bring books to my friends' homes to show them something fascinating, but they wanted to play with dolls. The only story book I could tolerate was the Bible, and I continually questioned the veracity of many of those stories, much to my parents' and pastor's chagrin.

A girl's schooling was woefully neglected in those years, but I was fortunate to have had a family that encouraged it. After my parents died, G.K. made sure I had an excellent education at Georgetown Visitation Convent in Washington, DC. Their motto was: "Be who you are, and be that well." I have kept that motto, I believe.

Lying awake far into the night, I thought about Wash's hand on my arm, patting me into calm submission, and wondered whether anyone would have done that to a man.

Diane Vogel Ferri

Chapter 4

The day may be approaching when the whole world will recognize woman as equal of man.

Susan B. Anthony

The men in our parlor were not the only ones to doubt the feasibility of such a monolithic bridge. For years, the citizens of New York and Brooklyn had been demanding a more efficient way to cross the East River between the cities. The only way to traverse the cities was by the Fulton Ferry. At times, it took hours to get on the ferry because of the growing population of the two cities. The discussion had been going on since the turn of the century, but especially after the winter of 1867. That winter, the river froze so solidly that the population of both cities crossed it by simply walking over the ice. Even carriages went across! But, eventually, the ice was too dangerous to travel.

Wash and the other engineers faced plenty of criticism and doubts about the immensity of the project, as it was to be the largest bridge in the world. Wash moved forward, despite the unyielding fault-finding. The first caisson had been built at the shipyard and would be moved down the river to the place where the first tower would be built. People were not aware of the other suspension bridge, the largest in the world to that point, that my father-in-law had built in Cincinnati.

We were astonished when three thousand citizens turned out on March 19, 1870 to see the dropping of the first caisson into the water. The deck of the caisson was covered with machinery, and lines were connected to a steamboat in case of trouble. Heavy wooden rams had been built to help push the enormous structure out. The next day, Mr. Kinsella's *Eagle* reported that a large number of people had come out that day because they did not believe such a massive structure could be dropped into the water without incident, and that they had to see it with their own eyes.

The King's County Democrats took the opportunity to create a festive event that day. There were speeches and bands, and people strained to watch the first caisson descend. It hit the water perfectly, with just enough speed to overcome the water resistance. The air chamber worked perfectly, keeping the front side from sinking. The deck never even got wet. The crowd cheered, and Wash and I stood hand-in-hand watching as well. All proceeded as the chief engineer had calculated, and many came over to congratulate him.

The dredging for the final site of the first caisson was behind schedule, so shortly after the caisson dropping, Washington traveled to St. Louis to visit James Buchanan Eads, whom he considered a genius. Eads was the chief engineer of a bridge being constructed over the Mississippi River. Wash took Horatio Allen, a consultant on the project, with him. I missed Wash even though the trip was only for a week. I never got used to our absences from each other, and I don't think Wash did either. It was as though we'd been apart for months.

Our reunion was tender and loving. Our unrehearsed rhythms, the intersecting of our bodies, brought out something primal and holy in me. At times, I would forget where I was, who I was, as if we were one person in a time spent out of time. The Bible states that two shall become one, and I reveled in that gift in our life together. I wished for a woman friend close enough to share those revelations with in confidence. I believed our love was unique and rare, but I was unaware of what others experienced.

Little John awoke that night. As his small footsteps pattered down the hallway, I rushed to clothe myself. We laughed and opened our arms to our little son, and the three of us fulfilled my greatest wish for a family. After John fell asleep, Wash gently carried him back to bed and rejoined me under the covers.

"What else have you learned about the illness?" I had been quietly concerned about continued speculation about the dangers of the work in the caissons.

"I discovered that the same morning we dropped the first caisson, a man in St. Louis died from the mysterious caisson disease after only two hours in the same type of chamber."

"Oh, no. What will that mean for the project?"

"Eads thinks that it's a freak occurrence. It was just the one man, so he's going forth as planned."

"Is that good enough for you, Wash? These men will be your responsibility. I heard you give your word that it would be safe."

"You heard that, did you? How did you hear that?" His arms pulled me in closer, and I could feel his smiling face next to mine.

"Oh, on the day all those men were here arguing with you."

"I knew you were outside the door listening—that's my Emily. You can't tolerate not knowing something, can you? Let's get some sleep now. I'll fill you in about what I learned from Eads in the morning. In only a few weeks, the work will actually begin once the caisson is launched and towed into place tomorrow. I can't believe it's finally happening."

Wash fell asleep promptly, but I lay awake contemplating the work ahead. My heart began accelerating in that familiar way when I could not contain my frustration. Earlier in the day, when John was napping, I sat in the parlor with a cup of tea, to read the current *Hearth and Home* magazine, edited by our pastor's sister and my friend, Harriet Beecher Stowe. In it, she wrote:

> *The position of a married woman is, in many respects, precisely similar to that of the Negro slave. She can make no contract and hold no property; whatever she inherits or earns becomes at that moment the property of her husband. Though he acquired a fortune through her, or though she earned a fortune through her talents, he is the sole master of it, and she cannot draw a penny. In the English common law a married woman is nothing at all. She passes out of legal existence.*

Those words boiled my blood. Harriet's sister Catherine had spent years advocating for women to become school teachers, saying it was natural for women, not men, to educate children. She was instrumental in establishing schools for training female teachers in western cities. I certainly applauded her efforts, but what was the purpose of a vocation in which one cannot earn a living? How does the teacher's pay belong to her husband? These accepted practices were absurd.

What if I, Emily Warren Roebling, desired to become a civil engineer? This opportunity would not be open to me, regardless of my knowledge of math and the sciences. It was a wonderful thing to have a husband who acknowledged my gifts, but of what use could they be when the only employment open to women was teaching children? I loved my little son dearly, but I did not find fulfillment in being with other people's children. I knew that about myself without doubt.

These unanswered questions kept me awake, and my only recourse was to breathe deeply and pray. I asked the Lord to guide me in my understanding of my place in the world and in the life He had given me, grateful for all the privilege I had enjoyed since childhood. But it was my belief that it was God Himself who had given me a keen discernment of the world. Why would He not expect me to use my gifts to my utmost? It was the wee hours of the morning when my brain, at last let me rest. That question would remain until morning, and the morning after that, and all mornings to come, I was certain.

Diane Vogel Ferri

Chapter 5

A proper wife should be as obedient as a slave.

Aristotle

Brooklyn in May looked as if the pale green of watercolors had brushed over the landscape. The ambrosia of lilacs slivered the air. The first light shadows were cast on John and me as the spring sun enveloped us in its balmy warmth and reminded us of the approaching summer.

  John skipped excitedly next to me down a path of effusive pink magnolia blossoms. He exclaimed as a robin hopped down the path in front of us and a chipmunk scuttled under some leaves. I struggled to hold his hand as we walked the few blocks to the site beside the Fulton Ferry slip. My eyes scanned the vast panorama. I never tired of the glorious waterway, the throng of vessels gliding in every direction, the thrilling backdrop of the bustling cities.

  In the distance we could see several tugboats pulling an enormous chamber down the river, which was a wonderful sight to behold. It had traveled four miles to be placed at the site of the first tower: the true beginning of the Brooklyn Bridge.

  John clapped his hands when he saw his father serenely standing on top of the first caisson, taking a ride down the wide, imposing river. It looked like a war leviathan, the deck strewn with tackle and various pieces of machinery. Crowds clustered around as the crew tied it up one block above Fulton Street. People's doubts, fears and enthusiasm seemed to all coexist that day.

I had purchased a new rabbit fur-trimmed hat and stole for the occasion, but it was much too spring-like to have worn them. Instead, I chose my royal blue silk hat with the peacock feather and matching dress with the extravagantly large bustle and multiple overskirts. A white parasol kept the spring sunshine off of my face. My long brown hair was coiled up tightly with as many pins as I owned to keep it safe from the fierce gusts off of the river.

The skyline of New York stood out crisply. A warm breeze arose from the East River and we could smell the mixture of coffee and molasses from nearby factories. Wash valiantly stepped off of the caisson and greeted those nearby. He scooped John up in his arms and hoisted him onto his shoulders. We were joined by Mr. and Mrs. Kingsley. Mr. Kingsley was the main contractor on the project and had dedicated himself wholly to working on the bridge. We strolled down to Sixth Street to witness the placement of the caisson, which was another great success and cause for celebration. At the luncheon following the launch, Mr. Kingsley was asked to make a speech, but instead requested a toast to the health of Washington. Of course, there were calls for Wash to make a speech, but my unpretentious, humble husband would do no such thing. Loud cheering prevailed, but neither threats nor blandishments could coerce a speech from him. His face flushed and he smiled, trying to hide his embarrassment. He never liked to be the center of attention. I was the outspoken one in the family. Somehow, this dichotomy worked for us, and we admired each other for our unique and opposite qualities.

The East River is not truly a river, but a salt water tidal estuary that connects upper New York Bay to Long Island Sound. Strong fluctuations in the current are accentuated by its narrowness and varied water depths. At times, it could be turbulent. A Dutch explorer called it Hell Gate. Washington Irving, a dear friend of my father's, said the tide sounded like a bull bellowing for more drink at half-tide! The large rocks in the riverbed made it difficult to navigate, and Congress had ordered the use of dynamite to break up the giant boulders for easier and safer transportation. Nevertheless, it was a magical waterway where blue herons, cormorants, and egrets abounded. Turtles lazed on the banks, and spring peepers and bullfrogs created a cacophony on summer nights. On our many afternoon walks, I employed the river to teach John as much as I could about nature.

"Mama, look!" John squealed as he knelt down to touch a nearby rock. "Lights, blue!"

"Yes, the shiny bits look like lights coming from the stone, don't they? And you are correct, that is the color blue. Good for you, dear."

"Give it to Papa?"

"Yes, let's take it home and Papa will save it in his mineral collection."

John sprinted ahead of me to another rock he'd found.

"Papa says some of these are garnets. It will be beautiful after he has polished it. Let's save that one, as well. I'm sure your papa will give you an adequate lesson on mineralogy when he is able."

Like me, my husband had multiple interests. His mineralogy collection was considerable, but I doubted whether he would have any time for his hobbies in the coming years. I, on the other hand, continued to experience frustration at my lack of opportunities. Until my marriage, I had been a formidable horsewoman, but Brooklyn was not conducive to equestrianism, and I missed it intensely. Needlework was insufferable, and we had a cook and other servants to help with housework. My most satisfying pastime was reading and writing, but what I read often set my mind afire instead of calming it. Every night I eagerly anticipated Wash's return home to learn of the progress at the site, to have an adult conversation, to expand my mind.

"What is the report for today?" I had asked one night, about a month after the caisson had been set in place.

"Forty men are in the caisson eight hours every day. Mr. Young is in charge. There are many more boulders to remove than we expected. No one has ever attempted to sink so large a structure into the earth as our caissons, Em. It seems there is no place more difficult to do that than the East River."

"Are you discouraged?" I asked.

"In a way, yes. The progress is much slower than I had planned. We cannot allow the newspapers or the public to become aware of these difficulties. Thousands of people show up every day to watch whatever they can see. I can't afford to fight the public or have them lose faith in this project. I need all of my energy for the work. And we need the two city governments to finance all of this, of course."

"Yes, I understand. It's constantly in the papers. It's the most exciting thing to ever happen here, all because of you and your father. I'm so proud of you."

"Did you see today's paper yet? One of our mechanics gave them an interview describing what it's like in the caissons. It may have an impact on the public's opinion."

"I haven't read it yet, I'll retrieve it from the parlor." I touched his shoulder as I walked by, hoping to convey my support. Although Wash was capable and knowledgeable, he had never asked for the job. His father was a healthy, strong 63-year-old when he died. It had been expected that the bridge would be completed with him as chief engineer, not Wash.

"Here is it." We spread the paper out across the table.

"Farrington, the mechanic, says he gets a confused sensation in his head, that it's weird and unnatural." Wash said, "He says his pulse accelerates, then falls, and the heat is like Dante's inferno. It's difficult to speak, and the noise of the hammers, drills, and chains is confounding." He looked up at me. "Well, that's sure to rile everyone up, isn't it?"

"I hardly think it would be an easy or pleasant experience," I replied, "It's work, after all. You worry too much. These are grown men, and they have chosen to take these jobs." I looked over to see Wash staring blankly out of the window. We were silent for a bit, imagining the unexpected consequences of this massive undertaking, until John threw his dinner plate on the floor and momentarily relieved the tension. Both Wash and I knelt to clean it up while John laughed at the sight of his parents together on the floor.

"There is nothing pleasant about it," he said. "The physical exertion is unnerving, the noise is sometimes deafening, the lighting dim, the air pressure unnatural."

"Has anyone gotten sick?" My stomach clenched at the thought.

"Men have been calling off," Wash conceded. "It's clearly a dangerous, and sometimes frightening job. If the caisson is unused for even a short time, it will stop settling and put us behind even further."

"Has anyone quit?"

"Yes, several have quit, but there are dozens of unemployed men, anxious to take their places. Immigrants are desperate for work. I hear multiple languages every day. They are hard and loyal workers, and this job pays better than most."

"This project is providing wages for needy families. It's a wonderful thing for both cities," I added with a light-spirited voice, hoping to brighten my husband's mood.

The morning sun was sizzling on the horizon when the frightening sound of an explosion awakened us. Observing the Sabbath, no one should have been working inside the caissons on a Sunday morning. I went to John when I heard his cries, and Washington ran out of the door in his sleeping attire. I put down my crying son, donned a robe, and gathered some clothing for Wash. The nanny did not come on Sundays, so I rushed down the street with John in my arms and banged on the door of my neighbor Mary. Her whole family had been awakened by the noise as well, and her little ones were gathered around her. She quickly took John into her arms and asked me to return as soon as possible to tell her what was happening. I rushed through the city streets with Wash's clothing crumpled in my arms and his shoes in my hands. There was shouting and complete chaos as people ran out of their doors.

"My God, what happened?" I heard Wash shout as I approached the scene.

"It was like a volcano, like the river exploded! Stones, mud and water spewed into the air, probably 500 feet," one man screamed, as though his hearing had been destroyed by the deafening sound. I looked back to see people running out of their houses and up Fulton Street, panicked, screaming, babies crying.

"Is anyone hurt?" Washington yelled into the chaos.

"There were only the three of us!" One man shouted back. "We were on top of the caisson! It knocked me off my feet, Colonel. I saw Joe leap into the river, but then saw him crawl back out. Eddy is around here somewhere. I think we're all all right."

"Thank God," Washington said, "We need to get in there and see the damage. Will you help me?"

"Yes, sir," the shaken man answered.

"Wash!" I yelled. "Here are some clothes!" A man ran by, shouting, "This is no place for a woman! What the hell are you doing here?"

"Excuse me, sir. Would you please hand these to Colonel Roebling? He is need of his clothes. I'm sure he won't be home for quite some time." I held the bundle out to him and he took them from me.

"Mrs. Roebling, is that you?" another man yelled. "You need to get back home to your son. This is no place for a woman."

"Yes, so I've heard."

Later, I learned the damage was not as disastrous as Wash had feared. His caisson had withstood the staggering blow of more than 17,000 tons. The sediment in one shaft had settled to the point that the water no longer weighed enough to contain the pressure inside. On normal workdays a small stream of water was kept flowing into the shaft to avoid this circumstance, but that had been neglected. Although everyone was unharmed, Wash decided that the explosion had resulted from carelessness and overconfidence. From that point on he was determined to take on even more responsibility for overseeing safety precautions for building of the bridge.

When I went to the O'Connell's to retrieve my son, he was sound asleep on their sofa.

"Is anyone hurt?" Mary whispered.

"No, it seems as if there was some divine intervention on this Sunday morning. If the caisson had exploded on a regular workday, there might have been injuries." I said.

"Well, there are plenty of Irish Catholics around here and the Navy Yard, aren't there? 'Tis God's blessing that it happened this morning," Mary commented. "Would you like to leave young John here until he awakens?"

"Oh, that would be lovely, Mary. I will go home and get dressed, then I will return in a bit to retrieve him."

It was barely six o'clock in the morning and the entire city of Brooklyn was already distraught before the day had even started. I walked to my house, feeling dejected over the project and disheartened for my husband with the mishaps and injuries that had already occurred. As I got dressed, the words *this is no place for a woman* gnawed at me so much that I pulled my journal from the bedside drawer, and wrote:

> *I am more determined than ever to give of myself to women's suffrage and equality. It is infuriating to be told there is no place for me on the construction site of this bridge. I have been involved in every aspect of it, and understand precisely what is going on. Wash keeps me informed every step of the way. I certainly know where there is danger and where it is safe to be as much as any male worker. I intend to continue writing for publication as soon as possible. There is only so much a woman can pour out in her personal journal. I have things to say that need to be read. Only two years ago the 14th amendment was protested under the leadership of Mrs. Susan B. Anthony and Mrs. Elizabeth Cady Stanton for the lack of protections and equality for women. We still have a long way to go, and I am determined to make my mark.*

I made a cup of tea to calm myself and tried to read from my new edition of *Leaves of Grass*. I intended to read it thoroughly, since Mr. Whitman had been a neighbor of ours, years ago. Although too distracted to read much, one verse caught my eye:

> *These became part of that child who went forth every day, and who now goes and will always go forth every day.*

I wondered what John's childhood was like for him, and whether mothers were ever relieved of guilt on any given day of motherhood. We do not merely create a human being at birth, but we continue to create them every day of their young lives, choosing what they will see and hear and understand. My devotion often was torn between my husband and son and the desires that haunted my mind and demanded fulfillment. How would it all work together for a woman? Wash was a wonderful father, and I knew that because my own father was faithful, true, and attentive to all of his children. I knew what a father could be, and perhaps it is why I had chosen Washington as my husband at such a young age. But that did not mean that I didn't question what was right for my son, my only child, every day. I was of sound mind and strong body, as was Wash, but I still worried that, one day, I might not be there for John, just as my parents had left me too soon.

When Mary opened the door, I saw John sitting at the table with the family. At the age of three, he appeared so big, no longer my baby. Mary's five youngsters were trying to entertain him with silliness, and his laughter filled their tiny dining area.

Mary's husband, Dennis, suddenly burst into the room in his nightclothes, yelling about the noise. I laughed aloud until I saw that the rest of the family had turned solemn. Dennis took a pot from the counter and held it over the children as if he intended to strike them with it. His own children cowered in fear, and I rushed to John, picked him up, and pulled him to me.

"Dennis! What are you doing?" I shouted. I looked at Mary, and she was trembling with fear.

"None of your goddamn business what I'm doing, Dennis bellowed, "What are you doing here, Mrs. Roebling?"

"I don't appreciate your language in front of the children, but to answer your question, your wife was kind enough to watch John while I left to bring clothing to Washington. He rushed to the bridge. Didn't you hear the explosion earlier this morning?"

"I didn't hear nothing." He didn't ask about the explosion, but turned toward Mary. She was already serving him coffee. He grabbed the cup from her hand, spilling the scalding contents on her arm, and she gasped, then put her hand over her mouth.

"Mary, are you all right?" I started towards her but Dennis blocked my path. I backed up, astonished at the scene.

"Mary, I thank you very much for allowing John to stay with you this morning. Thank you, too, children. Goodbye." I let myself out, sickened with worry for my friend. She had never shared any such incidents with me. It was clear that Dennis had been recovering from a night of drinking, and that was, too often, the beginning of bigger problems. I promised myself that I would check on Mary as often as possible and invite the children to come and play with John whenever time allowed. I did not know what else I could do.

Mary and I had met frequently while pushing carriages with our little ones through the neighborhood. Although she lived a few streets over in a poorer section of town, we immediately struck up a friendship, as John and her little Daniel were of the same age. I admired her calm demeanor while tending to five little ones, and asked her advice often. She seemed to enjoy sharing her experiences as a mother. I did not have my own mother to consult, and my sisters lived in towns far away.

Chapter 6

When the perfected East River bridge shall permanently and uninterruptedly connect the two cities, the daily thousands who cross it will consider it a sort of natural and inevitable phenomenon, such as the rising and the setting of the sun, and they will unconsciously overlook the preliminary difficulties surmounted before the structure spanned the stream, and will perhaps undervalue the indomitable courage, the absolute faith, the consummate genius which assured the engineer's triumph.

Thomas Kinsella
The Brooklyn Eagle

John and I walked to Prospect Park as often as possible. It bustled with activity and people to observe. John sat happily for a time in his carriage, clutching his favorite stuffed horse as we walked along the lake. When he got restless, I lifted him out and let him walk alongside of me.

In good weather, one could watch people practicing archery or playing croquet on the lawn. John never tired of watching the toy sailboats on the pond. The massive trees were a haven of shade on a steamy summer day. There were sturdy wooden benches to rest upon and hundreds of bird houses that attracted all kinds of birds. Even in winter, people skated and practiced ice baseball on the lake.

The city continued to build bridges and walkways and improve the park every year. It was an oasis in a place that was rapidly becoming overcrowded and noisy. John and I were just returning from our walk when I was horrified to see some of the workers helping my husband out of a carriage. He always walked to and from the work site which was such a short distance from our home. Two men helped him into the house and said that he'd all but collapsed when coming out of the caisson.

"You were in the caisson all day?" I asked.

"Yes, repairs were needed. We can't afford to lose any more time. The men have Sunday off," Wash whispered.

I turned toward the men. One of them advised that I rub Wash down with a combination of salt and whiskey to get his circulation going again.

"You don't think…," I couldn't finish the thought. I turned back to Wash. He didn't seem to be in any pain, which reassured me, but he could barely stand as I helped him out of his filthy clothing. He'd been in the caisson for more than eight hours, and he seemed short of breath.

"Have you been having trouble breathing, dear?"

He nodded, "A little. I just need some rest."

"You must get in bed now. I'll bring you something to eat."

"I'm not hungry. I need to go back early in the morning." He lay in the bed like a fallen statue, unnaturally stiff.

"You'll do no such thing if you aren't up to it. Why are you lying like that? Are your muscles sore?"

"No, I…," he attempted to sit up, but stopped and fell back rigidly like a board.

At eight o'clock, someone knocked on the door to inform us that there was fire in the caisson. Washington practically leapt out of bed and started to dress. I couldn't believe my eyes. He seemed quite able to prepare himself and leave the house after a short rest, so I let him go—not that I had a say in the matter.

It seemed he had just left when I heard fire engines thundering through Brooklyn toward the river. I looked out the window to see hundreds of people frantically chasing the fire engines. I could hear the warning bells from the work site. I couldn't stand by, doing nothing. John was in bed, so I ran to Mary's and asked her eldest daughter Bridget if she would stay with John. We ran back through the uproar in the crowded streets. Bridget looked terrified, but I assured her she would be safe if she stayed in the house, and that the fire was nowhere near us, but in a caisson. She blankly stared at me, and I realized that my words had made no sense to her. Nevertheless, I ran out the door to find Wash and see what I could do to help.

As I approached the site, I heard people speculating that the caissons had been blown to pieces, that men had been killed, that the bridge project was over. I'd lived long enough to know not to believe wild guesses. I found Wash, thankfully, not in a caisson, but out in the open air looking concerned, but safe.

"The caisson had to be flooded, I had no choice," he shouted over the noise.

"No one was hurt?"

"No, I ordered everyone away first."

People in the crowd seemed disappointed not to see uncontrollable flames and smoke. There was really nothing to see at all. No one had been killed, yet the crowd seemed to crave a disaster. By morning, it appeared that the whole of Brooklyn had come to inspect the scene.

"Just think what would have happened if it had been a regular workday? Hundreds would have been killed!" I heard one woman comment in passing. Wash and I just grabbed each other's hand and shook our heads at the foolishness of some people. My relief was great that night, and I said a prayer of gratitude for the safety of my husband and son and all those who toiled on the great bridge.

The next day, several men arrived at our home, angry and discontented over the mishaps. I did not believe that Wash was feeling revived enough for the confrontation, but I knew he could not be talked out of addressing the problems promptly.

"Colonel Roebling, you are in charge here, are you not?" General Slocum, one of the stockholders, demanded, looking directly at me as if he expected me to take my leave.

"As you well know, I am the chief engineer, General," said Wash confidently. "Mrs. Roebling is involved in every aspect of the project, as well."

"How is it that these accidents continue to occur under your leadership?" Slocum continued.

"We cannot continue to gain the public's support when one mistake after another is written in the papers every day! The public only reads about the errors, not the progress," Mr. Davis said.

"I cannot control what is printed in the newspapers," Wash reasoned. "Surely you understand that, Mr. Davis. If people are not able to see the progress with their own eyes, then they are not paying close attention."

Mr. Davis's face fell as well as his argument.

"These caissons, we knew they were experimental from the first," Mr. Thurber said, slamming his hand down on the table.

"No, no that is not correct, Mr. Thurber! I informed you from the beginning that they have been in use in other parts of the world. Mrs. Roebling and I studied them in Germany."

"Yes, but you have not used them before, have you?"

I saw my husband's hands begin to shake almost imperceptibly.

"Gentlemen" I said calmly, "as disheartening as these calamities are, they are, of course to be expected, are they not? What great undertaking in history has not been rife with problems? What progress can be made without errors and risk? Did you expect differently? Truly? Human beings are flawed, and Colonel Roebling, although completely in control of this project, is not present at the site to oversee every single worker at every single moment. That is simply not possible. I'm sure you are able to understand that. We have hired the most capable men to oversee every detail of the construction."

There was a silent moment, then Mr. Kingsley spoke up.

"Mrs. Roebling is correct. There have been no lives lost."

Wash looked in my direction, and I understood that he was allowing me to engage my diplomatic abilities; that he had nothing else to say.

"The fire marshal reported to us just this morning that he inspected the caisson and would not have even known that the fire had occurred. So all is well, is it not?" I concluded.

Of course, that was not in the papers. But, the next day the *Eagle* described the event as:

> "Men, muddied by splashing liquid clay, dampened by the streams of a bursting hose, made their difficult way over all obstacles, climbed upon the elevation whence the water shaft is accessible, and looked down only to see the unrevealing surface of the column of muddy water, with which the shaft is filled. The bursting of the hose sent up a spectacular plume of spray upon which sunlight played, forming a beautiful, clearly marked rainbow, with a fainter one reflected on the mist and spray from the streams."

At least the reporters were able to bring out the beauty of something, for once.

The same reporter described our own Mr. Kingsley: "He appeared calm and collected and preserved well in his equanimity, but a few words of conversation showed him to be anxious for the work." If only the calmness of those level-headed men could be reported more often.

George Templeton Strong, a noted diarist, wrote, "Caisson of the East River Bridge was severely damaged by fire yesterday. I don't believe any man now living will cross that bridge."

What nonsense. I managed to hide that one from my husband.

Time had been lost, but no lives had been sacrificed, and there had been no serious injuries. The engineering staff had stayed true to Washington's direction and vision. With the first caisson in place, the public was beginning to show a little faith in the massive project. There was finally something positive to read. Thomas Kinsella wrote on the editorial page of the *Eagle*:

> *America has seen nothing like it. Even Europe has no structure of such magnitude as this will be. The most famous cathedrals and castles of the historic Old World are but pygmies by the side of this great Brooklyn tower. And it is our own city which is to be forever famous for possessing this greatest architectural and engineering work of the continent, and of the age*

Diane Vogel Ferri

Chapter 7

Womanhood is the great fact in her life; wifehood and motherhood are but incidental relations.
                                        Elizabeth Cady Stanton

Although our marriage was secure, it was not as if we did not have our occasional difficulties. Wash was so engrossed in his work that, sometimes, I had to remind him of his family waiting at home to see him, of the promise he had made after his father's death. We had one rather upsetting quarrel about this, and it seemed to provide him with more awareness on the matter. If he was going to be extremely late or miss dinner, as he often did, he sent a messenger to let me know. Many a night, John ate dinner and prepared for bed without seeing his father, but when they were together, Washington gave John his utmost attention and affection. Times of separation were to be expected, I supposed, but I sometimes wondered why the female always carried the full burden of children. First, we must sacrifice our bodies, which never return to their youthful shape, and then our time and ambitions, should we have any. Although a child had two parents, there never appeared to be equality in that regard.

On the evenings when Wash was not to be home before John went to bed, I always read stories from the

Bible to him. John loved to hear about the animals on the ark and about the Three Kings bringing gifts to the baby Jesus on Christmas morning. One night, I read the story of the Good Samaritan, and John could not understand why people would walk by someone who needed help.

"You wouldn't do that would you, Mama?"

"Of course not. But people can be unkind to each other."

"Why didn't they help that man on the road?" he asked.

"Because he wasn't like them. There are all kinds of people in the world, and sometimes people don't like each other because they look different."

"You look different from me, Mama, but I like you."

"I like you too, liebchen." I treasured these moments, and pondered them in my heart.

"Mama…," John began to cough, and could not stop.

"Oh dear, let me help you up." I pulled him upright and patted his back. The coughing ceased, but his breathing was shallow and labored. I sent for the doctor, who arrived an hour later. John was breathing better, but still weakened by the event.

"Mrs. Roebling, is your husband here tonight?"

"No, he's still at the bridge, I'm afraid. Why do you ask?"

"There is a matter of John's health to discuss. His father should be here," the doctor said, shaking his head slowly.

"Are you disparaging our family situation and my husband's role as a father, or do you have something grave to inform me about, Doctor?" I asked.

"Neither, really," he looked up at me quizzically. "Have you been told that John has a weakened heart?"

"When he was born, there was some stress put on his heart, I was told, but he has been perfectly fine since then." My own heart was throbbing. I breathed deeply to calm it, but I felt frightened, and did, indeed, wish my husband were by my side.

"I do not mean to frighten you, Mrs. Roebling. I do not think it serious at his young age. But excessive coughing and overexertion may trouble it from time to time."

"He was playing outside vigorously this afternoon. Does this mean he cannot run and play as other boys?"

"No, not at all. Provide exercise and healthy food for him. If this happens again, please call me, but I expect he will be fine. Shall I contact your husband to explain all of this?"

"I assure you, I understand completely, and am capable of informing him myself." I said, but knew I would not bother Wash with it yet. There were too many other problems for him to think about at the work site. Besides, I was certain that John would have no more episodes, and would grow and play as other children.

Most evenings, I wrote by candlelight after John was sound asleep. I wrote about all the childlike wonders of my son and his fleeting innocence to keep them safe in my soul's memory. My life was lovely, compared to my dear friend Mary. Dennis was taking out his frustrations, whatever they were, on her and the children. My feeling for him was mostly anger, but maybe he was like the man on the road in the parable: unlovely, but still worthy of help.

Mary O' Connell was always on my mind. I wondered how she managed to care for five children when I had exasperating days with just one. Although they had a warm, cozy home, it was small for seven people. They rented the lower half of her cousin's house down the street from us.

I thought back to our first meeting. John lay in his fancy new baby carriage and we were strolling down Hicks Street. As we rounded the corner onto Poplar Street, Mary was pushing the carriage in the opposite direction, and neither of us was watching our path. I was peeking over the hood to see whether John was asleep. Mary had left her carriage momentarily to scold another one of her children to stop running ahead. The hedgerow blocked our view of each other.

"Oh! I'm so sorry!" I said after our carriages gently collided.

"Oh, 'tis all right. 'Twas my fault, I'm sure," Mary said, frowning at the little one grasping her hand. "This little lad was trying to get away from me!"

I bent down to the child and said, "You must listen to your mother, isn't that so?"

"Yea, Mum," the curly-headed child smiled up at me.

"He's just lovely," I looked up at Mary. "I'm Emily. I live down Hicks Street a way."

"My name's Mary, ma'am. This is Timothy, and me baby is Siobhan."

I was taken with Mary and her children immediately. Her Irish accent enchanted me. She looked like a waif, dressed shabbily, as were her children. My first thoughts were of having a friend, but one who might need my help. I had no women friends to speak of, no one to talk with about the challenges of motherhood. John was just beginning to toddle around the house, and his energy knew no bounds.

"You must be very busy with two little ones," I said.

Mary looked warily at my stylish new baby carriage, her eyes traveled the length of my dress.

"Oh, I have five altogether. My Bridget is watching the others so I could get Timmy and Siobhan out of the house for a bit. 'Tis such a lovely day."

"Five! That's wonderful! What a houseful!"

"We have but a tiny place to live, but these little ones bring me joy, to be sure."

"I'm sure they do. Please come for tea one day. I would dearly love to have some mothering advice from an expert."

"Oh, I don't know," Mary hesitated. Then Siobhan let out a piercing wail, and Mary never finished her answer. In the coming months I repeatedly attempted to make her acquaintance, but Mary was evasive. Looking back, I understood that our opposite stations in life made her uncomfortable, but at that time, I was not aware. I took my privilege for granted in my younger days.

"Mary, are you here?" I knocked softly on the door, hesitant about Dennis's presence.

"Hello, Emily, how are you? Please come in. Would you like a cup of tea?" She looked very tired. The three older children were at school, the youngest was asleep, and the other little one was playing quietly with some wooden blocks on the floor. Dennis was nowhere in sight, so it seemed a good time to be there.

"That would be lovely. How are things around here?"

"What do you mean by that?" She turned and glared at me.

"I just wondered how you and the children were faring. It's almost Christmas, and the little ones must be excited."

"Well, it will be a meager Christmas here, I'm afraid. We have so little extra, even though Dennis is working such long hours. It seems we are all sacrificing for this bloody bridge."

I smiled, then realized she was very serious.

"Do you have concerns about the bridge?"

"Of course! Don't you? Dennis tells me of so many injuries happening! Men are risking their lives for that ridiculous bridge, and for what? So people like you can go to New York and shop? What if one of those injured was Dennis, Emily? What would I do with all these children? I would be out in the streets!"

"Washington is doing everything he can to prevent any deaths or injuries." I knew my words were of little help. Washington could only do so much in the way of safety. The workers all were informed of the risks when they were hired, and most were unconcerned because they needed work so badly.

"I'm sorry you feel that way, Mary. I thought you and Dennis would be grateful for the regular wages. There will be employment for so many men for years to come because of this project. It was my father-in-law's dream."

"What do I care about his bloody dream?" She sat across the table from me and began to weep.

"Mary, what can I do to help you?"

"We don't need your help, thank you very much."

"But we're friends. Please help me understand what you're distressed about."

"If you must know, I am with child again." She looked up at me, "I don't want this baby." She hung her head as if she were a criminal, and began to weep sorrowfully. "I can't take any more. My littlest is only a year old! I'm so tired. I've heard that there are new ways to prevent these things from happening, but Dennis won't even discuss it. He says it's God's will to have as many children as He gives us. Do you believe that?"

"No, I certainly do not," I said, rising to go to her. "If you are choosing to be done with childbirth, that should be your choice, not Dennis's, or even God's. We are human beings with limits on our capabilities. When people say God won't give us more than we can handle, I say, rubbish! God gave us brains and free will and choices."

"Maybe men have choices," she replied.

"Yes, a wife's disabilities are great. How far along are you?"

"I have not even felt a quickening yet, but I know the signs all too well."

"Please think about what is best for you and the other children. I will find someone to help you if you do not want this baby to be born. There are ways to stop it, but it must be very soon."

"Oh Emily, my dear friend. Why are you so kind?" She sobbed, picking up the hem of her ragged dress to wipe her tears. "I don't know what to do."

"Then you will think on it and let me know, dear. Just don't wait too long."

Mary's littlest one, Siobhan, toddled over, and she took the child in her arms.

"I love my babies, every one," she said through her tears.

"Of course you do! No one would think otherwise. You must not berate yourself for these feelings." I said helplessly. "Mary, would it be all right if the children came to my house for a visit today? Maybe they would enjoy playing with John."

"That would be fine," she said sadly, as she enveloped little Siobhan in her arms.

John had too many toys for his own good, and I hoped he would be kind and share them with the O'Connell children. Every time I left Mary's house, I suffered feelings of guilt over all that I had and that they did not have. Their children had so little to occupy their time and it made Mary's days much more difficult. There were brief moments of envy as I yearned for another child, a child that did not want to come to us.

Shopping in New York was exciting, and soon there would be a bridge to get shoppers there quickly and easily. The Schwarz Toy Bazaar was a delightful place for children, and I indulged my one and only child a bit too much when we took the ferry to New York. It was time for John to learn to share before, as an only child, it was too late. If I devoted myself to my son's knowledge of the teachings of the Bible, he needed to see his parents live them out in life.

Mary's children appeared quietly at the door. After I led them into the playroom, they seemed hesitant to touch any of the unfamiliar toys they encountered at our home. My heart swelled with pride when John picked up a toy train and handed it to Daniel. Because of my love of horses, John had a large collection of wooden ones. One was mechanical, so I wound it up and it moved across the floor. The O'Connell children stopped short and watched in wonder. Soon they were all on the floor, building towers and playing with jacks, dominos, and puppets.

"I'm sorry we don't have many toys or dolls for girls," I said to Bridget and Deirdre. "Maybe you would like to come to the library with me and choose some books to read."

"Oh, yes, Mrs. Roebling, I love to read. I wish I could go to school every day!" Bridget said.

"Why can you not go to school every day?"

"When Mama is sick, I have to stay home and take care of the littles," she said without remorse or self-pity. "Sometimes I can't...."

"You can't what, dear?"

"My father doesn't think I need to go to school. He wants me to stay with Mama and clean and cook. I only go when he is not home in the morning. He doesn't believe in girls going to school. My mother tells him a lie...." She stared at the floor as if it were her fault.

I struggled to remain calm, so I did not make the poor child feel worse than she already did.

"You can walk down here and visit our library any time at all, dear," I said. I put my hand around her shoulder and led her into our bountiful room full of books, feeling ashamed of my wealth. Her eyes widened, and she did not hesitate to pull books off the shelf, her face bright with joy. It did my heart good.

"Thank you, Mrs. Roebling," she said, without looking up. She started to read, *Alice in Wonderland* to her sister.

I intended to have a word with Dennis as soon as possible. He reminded me of my own brother, Nathan. Nathan had bullied me through most of our childhood, and was jealous and angry toward girls. I could never understand his disrespect—our mother and father exhibited only love and companionship for each other. I would amuse myself on the floor with something or other, and Nathan would come by and stomp on it. If we were outdoors, running around, he would grab my arm and twist it painfully. He had a way of doing cruel things when no one else was watching. It seemed as if Nathan wanted to control my actions and punish me for them at the same time. When I asked him why he was being so mean, he would deny doing any of the things I had accused him of, and my parents never saw any of it. It was not that they didn't believe me, but they had no evidence and thought Nathan was a kind, gentle soul. What made him think he could do those things to a sister and not a brother, I would never know.

As we grew older, my only choice was to stay away from him and hope he would leave me alone. What his actions accomplished, I never understood. It was sad because family was the most precious thing in life, and I often missed Nathan, despite his cruel ways.

Chapter 8

When a woman has scholarly inclinations, there is usually something wrong with her sexual organs.

Friedrich Nietzsche

Wash and I enjoyed the company of our pastor, Henry Ward Beecher, and his wife Eunice. We frequently invited them over for dinner during the holidays. Henry was striking looking, with pale hazel eyes and blond hair streaked from the sun. He had little hair anywhere else, no eyebrows or beard to speak of, but a mischievous smile that engaged people who met him. Henry's fame had continued to grow over the twenty-four years he had been pastor of Plymouth Church in Brooklyn. Thousands of parishioners thronged to our church each week in hope of claiming a seat in the sanctuary and not being turned away. Henry's fiery preaching and strong leadership drew people from all over the world. He boldly supported social reforms such as women's suffrage and temperance. He could be controversial, as well. Henry was one of the few pastors who championed Darwin's theory of evolution, stating that it was not incompatible with Christian beliefs.

But Henry's charisma and fearlessness caused abundant rumors as to the state of the Beecher marriage and Henry's way with women. One journalist wrote that "it was standard gossip that Beecher preaches to seven or eight of his mistresses every Sunday."

I refused to submit to hearsay, and had only sympathy for them as they suffered the loss of four of their eight children in past years. What marriage wouldn't be strained with that kind of grief and loss?

"I read about another great blowout," Henry mentioned at dinner.

"Yes," Wash responded. "I was in a remote part of the caisson at the time. Half a minute elapsed before I realized what was occurring. I groped my way to the supply shaft where the air was blowing out. I was trapped with a few other men. It was a deafening noise. Water came rushing in, and the lights went out. Men were panicking, tripping, falling over each other in the darkness, water up to their knees in a heartbeat."

"How frightening!" Eunice said. "What happened?"

"Shush, Eunice, the man is trying to talk!" Henry frowned at his wife.

"The lower door had been blocked, and was not closing." I explained. "Wash kept a cool head, determined what had happened, and in fifteen minutes, air pressure was restored to the caisson."

Henry looked from me to Wash in astonishment. Apparently, women were not permitted to show knowledge when he was present. Wash was smiling and nodding at me to continue.

"What's wrong, Henry? Cat got your tongue?"

"Well, I ...just...."

"I don't think we've ever seen you speechless, Reverend!" Wash laughed heartily.

Eunice was clearly enjoying the moment. She was a lovely woman, but had recently written some articles that asserted that the place of labor for all married women was in the home. While that was agreeable to many, I did not think such a statement should apply to all women. But, two people did not have to agree on everything to be friends.

"Eunice, would you come into the kitchen, and help me with dessert?"

"Of course!" She practically jumped out her chair. In the kitchen we giggled like schoolgirls.

"Oh, Emily! You have such a way about you! I wish I could be more like that."

"How can you, when your husband shushes you? My goodness, I would not put up with that if I were you," I said.

"I think every marriage has its own arrangement, and that is ours, I'm afraid," Eunice replied.

"I know you do not have the kind of marriage Wash and I have, but do you find any happiness, dear?" I asked, touching her arm gently.

"Henry does a great amount of traveling. He meets many people. I'm afraid I am the least interesting of the people he knows," she said forlornly.

I drew close to her. "Are the rumors true? He's a pastor, for goodness sake!"

Eunice turned away from me abruptly and walked back into the dining room without a word. My curiosity had gone too far.

When I reentered the dining room with a tray of chocolate cake, I looked over at Eunice. She would not look my way, but occupied herself in smoothing out the napkin on her lap.

"I'm about to begin a lecture tour," Henry blustered.

"Yes? And what will you be lecturing on?" Wash asked.

"Yale University has established The Lyman Beecher Lectureship, based on my father's teachings. I will be teaching courses."

"My, what will Eunice do while you're gone?" I interrupted in as innocent a voice as I could muster.

Wash intervened, "I'm sure Henry has made sufficient arrangements for the family, Em."

"Perhaps," I replied, doling out large slices of cake.

"I am planning a visit soon to the men working on the bridge," Henry changed the subject. "A shepherd must be among his flock."

"You have many parishioners at work there," Wash said. "I'm sure they would welcome some encouraging words from you, Henry."

"Sympathy with the people, insight of their condition and a study of moral remedies will give you all you need to lead them into the light, Washington. You are a leader, just as I am. I seek to change people's lives, not their minds. You are changing lives by the very brilliance of your bridge and all the working families for which you are providing employment."

"I appreciate that, Reverend. I had not thought of it that way. This is why President Lincoln said no one has so productive a mind as you."

"Religion must adapt to the changing times."

"How does the Protestant religion accomplish that, Henry?" I asked.

"The Civil War did great damage to our society, and it is incumbent upon us to repair that damage through the continuing work of women's suffrage, the assimilation of former slaves into our society, and teaching the love our world yearns for."

"It is a great relief to hear you speak of the need for women's equality. Some would argue that the Bible opposes such a thing," I said.

"The Bible teaches us that our Lord is a God of love and mercy. Social reform is nothing more than loving God's children, whether male, female, slave or free, old or young! The aim of preaching is to gain, hold, mold, and fashion the heart of men to the noblest dispositions and best conduct."

"And women, of course. You never cease to preach, do you Henry?" I asked. "This is why Plymouth church draws the biggest crowd in Brooklyn every week. I've heard that we are the nation's largest church."

"You are correct, my dear Mrs. Roebling. Now where is that delightful chocolate cake? I believe I have worked up the taste for a second helping!"

The Christmas season always brought much-anticipated activity. Decorating our home was a joy for me. Traditionally, we had an eight-foot tree for the parlor. John and I would decorate it with shiny ornaments and candles. Evergreen garlands were strewn about the house, and the smell was heavenly.

Christmas trees were not common when I was a child. Wash and I spent two years in Germany, and it was there that we saw the most glorious Christmas trees and decorations. I brought a collection of glass ornaments back with us, and, every year, looked forward with surprise and delight to carefully unwrapping each one. It was only recently that Christmas was deemed a national holiday in

America. It put some joy in an otherwise dismal time of year.

John was of an age to form lifelong memories. Wash and I were still hoping there would be another child on the way by then, but it was not meant to be. I trusted God to bless me with what He wanted me to have. I believed He had other endeavors in store for me. I loved being a mother, but always seemed to need more. I would not admit that to any of my friends, who appeared to be completely fulfilled by their children. Feeling like a pariah as a woman, I was somewhat comforted by the *Women's Journal*. Mary Livemore wrote: *"Above the titles of wife and mother, which, although dear, are transitory and accidental, there is the title 'human being,' which preceded and outranks every other."*

Some women appeared to have little interest in simply existing as a human being, not just a woman who serves others, day after day. Darwin's work in biological determinism stated that the two sexes were polar opposites in character and nature. Men were suited to the public life and women, to the private. Why, then, was I always drawn to public events and the activities of society? On some Sundays, while listening to Henry go on and on at the pulpit, I daydreamed about being the one to preach. There was so much to say! In the matter of gender, why were the characteristics mutually exclusive? For example, why were men encouraged to have sexual experiences before marriage, but not women? How on earth were intimacies to occur without both parties?

Once, I had sought out the advice of a physician on the matter of conceiving more children. He told me that when women were too scholarly, it led the uterus to become dysfunctional. How in the world does that make any sense? Are the brain and women's reproductive organs connected somehow?

The notion that men were superior to women in every way was discouraging. I was capable of comprehending the science behind the building of the bridge. Mary was capable of raising her five children with little of Dennis's help. How was that inferior?

John's fourth Christmas was memorable. He found enjoyment in every little detail of the season. A beautiful veil of snow began falling at the beginning of December, and did not cease. We were outside one day, building a snowman together, when a large sleigh went by filled with freshly cut Christmas trees. John started running after the sleigh, and we, after him! He was so excited that we followed the sleigh to Fulton Street to buy a tree that Wash dragged home. It was a season of sleigh rides and caroling and John asking to hear *'A Visit From St. Nicholas,'* each evening after dinner, which Wash was obliged to do every time he was home.

Plymouth Church was lit with hundreds of candles for the Christmas Eve service, and the aisles were full, as well as the seats. I never failed to appreciate the beauty and history of our neighborhood church. The pews were arranged in an arc before the pulpit on both levels, and it was considered very modern to have a church designed in such a way. Our organ was the largest in the United States, and we were the first to have printed hymnals with words and music on the same page. Some Sundays, my mind wandering, I would imagine Abraham Lincoln praying there before his candidacy for president, or picture the runaway slaves hidden in the darkness of the church basement.

Every Sunday crowds gathered outside in hope of hearing Henry. I had heard it said that up to 3,500 persons sought admission to our services. Many had to be turned away each week, but especially so on Christmas. Henry often asked that the regular parishioners, such as we, not return for Sunday evening services so there would be room for visitors. Henry had been pastor of the Plymouth Church since 1847, and people never tired of his fiery, spirited sermons.

Amid the candlelight, we sang, *It Came Upon a Midnight Clear*, my favorite, as well as *Silent Night* and *We Three Kings*. Reverend Beecher gave an inspiring sermon, retelling the Christmas story, but, as usual, he managed to shock a few parishioners with his particularly distinct opinions:

"I do not believe that human fate is preordained by God's plan, but by a faith in the capacity of rational men and women to purge society of its sinful ways. This sacred night, I give you the gospel of love. God's love is what leads us, not sin. What kind of loving God would send his children to the fires of Hell? No! He created us for his enjoyment and for ours, as well, while we are here on this earth. And that love includes those who have been enslaved and oppressed in this country. Our former slaves, men and women both! We must reach out to those now set free. We must seek equality for our women because God loves all of his creation! This is why He sent His son on Christmas day to be our Savior. Merry Christmas to all! Go in peace."

His comment about the equality of women seemed a bit hypocritical to me, but nevertheless, I was inspired by his message.

Christmas morning was a joy, despite only one child's belief in St. Nick. John opened his many presents with great enthusiasm, and when he was done, he asked, "More?" Washington laughed and suggested that they begin to play with the ones he had. They set up stack after stack of colorful blocks, and every time Wash knocked them down, there were gales of laughter from my two boys. I went to help the cook prepare the turkey and set the table for the Beechers and their four children.

Dinner was merry with all the children, but Eunice remained quiet for most of the evening, and was difficult to engage in conversation. Henry, on the other hand, never stopped talking. He regaled us with stories of his many travels. He spoke admiringly of Edna Dean Proctor, an author with whom he was collaborating on a book of his sermons. Eunice's face soured whenever Henry spoke her name, and it seemed clear why there were so many rumors surrounding the couple.

"Children, I was forbidden to celebrate Christmas as a boy. I never heard of Santa Claus or hung up a stocking. I feel bad about it to this day! A little love is what I wanted."

"You can't get love for Christmas, Papa," said one of the Beecher children.

"Well, of course you can, son. The birth of Jesus is our gift of love!"

"Henry, I have heard that you have become the president of the American Women's Suffrage Association."

"Yes, I have. A very high honor, indeed."

"I'm sure it is, but wouldn't a woman be better suited?"

I felt a hand on my arm, and knew my patient husband was asking me not to continue the conversation. It was for the best, as I could get a little overwrought when it came to issues of women's equality. At least we had a respected and accomplished man on our side in Reverend Beecher.

As we prepared for bed that night, I told Wash about my observations about the Beecher marriage and Eunice's reactions every time Henry brought up a woman's name.

"Oh, that's ridiculous, Emily. He's a preacher, for goodness sake! Why would he risk his family and career for another woman?"

"Well, he did emphasize in his sermon last night that we are here on earth to enjoy ourselves." We fell into bed laughing about the absurdity of it all and the joy in our trust for each other. Wash took me in his arms, and after such a busy day, we fell asleep within minutes of extinguishing the candles.

Chapter 9

The mother at home, quietly placing the dishes on the supper table;
The mother with mild words—clean her cap and gown,
a wholesome odor falling off her person and clothes
as she walks by.

Walt Whitman

There was frantic banging on the door, and someone was calling for me. It was Bridget.

"Mama needs you! She's in a bad way. Please come, Mrs. Roebling!"

"Where is your father?"

"He never came home last night."

I pulled my robe on over my nightclothes and ran out the door through the snowy street in my slippers. Upon nearing the O'Connell house, I could hear Mary wailing. The youngest children were crying in fright, and I told them it would be all right. I went into the bedroom and closed the door behind me. Mary was bathed in blood and writhing in pain.

"Mary, what is happening?"

"The woman down the street gave me something to end this, but I didn't know it would be like this."

"What do you mean, gave you something? Oh, it doesn't matter. Have you lost the baby?" That seemed a foolish question. Mary began to sink back onto the bed in some relief.

"Are the pains subsiding?"

"Yes, I think it is over. Oh, God what have I done?"

I comforted her briefly, then opened the door to the faces of the frightened children and told them their mother would be all right, but that they needed to be quiet and let her rest. Bridget was a great help in cleaning up her mother and the bedclothes. While we were getting Mary into a clean nightgown, Dennis burst in the door, mumbling incoherently.

"Well, while you were gone, your wife miscarried the baby, Dennis. You should have been here. She could have died."

"You don't tell me what to do!" he thundered, suddenly awake. "What did she do to kill my child?"

"Have you no compassion for your wife or concern for her health?" I looked at the children hiding in the shadows of the dimly lit kitchen and knew that this conversation would need to wait.

"I will send for Dr. Wilding," I began, but Dennis had disappeared into the bedroom. I heard Mary sobbing and apologizing to him. Apologizing! I found coats for the children and brought them back to our house in the hope that they would not hear any more of their father's cruelty.

Mary's five children were so polite and quiet that I yearned to hear them create a fuss as they had on other visits, but they asked for nothing. Great fear was reflected in their eyes, and it broke my heart to imagine children living in distrust. Childhood should be carefree and exuberant, a time before the cares and responsibilities of adulthood arrive.

"Children, you must play with the toys!" I said merrily, trying to help them forget their worries.

"Oh, no, Ma'am. We might break them. They're new, from Christmas," said little Timothy.

"Well that's what they're for! John can always get more toys." I realized what I had just said—that my son could have all the toys his heart desired. "You know children, we only have one child at this house, so we are happy to have you visit us. These toys have been lonely for you to come back and play with them!" With that, the little ones laughed.

"Please have some fun, and I will fetch some Christmas cookies for us to share also."

I left the room so the children would be comfortable, but felt bereft. Mary's young ones had so little, and we had so much. The sight of so many siblings made my heart yearn for another child once again. What would it be like to have this immense house filled with the laughter of children?

That was the one thing, with all of my money, I could not have, could not buy. For that, I was the poor one.

Diane Vogel Ferri

Chapter 10

The demand for equal rights in every vocation of life is just and fair; but, after all, the most vital right is the right to love and be loved.

Emma Goldman

The snowflakes outside the window made a silent journey in their free-fall to earth, circling slower than gravity would allow. Staring motionlessly, I watched as a tuft released itself from a branch and was carried out of my sight on the breeze. The sheltered abundance of winter could be comforting, but the dark months of 1872 were long and dreary, leaving me depleted of joy, as gloomy days often did.

That February had been unseasonably warm, a turn from the sallow gray of the snow and sky. That night, the snow came down in wet, heavy clumps for hours, then promptly froze. In the morning, the sun created a fairytale picture, with twinkling gems of ice gleaming on every tree from bough to twig. John, Wash and I were sitting down to breakfast when the thuds and thumps began. We looked out the window to see branches large and small breaking off and falling to the ground. The willows, birches and pines were the first to go. By mid-morning, the neighborhood looked as though a hurricane had gone through. Bushes were flattened and trees denuded, limbs amputated. The melting was welcome, but the streets were debris laden all day, so Wash decided to stay at home for the morning.

We read six newspapers every morning at breakfast, and shared stories of interest with each other. This was a way for John to learn about the world as well as a way for Wash and me to exchange thoughts and ideas.

"Have you read about the terrible murders in our own Brooklyn?" I asked Wash.

"No. Murders? Are you sure that's something to discuss right now?" He asked nodding in John's direction. I shooed John off to the nanny.

"It says that a young woman named Fanny Windley began working in a Brooklyn factory at age eight! Isn't that awful? At fifteen, she was seduced by her 45-year-old employer, a George W. Watson. He tortured the poor girl for more than two years with his advances. Then, on the stairway of the factory, she shot him to death! Now the jury must decide whether this act was first-degree murder or if Fanny was under a weight of grief that could not be resisted. Certainly, they must not convict the poor thing."

"Em, she murdered the man," Wash said calmly, looking up from his paper.

"Do you know what it's like to have a man have his way with you without your consent? Or to be bullied by someone bigger than you? Well, that's a foolish question. Of course you don't. You're just a man!"

I looked up to see Wash trying to suppress a smile.

"Well, here's another interesting development," I looked over at Wash. "Victoria Claflin Woodhull intends to be nominated by the Equal Rights Party for the first woman presidential candidate!"

"That's ridiculous," Wash said, quietly returning to his paper.

"Why is it ridiculous, just because she's a woman? Because it's the first time for something? You, of all people, should understand that the first time for anything is a necessary challenge. Look at all the speculation about the enormity of the bridge. Most people say it's impossible, just because it's never been done before."

"Yes, touché, dear. You are most certainly correct and I take your meaning."

"Thank you! I hope you mend your thinking on such possibilities for women. It's something you and every other man shall have to get used to." Wash did not look up, and I could see that the discussion would go no further.

"What's happening with Boss Tweed?" I asked. Mr. William Marcy Tweed was head of Tammany Hall, the democratic political organization, and on the executive committee of our Bridge Company. He was instrumental to the early stage of the bridge project, by winning the backing of the New York aldermen, and he was a major stockholder. The newspapers were obsessed with rumors of corruption. He was accused of skimming money from the city's bridge contracts, among others.

"He is one of largest landowners in New York and director of the Erie Railroad, and the papers are having a field day with their insulting caricatures of him. Look at this one," Wash pointed out a cartoon depicting Tweed as grossly overweight, which he was, and his face was a bank bag with a dollar sign on it.

"Aren't you concerned about the money he may have stolen from the other bridge contracts?"

"I can worry about it, but there is nothing to be done until it is proven and justice is rendered."

"He's done so much for New York, so charitable, such a good father to those eight children. How can someone like him be so corrupt?"

"We don't know that yet, Em. You know the newspapers deal in postulating and rumor mongering on a daily basis. Anything to sell more papers."

"Yes, you're right, of course. We just don't need any more bad publicity for the bridge."

Late in the day when the streets were cleared and it was safe to go out I took the opportunity to go to the bridge and observe the progress. Approaching the work site, I saw my husband standing alone, looking distressed.

"What is it?"

"Some of the caisson workers are beginning to have serious physical effects. They are at a depth of more than fifty feet now. I intend to enlist a doctor to be here at all times. I've spoken to Dr. Andrew Smith. He is a former army doctor, a surgeon and a throat specialist. He has informed me of further complications and symptoms of caisson disease."

"Caisson disease?"

"Yes, that's what Dr. Smith is calling it. It used to be called 'the bends.' You remember when I suffered some minor symptoms."

"Yes, of course, but they were temporary."

"For me, they were, but some men suffer permanent damage. Now that the caissons have reached a considerable depth, some serious effects are occurring. The pressure inside the chamber is twenty-four pounds.

Dr. Smith has entered the chambers himself and has noted that his breathing was more rapid. He wrapped a steel tape about his own chest, then compared the measurements he got when breathing inside the caisson with those taken up on the surface. Under pressure, he found his chest expansion was nearly twice what it was normally.

"That sounds terribly dangerous."

"He also observed that the men coming out of the caisson all had a pallor that lasted twenty minutes or so, and their hands were slightly shrunken, and the tops of their fingers were shriveled."

"As if they were under water for an extended amount of time," I said.

"Precisely. Some of the men were running fevers while under pressure as well."

"What other discoveries has he made?"

"He took a dog down there yesterday. He left it there for seven hours then went down, killed it, took a blood sample, and carried it back up to detect changes in the oxygen content and dissected it to look for organ damage."

"Oh, well, that's unfortunate, poor dog. I hope it was worth a life!"

"No, apparently it proved nothing," Wash shook his head. "Dr. Smith has prepared a set of rules that I will be giving the men to prevent further symptoms."

"What kind of rules?"

"He suggests eating beforehand, especially meat and warm coffee and very little alcohol. They should rest, and not take exercise after coming out of the caisson, get eight hours sleep, never enter the caissons if they are not feeling well—things like that."

"Those seem sensible, I suppose. Nothing different than living a healthy life."

"I'm afraid that's all we have to go on right now. I don't think it's enough. I continue to feel great responsibility for the health of my workers. They have families to provide for. I am at a loss as to what else can be done. It will take another year and another half a million dollars before we reach bedrock. Thousands of hours, hundreds of men sacrificing for my father's dream."

"Really? Another year?"

"Yes, and dozens of men have already suffered sickness. Dr. Smith tells me that, due to the formation of nitrogen bubbles in the bloodstream upon decompression, this disease can cause all manner of life-threatening conditions. I've seen men come up retching, unable to walk or stand for a time, sometimes with excruciating pain in their limbs. How can I keep doing this to good men?" We were silent for a while. I simply held his hand.

"Maybe the second caisson doesn't need to go to bedrock," he said suddenly. "They brought up fossils from the riverbed for me to examine, and I have determined the foundation under the river hasn't shifted for millions of years." He looked at me as if searching for an answer in my face.

"Are you sure? You mean the New York tower will stand on sand?"

"Yes, yes, I have made my decision. If it hasn't moved in millions of years, I think we can safely say it won't in the next century, either."

My husband looked purely exhausted, so haggard and tired. His skin drooped unnaturally, his hair unkempt and need of a trim. There were traces of gray in his beard, and he was only 35 years old. How could I have overlooked this change in him? Both of our lives had been consumed by the building of this bridge, just as with my friend Mary, but at what cost? I did not intend to lose my Wash over a bridge, yet it was not our choice to begin with. No one had expected John A. Roebling to succumb to death after a foot injury. From then on I became determined to be of more help to my husband.

But then it happened.

A week later, after several hours in a caisson, Washington came out and completely collapsed. He thought he had been in the caisson for a short enough period, but he was wrong. Throughout that night and next day, his pain was so excruciating, his cries so hideous, despite the injections of morphine Dr. Smith had administered, it appeared that my husband was going to die. He lay in the same bedroom in the same house on Hicks Street where his father had died. I was frantic with fear, but tried to appear calm for Wash and John.

For several days, we had assistance around the clock. Wash was essentially paralyzed, but still in tremendous pain. He could do nothing for himself. When I went upstairs to sit with him, he insisted that it was temporary. No one else believed that, including me.

"The secret," he said, "is to keep off fear, to simply determine not to have it."

"You are a highly intelligent, sensible man. How can you believe that the power of the mind is stronger than the body?" I asked. "I know that was your father's theory, but it did not work for him." I despised saying so to my eternally optimistic husband. Sometimes my realistic thinking could be cruel, and I was furious with myself for it.

"I can help. You know very well that I am able," I said.

"What do you mean?"

"With the bridge, the engineering, of course."

"Oh, Emily, I don't know."

"Why do you hesitate? Did you not believe your own words when you told the men in our parlor that I was as capable as any man? When you told me I knew more about the caissons than some of the men there that day?"

Just then, Wash's face changed from concern to a grimace. I had said too much, been too forceful, thinking of my own pride, my own need to feel important and accomplish something. My husband's condition was delicate, and the doctor had asked me repeatedly to not upset him. Yet, I pushed forward with my own selfish notions.

"You know," I said calmly, "There are many men who can assist in your absence. What if I am just a liaison? A communicator, when needed?"

Wash's face relaxed and his body loosened before my eyes. I decided to stop talking and let him rest. His eyes closed slowly, and he slept soundly that night.

The next morning, a messenger arrived at the door.

"Mrs. Roebling, bad news," he said, and handed me a sealed envelope.

"Well, thank you, in any event," I handed him a coin and closed the door. The envelope was addressed to Wash, but I ripped it open. It was from Dr. Smith.

Washington,

I will be visiting you this evening, but I wanted to inform you immediately of the death of one of your workers. He was a German immigrant named John Myers, about forty years of age. Myers worked just over two hours this morning and came up to rest by my directives. He was outside nearly an hour when he complained of not feeling well and headed toward his boarding house. It was reported back to me that he collapsed and died on the stairway to his room. I intend to perform an autopsy to determine the cause of death.

Dr. Andrew Smith

One week later, Dr. Smith informed us that the man's brain, heart, and kidneys had been in perfect condition, but his lungs were congested to an extreme degree. Upon learning this, Washington rose from his bed and returned to work, to everyone's amazement. I visited the site more often than I previously had in the hope of glimpsing my husband out in the open air, not imprisoned in a caisson. I requested that one of the workers privately inform me if Wash had been in a caisson for more than an hour. To my knowledge, my husband never discovered this small betrayal.

That entire summer involved constant setbacks. Wash was as stubborn as his father, who had refused to believe his injury was life-threatening. Very few people noticed Washington's pain or disability. He was so focused on the job at hand that all the workers continued to take him at his word when he said he was fine. They all were fond of, and greatly respected Colonel Washington Roebling, as did I.

By November, the Brooklyn tower reached a height of 145 feet, which extended past the level of the bridge deck. The archways began to appear, majestically thrusting towards the heavens. It was a hopeful and heartening sight for us, as well as for the entire city.

It was not until another Christmas season came that Wash had no choice but to accept his condition. He was no longer able to go to the work site, and his secret was revealed. He experienced sudden, violent cramps, dizziness, vomiting, pain, and numbness. His pain was unaffected by the many injections of morphine Dr. Smith gave him. He tired rapidly, and was unable to eat or rest. The doctors told us there was almost no possibility of full recovery, and Wash obsessed over the notion that he might not live to see the bridge completed.

I had no choice but to take his place, to be his eyes and ears.

In addition to all of the hideous physical ailments my husband suffered, he became extremely irritable and distraught over the slightest problems. I was the only person who could deal with his moods and profound gloom.

When a contractor or foreman appeared at the door, I did not take him upstairs to the bedroom, but ushered him into the parlor and insisted that he tell me why he was there. Soon, men were bringing me full reports of the day and were beginning to ask me questions. Instead of pretending to relay the information to Wash, I answered them myself. If the man refused to accept my answers, I excused myself, ascended the stairway, waited in the hallway, and then returned with the same answer.

The men never suspected that I had not consulted the chief engineer.

Diane Vogel Ferri

Chapter 11

Hold yourself responsible for a higher standard than anybody expects of you. Never excuse yourself.

Henry Ward Beecher

Work had slowed down without the chief engineer's presence that winter. A profusion of snow had blocked streets and the river was choked with ice. Assistants would show up at the house regularly, but although I allowed him to try, Washington had difficulty carrying on discussions of any length with them. His patience was short, his frustrations long, and I seemed to be the only person he could tolerate for more than a few moments. His eyes began to fail, and we feared he was going blind, but daily communication was of great importance. Each morning and afternoon, I sat at my husband's bedside as he dictated his directions to the foremen and crews. Henry Murphy reported that money was running out, and suggested that foremen's pay be reduced by half.

"Em, please write this reply to Henry."

> *I do not myself think it a fair arrangement to put any of these gentlemen on half pay. They are not like day laborers who can be picked up at any time — they have to*

devote a great deal of thought to this work when they are away from it as well as when actually present at it.

"Will you read that back to me, dear?"
"Of course."
Later that same day he asked to dictate another letter to Murphy.
"Oh, Wash, please rest for the day," I implored, but he had too much on his mind and could not rest.
"There is a matter of awarding the contracts for the iron links that will attach the cables to the plates at the bottom of the anchorage that must be settled," he insisted. "Write this down, dear."

I do not think the Brooklyn Bridge is the proper kind of a structure to experiment on. Last, I desire to say that if the rule is invariably adhered to of giving all contracts for supplies to the lowest bidders irrespective of all other considerations, I hereby absolve myself from all responsibility connected with the successful carrying on of the work.

"It sounds to me as if you are expecting some trouble."
"They want to award the contract to the Passaic Rolling Mill to save money, but the company has never even attempted such a thing as this before. I will not be a party to such folly. I will not be connected to them financially, politically, socially, or in any other way!"
Washington's fury continued throughout the evening. I sharpened pencil after pencil as we tried to express his wishes in long letters to the people it

concerned. All of this served to further my understanding of the building of the bridge and its complexities.

Only days later, Henry Beecher paid Wash a visit as pastor and friend. I led him to Wash's study to find him writhing in pain, his face contorted in a monstrous grimace.

"Washington, what can I do to assist you, my friend?" Henry looked aghast at my husband's condition. I went to Wash's side and tried my best to soothe and distract him.

"It will pass soon. I'm sorry, Reverend, that you had to witness this," I said, putting a warm cloth on my husband's forehead.

"Nonsense! I will offer a prayer! Dear Lord, your humble servant Washington is suffering and in need of immediate comfort and strength. We ask that you calm his mind and allow him to continue his great work here on this earth. Your Holy Word tells us that suffering produces perseverance, and perseverance, character, and character produces hope! Hope does not disappoint us because You Lord have poured out Your love on us and on your servant Washington. Amen!"

"Thank you Henry," A tranquility had overcome Wash. His eyes were closed, but his breathing was steady and strong, his face placid. Henry was looking out the window at the activity at the bridge site. He then closed his eyes and whispered further prayers for my husband. Wash slept peacefully that night for the first time in days.

In April, I convinced Chief Engineer Roebling to take a formal leave of absence. The doctors insisted that the only chance he had of recovery was to get away from his bridge. I called many of the foremen to the house to assure them that he would return as soon as possible and gave them detailed instructions for while we were away.

We decided to travel back to our beloved Germany to the hot springs in Wiesbaden. I was not certain that my husband could endure the trip, but we had to take the chance. His doctor concurred.

Traveling to Europe was a terrible ordeal for Wash, but we held high hopes that it would be worth it. We enjoyed the solitary time with John, who was now a lovely five year old and delightful in every way. Wash began teaching him new words, developing his vocabulary, and how to add and subtract. He talked to our son about engineering, and on good days, they searched for additions to Wash's mineral collection.

Wiesbaden was famous as a city planned for luxury and known as a global spa. On the ship, I read to John and Wash about the history of the city. The name came from the term *wisibada* meaning "baths in the meadows." The Romans had established the baths in the first century. People traveled from all over the world for their healing powers. There was a great amount of social intercourse and sophistication, but we were much more interested in getting Wash well enough to return home. I could not deny that I was attracted to the society and beauty of the city. I yearned to get dressed up in exquisite finery and attend a ball, but I reserved my energies for my family. It was difficult not to imagine what our lives might have been if John A. Roebling had not died—something I constantly struggled to rinse from my brain.

Wash dictated his letters to the bridge contractors and could not be talked out of doing so, although the directives he left were more than adequate. He had a daily regimen of time in the warm, soothing water at the hot springs, and while he found it relaxing, it did not appear to heal his infirmities.

On sleepless nights, we'd discuss our return to New York and all that awaited us. Talking about the bridge was still thrilling for Wash, and I would see his eyes light up in optimism that he would indeed live to walk across the bridge in triumph, something his father had dreamed of as well. We made practical decisions about John's schooling and buying a new home closer to the bridge. Our dreaming went so far as to list destinations we would travel to when the bridge was completed and Wash was well again.

We continued to read all the newspapers and reports we could find in Germany. While we were gone, Boss Tweed went to trial, was convicted of 204 counts of embezzlement, and sent to jail. The murderous Fanny Windley of Brooklyn went to trial for the second time and was released on $2,500 bail. She was defended by a woman named Kate Stoddard, which interested me. After failing to post bail, Fanny had disappeared. I didn't know what to make of it all. I was glad to see a woman defending a woman, but what had happened to Fanny? Her life was over because a man used her up as a girl before her life had started.

News of our friend Henry Beecher also made its way across the ocean. One of the women at Plymouth Church, Elizabeth Tilton, was reported to have confessed to an affair with Henry, to her husband, Theodore. Theodore accused Henry of seducing his wife and was suing Henry for "alienation of affection" and "criminal conversation." Our own spiritual leader was going to trial for committing adultery with Mrs. Tilton! What humiliation our friend Eunice was facing.

"Do you believe these allegations?" I asked Wash.

"I don't know what to believe. Henry is a friend who has brought me great strength and comfort. His prayers by my bedside calmed me. He has been a faithful servant of Plymouth Church for many years. This woman is ruining Henry's life and reputation."

"Do you think this woman, as you call her, has no life of her own that will be ruined? Or is it all her fault?"

"She is the one who has made the claim, Em. Even if it's true, she should have kept her mouth shut."

"I'm surprised at you. It takes two people to create this kind of mess, does it not? He's being accused of seducing her, you know."

"Being seduced and succumbing are two different things."

"Maybe it's the husband, this Theodore Tilton, who should have kept his mouth shut. Perhaps he was not making Elizabeth happy, and now he wants to blame his awful marriage on someone else," I said, folding my arms.

"Does that give her the right to break marriage vows?" Wash looked at me sternly and frowned, folding the tufts of his eyebrows.

"All I am saying is that there are reasons that people stray. There is always a reason."

We returned from the resort on the Rhine River to Brooklyn six months later. Wash had experienced some brief spells of relief, but the warm alkaline springs did not bring healing, and our disappointment was acute. While we were gone, the towers were being completed, the anchorages built, and cable-making machinery had been assembled and set in position. None of this would have happened without Washington's detailed specifications and the devotion of his workers. It involved voluminous and tiresome correspondence, but it kept our spirits and our motivation high.

One day, we would cross the great bridge together with our son by our side.

Diane Vogel Ferri

Chapter 12

For that which I do I allow not; for what I would, that do I not, but what I hate, that I do.

Romans 7:15

I had written to Mary many times while we were away, but she never wrote back. When I called on her upon our return, Bridget said her mother had taken a job in New York.

"The days are very long for her, Ma'am. She has to take the ferry both ways. Sometimes the ferry is so crowded at the end of a workday, she must wait for it to return and pick up more people. She goes to bed as soon as she gets home."

"Are you caring for all the children, Bridget?"

"Yes, Ma'am. But 'tis all right. My father is sending money when he can."

"And where is your father?"

"He left some time ago. We don't know where he is, but he sends money. It just isn't enough for food and rent, so Mama had to find a job."

"Do you know why he left?"

"He was very angry with my mother for losing the baby."

"Oh, that's so unfair, isn't it? How can he blame her for … I'm so sorry, dear. Please come and get me if you need anything, and ask your mother to call on me when she can."

"Yes, Mrs. Roebling. I will tell her."

My heart was heavy for Mary, and Bridget as well. The girl couldn't be more than thirteen years old. Surely Wash and I would help with the finances if Mary would let us. But she was a proud woman.

Upon our return, the whole city was in an uproar over the Henry Beecher scandal. Elizabeth Tilton had confessed her affair with Beecher, and it became public when Tilton's husband told Elizabeth Cady Stanton of the illicit relationship. Stanton then repeated the story to Victoria Woodhull. Incensed over Beecher's hypocrisy and criticisms, Victoria Woodhull published a story titled, "The Beecher-Tilton Scandal Case" in her paper, *Woodhull and Claflin's Weekly*.

What a tangled web of folly! Not only had Henry been accused of committing adultery, but he had Woodhull arrested and imprisoned for sending what he considered obscene material through the mail. He had publicly denounced Victoria Woodhull for her advocacy of free love, and Woodhull, in return, pronounced Beecher a fraud as a man of God. It was a war of words, and not very Christian of our pastor, I feared.

His indignation reminded me of my own. Often wanting to be meek and holy, injustices could overtake my senses and cause me to be someone I did not want to be. As a woman, a certain decorum and comportment was expected. I often heard my father's voice in my head, "Be a lady, Emily." Although my husband never outwardly criticized me or tamped down my fervor, had I embarrassed him with my frequent outbursts? Did he wish his wife to be more like Eunice?

It was a horrid chapter in the lives of all those involved. Wash and I discussed our roles as friends of the Beechers, and how we would proceed in the future. Of course, Eunice was the victim in all of this, and although we were never close, she needed support in all of these matters. Was it not enough that she had stood by Henry's side through all his other controversial sermons and through criticism on his extreme views on abolition? He continued to travel the country, preaching even through the loss of four of their dear children. How much was one woman able to withstand? The thought that Henry would inflict any more suffering on the poor thing was horrifying.

Through the years I had heard many a story of Henry's infidelities but, being a personal friend, I chose to believe the best in him, and not be taken in by his fame or renown. His Sunday lessons on the "Gospel of Love" were appealing. But the tremendous amount of gossip and the years of Henry's prolonged absences from his family conspired to force me to face the truth about Henry Ward Beecher. The papers called him a prime example of Victorian hypocrisy. They were full of limericks and caricatures.

The Reverend Henry Ward Beecher
Called the hen a most elegant creature.
The hen, pleased with that,
Laid an egg in his hat,
And Thus did the hen reward Beecher.
               Oliver Wendell Holmes

It all seemed like a dark stain on Brooklyn. It was shocking to hear people make excuses for Henry and pity his suffering. They called his sins *alleged*. His flamboyance and controversial ways, however well-intentioned, had brought it upon himself. I did not know what to believe, but just because he was a famous man, it did not make him innocent or above reproach. Why did people refuse to see the truth about certain matters and defend someone who had hurt other innocent people, namely, poor Eunice. Worst of all, Plymouth Church would forever bear this mark. A pamphlet was widely distributed titled, "Wickedness in High Places," that asserted that Plymouth Church could no longer be regarded as the center of Protestant American virtue or as Brooklyn's answer to Tammany Hall.

Wash and I hoped to create a different reputation for Brooklyn. It must be known for its magnificent gothic bridge, not for the church of a famous fool.

There were so many other more worthy developments in America for the papers to focus on, all of which we appreciated even more upon our return from Europe. Railroads were connecting the states as never before. Mr. Eads had finished his bridge in St. Louis, and although it was not as glorious as ours, it was a major achievement in engineering. In Massachusetts, the Hoosac Tunnel had been completed. In New York, the Western Union Telegraph Building was the nation's tallest office building at ten stories. Carnegie had built the biggest steel mill on earth in Pennsylvania, and, of course, work continued on the bridge that would connect New York and Brooklyn forever.

Wash continued to suffer terribly. He had horrible headaches and pain in his joints. He was not paralyzed, as the papers so often reported, but his nervous system had been decimated. Any noise would startle him; bright lights hurt his eyes. The doctors called it *nervous prostration.* He was continually in anguish over the slightest things. This was so unlike his natural sanguine character and calmness of mind. He had nightmares about mistakes on the bridge and not being able to finish it. He blamed himself for his condition. On some days, he wanted to give up on everything, including his own life. Even so, he wrote to the papers, stating: *I am perfectly competent to take care of the Brooklyn Bridge.* Intellectually, this was true, but, emotionally, I was the one carrying the load. Even without the presence of the chief engineer, the bridge continued to rise. Wash's absence posed no enormous problems because his written instructions were thorough and clear. Each day, he dictated his wishes to me. I read them back aloud so he would be assured they were correct, and I had them delivered to the bridge site. Colonel Roebling was still in charge:

> *Above the arch is a spandrel-filling of various thickness of courses, and covered by a broad band-course at the line of the keystone. The space between the keystone and the cornice is occupied by a recessed panel. The interior space above the spandrel-filling is not all solid, but consists of three parallel walls, separated by two hollow spaces. The middle wall is 4 feet 2 inches thick, the outer ones vary from 4 feet 2 inches to 5 feet 3 inches in thickness, and the width of the hollow spaces varies....*

The newspapers repeatedly speculated on my role in the project and how the work had proceeded while we were in Europe. I was disinterested about receiving any credit, but when all my patience for their wild guessing was gone, I wrote:

> *It could never have been accomplished but for the unselfish devotion of his assistant engineers. Each man had a certain department in charge and they worked with all their energies to have the work properly done according to Colonel Roebling's plans and wishes, and not to carry out any pet theories of their own or for their own self-glorification.*

Dr. Smith appeared at our door one night, and reported to us that there had been 110 cases of sickness. He attributed them to compressed air that were severe enough to require his services.

"As a physician, I must inform you both about the multitude of ailments your workers are experiencing. Here are some notes I have made my notebooks:

> *Case 11 - E. Riley. Taken sick Feb 16th, one hour after leaving the caisson. Pressure 26 lbs. Epigastric pain and pain in legs. No loss of sensibility. Profuse cold perspiration. Pulse two hours after attack was 96. The pain, which was at first very severe, had by this time become much less. Gave him an ounce of brandy and a teaspoon of fluid extract of ergot. In 10 minutes the pulse had fallen to 82. Was able to resume work the next day.*

"But he was able to return to work, is that correct?" Wash asked.

"Yes, and he was willing."

"Go on," Wash said.

Case 13 - Henry Stroud, a diver by occupation, began work on the morning of April 2d. Half an hour after coming up from the first watch, was taken with numbness and loss of power in the right side, also dizziness and vomiting. This was followed by severe pain over the whole body. Excessive perspiration. Was treated with stimulants and ergot, and in five hours was well enough to return home.

Dr. Smith looked up at us with a grim expression.

"What else can we do, doctor?" I asked.

"I have sent some of the men to Brooklyn City Hospital. There is a young intern there named Dr. Walter Reed who is very interested in studying these patients. He is keeping notes on each victim, and gives his notes back to me. We have a number of theories we are working on."

"Yes?" Wash seemed to be calmer than usual on hearing so much disturbing news.

"I believe that when under pressure, the blood is not distributed according to normal physiological demands. It retreats from the surface to the center of the body and accumulates there until an equilibrium of pressure is produced. I think it could be adjusted to these unnatural condition if the pressure were experienced by degrees."

"So the longer a man stays down in the heavy air, the more the circulatory system will be affected. When the pressure is removed, suddenly, the blood vessels fail to assume their natural conditions." I suggested.

"That is correct, Mrs. Roebling. That is my hypothesis at this time. I will report the findings of Dr. Reed and myself as soon as possible."

"I have been quite sick, owing to the imprudence of remaining too long in the caisson. Everything was going well otherwise," Wash said sadly.

Chapter 13

No man is good enough to govern any woman without her consent.

Susan B. Anthony

Approaching the O'Connell house, Dennis's voice rose above all the others. I hesitated to go any farther, as they seemed to be in a quarrel and I was sure I would not be welcomed. But fearing that my friend Mary might need my help, and thinking of those poor children witnessing all the anger, I knocked on the door and Bridget opened it. She'd been crying.

"Oh, please help my mother, Mrs. Roebling."

Mary was on the floor in the corner with Dennis looming over her and yelling something about her being a terrible mother.

"You are a sinner, Mary O' Connell! You are going straight to hell!" He raised his hand as if to strike her, and I flew across the room and shoved him from behind toward the wall.

"What? Oh, it's you again. Get out of here! This is a private family matter."

"I will not, Dennis. Haven't you tortured this woman enough? Leave her alone, or I shall call the police."

"The police do not tell me how to handle my family matters."

"Your family! You have not even been here to provide for them, to help with the children you already have! You are no family man!"

"That is none of your business, Mrs. Roebling. Go back to your crippled husband and leave us alone."

"Where have you been? You had a job on the bridge with regular pay. That was meant to support this family, not your wife going into New York every day just to put food on the table and leaving your own child to do an adult's job."

"I was fired from that job, I'll have you know. Didn't your husband tell you?"

"No, I was unaware of that, but I'm sure it was for good reason. They can't have men coming to work drunk and endangering the lives of the others."

"You get out of here now, before ...."

Galvanized, I stood up taller and walked toward him to show I was unafraid of his drunken rage. "Fine, but I'm taking Mary and the children with me."

Dennis's stature deflated. He stood by helplessly while I gathered the younger children. Mary said nothing, but followed along as if in a trance. We walked back to my house and had lunch together. The younger children set right to playing with John, and it was peaceful for a bit. I did not press Mary to talk, but just let her be. After some food and tea, she appeared to be more like herself.

"I'm worried about Dennis. He's so overwrought these days."

"Mary, why didn't you tell me he'd been fired? I'm sure Washington was not informed of this. Was it the drink?"

"Oh, yes, just like his father before him." Her head was bent in shame, her hands busily smoothed out the wrinkles in her worn and stained dress. "He used to be so jolly, so much fun to be with. When Bridget was born, he was a good father, really he was. But now…."

I busied myself pouring more tea for both of us.

"I'd give anything to have Dennis look at me the way the Colonel looks at you."

"Oh, Mary, dear Mary. Does he do physical harm to you or the children?"

"He has, at times, but mostly he just threatens us. That is just as frightening to the children. For myself, I care not what he does, but it scares them."

"There is no reason for him to touch you in anything but a loving way. It is wrong. Wrong of him to hurt you, his wife, the mother of his children. Does he suppose he can do without you?"

"But what am I to do? There is nowhere that I can escape his wrath. I know his anger is truly at himself. I try to be a good wife. I try to understand but…." Mary began to quietly weep. "I can't cry in front of the little ones. It frightens them. They need one strong person."

I led Mary up to my bedroom and settled her into the bed, bringing a soft blanket, some warm milk, and my own handkerchiefs, and told her to weep as long as necessary.

"I know men believe weeping to be unnecessary and pitiful, but we know when it is needed. You can stay here as long as you want, and I will keep the children entertained."

"But they won't know where I am."

"I will tell them you're resting and you will return presently."

After a few hours, we sent Bridget back to the house and Dennis was gone, so they returned home with as much food as they could carry and some of John's outgrown clothes and toys.

The first bridge tower in Brooklyn was rising higher into the sky before our eyes. The freestanding masonry was a sight to behold and more magnificent than I had even imagined. There seemed to be fewer criticisms in the daily papers now that there was something tangible to see—a vision for the future. The stonework had suffered delays when quarries failed to deliver on time or weather hampered the work. The stone came from twenty different quarries in thousands of shiploads. The top of a tower was crowded with up to eighty men working there at one time.

In the cold winds of November, a magazine editor visited the base of the great arch and wrote that from the finished span "a perspective will be afforded which, for grandeur, will have no rival in the world."

Our Master Mechanic Farrington wrote to Wash and me:

There are times when standing on top of the Brooklyn Tower, one feels as completely isolated as if in a dungeon. Some years ago, I had an experience of this kind by daylight. It was in the early morning, when a dense fog covered the whole region, that having occasion to examine some machinery, I went on the tower before the time for commencing work. I shall never forget that morning. I found the fog had risen to within twenty feet of the top of the tower, and there it hung, dense, opaque, tangible. It was what you might seem to cut with a knife. It seemed I might jump down and walk upon it unharmed. It looked like a dull ocean of lead-colored little billows; vast, dead, immovable.

Two weeks after the confrontation at the O'Connell house, we were informed that a man jumped off the first tower to his death. We were not told of his identity until the next day.

It was Dennis O'Connell.

As soon as the daily messenger left the house with that information, I rushed to the playroom to find John's nanny. I asked her to go immediately to the O'Connell house to care for the children and I would be there with provisions within the hour. But before I could leave the house, the nanny returned, reporting that the house was empty. I had no knowledge of where Mary and the children had gone or the location of her family.

"What a terrible friend I have been to Mary and those dear children," I said to Wash.

"That is not true. You tried your best. We cannot intervene in the lives of others where we are not wanted," Wash said. "I'm ashamed of this, but I cannot help but think about how she is free of that monster, Dennis."

"I am afraid I was thinking the same thing. He will never terrorize Mary or those children again, but whatever will she do alone?"

"I just wish he had not chosen our bridge to end his miserable life," Wash added.

Chapter 14

Before winter shall drive the workmen from their positions we shall see the first strands of the great cable stretching aloft, spanning the river.

The *Eagle*

1876

It took two more years to complete the towers, and the bridge was halfway done at that point. Twelve men had lost their lives to the towers, and more dangerous work was ahead. A controversy arose over a report claiming the bridge would obstruct traffic on the river. Some called it a nuisance, saying it would hamper the commerce of the cities. Public hearings were held, and wild speculation once again threatened to stop the work. It was clearly too late to do that and there were just as many defending our bridge as there were detractors.

On some days, it could not be hidden from my husband. The only good news was that Boss Tweed, although convicted of many crimes, had not been successful in skimming money from the bridge's contracts, as he had done with other public works. There appeared to be no end to the improprieties and corruption of our acquaintances.

Amid celebrations for America's one hundredth birthday, the Beecher-Tilton trial filled both the papers and people's imaginations. Tickets were required to the trial, and although they were free, people were selling them on the streets. Not only were the cities of Brooklyn and New York enthralled with this spectacle, but the entire country as well. Henry Ward Beecher was so famous and so respected that the majority of the public refused to believe that he could participate in anything so heinous and sinful as adultery. The trial put Brooklyn in the spotlight for six long months, and I was sick to death of hearing about it. It had taken Reconstruction efforts off the front pages of the newspapers and had been deemed the most sensational trial in American history!

"Listen to this. The paper says that more than 3,000 people have been turned away from the trial. It's like a carnival! Vendors selling sandwiches and drinks and renting binoculars on the street corners! Have you ever heard of anything so distasteful?"

"This paper says that both Theodore and Henry have made very poor showings so far. Our dear reverend has disputed every one of the ninety-five witnesses called to the stand claiming poor memory nine hundred times! How long will the debacle continue?" Wash shook his head.

"The whole mess is so confusing and distorted in people's minds, I'm sure the jury will have difficulty coming to a true verdict."

"Perhaps Henry is regretting targeting Mrs. Woodhull's 'free love' theories in his sermons," Wash said, "Her advocacy of separating the state from matters such as birth control and adultery were no more controversial than many of Henry's own sermons. He made an enemy of her and that is how all of this started. She was only publishing the hypocrisy she saw in him."

"Does that mean you believe him to be guilty?" I asked.

"Have you never noticed how the women flock around him after church every Sunday? I have heard plenty of rumors besides this one. I don't know what to believe."

"Even his own family is torn. Harriet Beecher Stowe is supporting him, while his other sister, Isabella, is for Woodhull. A sad state of affairs."

After eight days of deliberation, there was no decision. No verdict. No conviction. Henry's supporters rejoiced in the streets. Henry called for the church to hold a final hearing to exonerate him, and it did. The Roeblings did not participate in that spectacle.

In the end, I did not care one whit which way it turned out. I just cherished the truth and desired to see it upheld, no matter whom it concerned. In the past, Henry had been kind, generous and inspiring, but he now appeared to be a pompous hypocrite, a self-serving man who had destroyed his family's reputation as well as the reputation of our city. My prayer was that someday Brooklyn would be known for the great bridge, not a farcical trial.

On the last afternoon of the trial, Mr. Kingsley appeared at our front door with more bad news. I led him up to the bedroom where Washington was resting.

"Washington, Emily, I'm afraid we have suffered two more deaths on the bridge, and I wanted to inform you in person before you read it in the papers."

"Oh, Lord, what has happened now?" Wash looked crushed and defeated.

"Mr. Reed suffered from epileptic fits, a fact that he concealed from us when hired. One of the other workers heard him groaning and then saw him just topple off the tower. The other man, a Mr. McCann, made a fatal mistake when he attempted to jump around an obstacle on the tower. A box of mortar was about to be raised, but hit him, knocking him off and into the river. We have not found his body yet."

Washington slumped over and I could not see his face or his reaction. When he looked up at us, there were tears in his eyes.

"What are we doing? How many more men will we lose? How many more families will be devastated by this bridge? Should we stop?"

Mr. Kingsley and I looked at each other, unsure of what to say.

"Washington, we cannot stop now. If we did, those deaths would be in vain," Mr. Kingsley said quietly. No one spoke for a few moments.

"Yes, I'm sure you're right," Wash mumbled. "We will carry on." But his words were not convincing. The obstacles past, present and future sometimes seemed too much to handle. The responsibility Washington carried was almost too much for one man. That is why I carried it with him.

That evening was a nightmare for us both. My husband's mental and physical distress was so great that I called on Dr. Smith to bring something to calm him.

"I am sorry, I do not have more to help you, Colonel," said Dr. Smith. "Our experience with treating

No Life But This

this mysterious disease is still limited." The doctor looked my way.

"What do you recommend?" I asked, feeling hopeless.

"The only thing I can offer is to urge you both to leave this area for the time being."

"I will not!" Wash shouted.

"I know you do not want to be away from the bridge," I said, taking Wash's hand, "but we have no choice. There is the Roebling house in Trenton. It is quiet and only a day's drive from here. I will arrange for a brief stay there. I promise I will continue to allow you your work and will use all of my abilities to communicate your wishes."

Every day, I was called upon to be nurse and private secretary to my husband. There were times I wished that I'd never heard of the Brooklyn Bridge, when I yearned to leave it all behind us and let someone else complete the work. There were nights, when I lay awake and stewed in my frustration over the tasks of the coming day, the letter writing, the clarifications, the time stolen from John and me. But the bridge had become my life's work as well, and if someone would have truly offered to take its burden from us I, most certainly, would have said no.

The family home in Trenton was tranquil and conducive to rest for both of us. John loved being outside, and examined the nearby woods almost every day, coming home with a netted butterfly, a captured dragonfly, a stone for Wash's collection, or a stick he'd turned into a play rifle. I, too, loved the serene surroundings, so different from the bustle of Brooklyn. Despite the peace, at times I felt my endurance waver. It was frightening because there was so much more to accomplish in life than the work left to us by my father-in-law. In addition to writing all that Wash needed, I wrote in my journal daily, and sometimes compiled essays that were sent out to newspapers and magazines. Only two had been published. The concentration writing took at any level could be overwhelming.

Day after day, I marveled at my husband's ability to keep everything in his head while so far from the worksite, his sleeves rolled up, his pocket-watch on the table next to him. As his body continued to weaken, his mind seemed not to have been affected in any way. His concentration on daily matters was unyielding, and his recall for facts and details, perfect. For anyone to suggest otherwise was quite upsetting. He did all his calculations in his head as well. Once I secretly double-checked one of his mathematical equations, unable to imagine how he had done it without extensive paperwork. I was a bit humiliated to discover that he had been correct without my validation. Nevertheless, at times he was prepared to give up on the whole thing. He even attempted, at one point, to resign, but his resignation was rejected.

One of his engineers, Francis Collingwood, was reportedly suffering from exhaustion. Wash dictated this letter to me:

> *Regarding your health my counsel would be sit down and keep quiet....Above all don't let a fake ambition lead you on to undertaking tasks that will only break you down all the more. You are no doubt beginning to find out, as I*

have found long ago, that nervous diseases are as intractable as they are incurable, and only through mental rest of all the faculties and especially the emotions can they even be palliated on the slightest degree.

"Please read that back to me, dear."

After his corrections and approval, John and I took a carriage to the post office almost every morning. Not only did this routine secure Wash as the continuing chief engineer, but it kept me as close as possible to the everyday workings of the bridge.

Unfortunately, even the distance between the bridge and Trenton did not prevent my husband from great distress over the least little thing. The newspapers constantly made wild conjectures about who was actually managing the day-to-day work of the project, often ignoring Washington's ongoing contributions. They even suggested that it was I, Emily Warren Roebling, who was the chief engineer, possibly because the correspondence was always in my handwriting.

There was an article in the *New York Times* that Wash insisted I read aloud to him.

HOW THE WIFE OF THE BROOKLYN BRIDGE ENGINEER HAS ASSISTED HER HUSBAND.

While so much has been written about the Brooklyn Bridge and those who have had a share either in planning or building it, there remains one whose services have not been publicly acknowledged. Since her husband's unfortunate illness Mrs. Roebling has filled his position as chief of the engineering staff, says a gentleman of their city well acquainted with the family. As soon as Mr.

Roebling was stricken with that peculiar fever which has since protracted him, Mrs. Roebling applied herself to the study of engineering, and she succeeded so well that in a short time she was able to assume the duties of chief engineer. Such an achievement is something remarkable. When meeting with bidders for steel and ironwork they were greatly surprised when Mrs. Roebling sat down with them, and by her knowledge of engineering helped them out with their patterns and cleared away difficulties that had for weeks been puzzling their brains.

"Well, dear wife, I believe it is time for me to resign," he said, grinning.

"Even though I did meet with the bidders last month, I hardly think that I solved all of their problems. Someone is exaggerating a wee bit," I replied.

"Just a *wee* bit though," Wash said.

"Does it bother you that I am given credit for your work?"

"No," he said pensively. "I believe we are equals in this endeavor, if you must know."

"I cannot imagine another man on earth who would be able to say such a thing."

"Maybe it's time for intelligent, capable women like you to be given the recognition they deserve," my husband said looking directly into my eyes.

"I continue to be reminded of why I married you, Colonel Roebling."

Chapter 15

Weeping may endure for a night, but joy cometh in the morning.
                                                    Psalm 30:18-19

As the seasons changed, so did my demeanor. The snow was relentless and often kept us housebound. One of my dark spells came about during that long Trenton winter. Throughout my life, they came like a ghost in my head every so often. If the days were too similar, too gloomy, if there was little to look forward to, I fell into a period of murkiness, blackness—a garden with nothing blooming, a shape-shifter in my own skin. Mealtime was a chore; sleep was elusive. My brain lost its normal functions of concentration and activity, as if cotton stuffing filled my head.

As much as I thrived on helping my husband, I became troubled by what my own life was, what I was to do with it. Only having one child left me the opportunity for too much pondering. We were fortunate to have household help and a nanny several days a week, but that left me time to ruminate about things that could not be controlled. My natural state was one of optimism and cheerfulness, so these spells were most upsetting. I was a proud woman, and liked to keep up appearances as a strong, capable female, so I never discussed these periods with anyone. My leaden pride insisted I would be fine in my own time. Washington often observed the changes in me, but seemed unable to offer any sympathy or help. Other times, he was so involved in his work that he hardly noticed.

A dark spell was like not being alive, but walking around in the world with no feeling. I looked at my son and did not feel the rush of love that normally flooded my heart. Staying in bed was preferable to rising with my usual exuberance for the day. I didn't know what to call it, but I noticed that it affected me more when there were many days of dreary skies, rain, or snow.

I awakened one night, and could not return to sleep, so I wrapped my robe around me and tiptoed down the stairs. I sat by the window and watched the halo of the moon cast lavender shadows about me. The mantle of purple sky held millions of stars that Washington loved to gaze at through his telescope. They appeared as little blinking messages to me. It was then, in the quiet, my lungs hollow, my mind a vacuum, that I heard the voice for the first time; *"There is more, there is more...."* My head jerked behind me as if a human presence were there. This voice—where did it come from? What did it mean? Was God speaking to me, reassuring me that there was more to my life than this despondency? I feared my brain was sick, and told no one about it.

"Dear, what is wrong with you? You don't seem like yourself at all these past days," Wash commented one morning as I tended to his dressing needs. I took a moment to respond, and he waited patiently.

"Do you remember after John was born? I couldn't seem to find joy in my new motherhood."

"I'm not sure what you are referring to. You had an extraordinarily long period of convalescence. The doctors in Germany feared for your life in the days following John's birth."

"I'm not speaking of that. It was a time of unexplained sorrow." I slid him into his crimson bed jacket and brought him a washing basin.

"I don't understand, Emily. I am aware that you are not fond of winter weather, but what have you to be unhappy about? Our son is healthy and strong. Is it caring for me that distresses you so?"

"No, I never want you to think that. I do not have the words to expound on the matter, or to justify myself."

"I do not ask you to justify anything. I just want you to be as you were."

"To be as I was? What was that, precisely?" I could not bear any more conversation, and abruptly left the room.

"Emily, please return!" I heard Wash call out as I moved down the long hallway away from him, away from expectations and explanations. I sent for the nurse to complete Wash's toilet for the day, and I retired to my study, but accomplished nothing. A shameful waste of a day, regardless of the morose conditions of the weather outside my window. In the afternoon, I retired to my bed and slept fitfully, ignoring my husband's requests for my presence. John was happily occupied in his playroom with the nanny and a new friend from the neighborhood. I was unneeded, unnecessary. In the evening shadows, I rose and went to my husband.

"I'm here," I said flatly.

"Emily, I have a suggestion. Something that might lift your spirits although I still don't understand your dolefulness. Why don't you visit G.K.? He seems to be the one person who can cheer you."

"G.K.," I murmured. My eldest brother was, indeed, a loving and bold presence in my life. Of all my siblings, he and I shared a special bond. We had not seen each other for months, although we consistently corresponded.

"What if I arrange a visit? You can return when you are feeling yourself again."

"Yes, myself again. I see that I am not needed here."

"That's not what I am saying," Wash started.

"G.K. is toiling along the Mississippi River at present. His reassignment to the Corps of Engineers has him working on the railroads. I very much doubt that he has the time to stop his work for a visit from his pitiful little sister just to raise her spirits."

I started to leave the room in frustration, but turned back to Wash and said, "Thank you for your concern. I'm sure I will be well soon. Be myself, as you say."

When spring finally bloomed around us, my melancholy and spirits lifted. I looked up into the untouchable heavens and remembered that I had breath and life. Gazing into the eyes of my son I saw God staring back at me. When we sat down to our meals, I gave thanks for the abundance of nourishment. There was not a single reason to be sad, and I was greatly relieved that the dark spell seemed to be over.

That summer, we took John on walks around the property and enjoyed carriage rides with too much food packed in our picnic basket. There was a small pond at the western end of the property where we could sit amid the beauty and watch our son explore. The sunshine was like a tonic, a reminder of the light in my world. We spread out a blanket in the shade of a tree by the river and enjoyed the peace and quiet together.

"What are you reading?"

"I'm reading about Sorosis," I answered, not wanting to be disturbed at that moment.

"Sorosis? I'm familiar with the botanical term. When did you begin botanical studies?"

"I studied botany in school, but this is the name of a women's club. I believe it is meant to refer to the Greek term for sister in this connotation."

"Sorority?"

"Possibly. Mrs. Jane Cunningham Croly initiated the group several years ago. I am just now becoming aware of its noble mission."

"What would that be?" Wash was carrying on the conversation, but clearly not taking it seriously. He had neglected to bring his own reading material and now intended to interrupt my reading time for his entertainment.

"Ask yourself how many organizations are composed purely of men. I'm sure you would be a member of many if your health had permitted you. Now ask yourself why women should not have professional clubs of their own. Do you think they would be admitted into the men's organizations?"

"Of course not; they're strictly for men."

"Yet you don't think women should have the same comradery?"

"Emily, dear, calm down! I said no such thing, did I? You are assuming too much."

"Oh, yes, I suppose you're right. I just thought you'd find it frivolous as so many men do."

"You still haven't told me its mission."

"It began with a woman attempting to infiltrate the all-male New York Press Club. Oh, listen to this, I think I remember reading about this in the *Times*."

"Mrs. Croly and a group of Sorosis members attempted to disrupt an all-male luncheon at Delmonico's by conducting a women's club meeting at the same location, albeit in a private room. Since women were not permitted to dine at Delmonico's without a male escort, it was considered scandalous. Delmonico's calmed the storm and promoted their progressive reputation by offering to host the Sorosis anniversary meeting every year!"

"That sounds…well, interesting. Something you want to be involved in?"

"The bridge, while a worthy task, has taken me away from so much I should have known about the world of women. According to this article, Sorosis has continued to gain influence over the past few years. Isn't that wonderful?"

"Hmm, hmm," my husband rudely started to hum in my presence.

"It says here that some men have even tried to join! Oh, listen to this. This was the response to those men:"

"We willingly admit, of course, that the accident of your sex is on your part a misfortune and not a fault; nor do we wish to arrogate anything to ourselves because we had the good fortune to be born women. Sorosis is too young for the society of gentlemen and must be allowed time to grow. By and by, when it has reached a proper age, say twenty-one, it may ally itself with the Press Club or some other male organization of good character and standing.

But for years to come its reply to all male suitors must be, 'Principles, not men.'"

I could not contain my laughter. Wash just looked in the distance as if he did not want to be associated with me. John came running up from his explorations to see what the fuss was about.

"Oh, your mother is just having a wonderful time all by herself," Wash told our son.

Diane Vogel Ferri

Chapter 16

With its princes of the lofty wire, the Brooklyn Bridge is now the cheapest, the most entertaining, and best-attended circus in the world.

The New York Tribune

On August 14, a telegram arrived in Trenton:

> THE FIRST ROPE REACHED ITS POSITION AT ELEVEN AND ONE HALF O CLOCK. WAS RAISED IN SIX MINUTES.

The first giant cables for the suspension bridge were in place. We were thrilled, and the rest of Brooklyn was as well. We marveled at the photographs in the newspapers. It was starting to look like a bridge, and crowds gathered daily to watch the progress.

"Have the papers arrived, Em?" Wash called from the dining room.

"Yes, here they are. I, too, am anxious to read about yesterday's event."

"Where is my magnifying glass, Emily?"

"It's right in front of you."

Wash furiously paged through *The New York Times* until he found what he was looking for. Our Master

Mechanic E. F. Farrington had decided to make the first crossing of the East River by using the bridge cables while riding in a boatswain's chair that was tied to an endless wire rope called "the traveler." We had heard that ten thousand people had watched from both shores.

"What does it say?"

"It says: *He went swinging out over the housetops between the anchorage and the tower, Farrington freed himself from the rope about his chest and stood up on the seat. He lifted his hat in response to the crowds below!*" Wash looked up from the paper.

"That man is daft, I say!"

"Go on! How I wish we'd been there," I said.

"People were running through the streets, shouting and cheering. He waved and blew them kisses. Sailing steadily all the while, his course was nearly horizontal at first, then he was beyond the sag and climbing sharply, almost straight up, a coat-flapping form that looked small and birdlike. In a little less than seven minutes after leaving the Brooklyn tower, he made a flawless landing on top of the New York tower. Then with no delay whatever, he was back in his seat again and on his way on the last leg of the trip down to the New York anchorage."

"Wonderful!" I said, "Let's see what this report says. I searched through the next paper in our pile.

"This one quotes Farrington as saying, "*The ride gave me magnificent view, and such pleasing sensations as probably I shall never experience again.*"

"It seems his escapade was worth it," Wash said, relaxing back in his seat. "In essence, he has proven the safety and security of the bridge. I know Farrington would not ask any worker to do something he would not himself do. He has proven to the public that the bridge will work. After all the years of doubts and fear, it will work." Wash put the paper down pensively. I wondered if he was feeling as left out as I that day.

We spent those years in Trenton writing our daily correspondence to Wash's assistants and watching our boy grow up to be a fine young man of ten. He was a constant delight and a blessing to us. As he grew, he became interested in our work for the bridge and attempted to learn all he could. Wash never suggested that the complexity of the engineering was above him, just as he never did with me.

"What is the definition of civil engineering, John?" asked Wash at lunch.

"Design, construction, and maintenance of the physical and naturally built environments," John peered up at his father and saw approval.

"Very good, young man. What types of things do you see in Trenton that have required civil engineering, then?"

"The roads, bridges, and…. railroads?"

"Yes! Well done, son," Wash clapped him on the back.

"Oh, Wash, stop testing the boy; he's only ten. Let him decide what he wants to learn," I said, smiling at my two men.

"I don't mind, Mama. I want to be an engineer just like Papa someday," said my handsome little boy.

"Well, you have plenty of time to think about that, don't you? How about returning to the school work that needs to be done for tomorrow?"

"I hate reading those stories!"

"How could you possibly hate to read about Tom Sawyer? A boy just like you!" I said.

"He's not like me at all. Why, Tom Sawyer doesn't live in a big house with servants and nice clothes. He gets into trouble all the time—and he lies!" John exclaimed.

"Well, that is true, You are a good boy, but at least I can see that you have been reading it. How about finishing your chapters and I will bring dessert to you in your study?" I said.

"All right," John said dejectedly. Nevertheless, he left the room and obeyed me as usual.

First Presbyterian Church in Trenton was not as famous or well-attended as Plymouth Church, but we looked forward to the services each Sunday. Going to church was a reason to dress up for a change and get Wash out of the house when he was agreeable. The light-filled sanctuary and the glorious pipe organ never failed to be inspiring for the week ahead.

Our pastor, Reverend John Minton, was not the dynamic speaker we'd had with Henry Beecher, and sometimes my mind wandered from the message of the day. I had a deep religious foundation, but as an adult, I still questioned some of its teachings, although my basic beliefs stayed strong. The Reverend was reading from II Corinthians 12:7:

> *"And lest I should be exalted above measure through the abundance of the revelations, there was given to me a thorn in the flesh, the messenger of Satan to buffet me, lest I should be exalted above measure."*

The dark spells were my thorn in the flesh, a ponderous weight to carry just as Paul himself had carried his unnamed burden. While being blessed with an abundant life, maybe, in the abyss of my sadness, the Lord was reminding me not to exalt myself, to remember humility.

> *"For this thing I besought the Lord thrice, that it might depart from me. And he said unto me, My grace is sufficient for thee; for my strength is made perfect in weakness."*

I had been blessed with an enlightened mind, a passionate heart, a love of learning along with impatience for the future. Nothing was enough for me, but here Paul was saying that it was wrong to exalt oneself above all measure, and that God Himself should be enough for each day. How could I balance the God-given gifts of my womanhood and be content in the knowledge that in weakness, we find strength?

"Em, you are unusually quiet today," Wash commented on our way home from church.

"The scripture this morning is still speaking to me, I think."

"Yes, the thorn in the flesh. I wonder what it was that Paul struggled with. Do you think it was of the body or the mind?" Wash asked.

"I believe they are one in the same. Either one causes an equal battle within oneself, do they not?"

"Yes, that is true."

"Remember when I spoke to the American Society of Civil Engineers a few years ago?"

"Yes, of course. You were the first woman to speak to a men's group such as that. They were all impressed with your knowledge of stress analysis, cable construction, and calculating catenary curves, I remember."

"But what was that for? What is the purpose of my knowledge?"

"I don't understand your question. You are asking what the purpose of knowledge is?"

"What its purpose for a woman is."

"Oh, Em, I don't know."

Sometimes my poor husband wearied of my constant questions and ruminating. I let the discussion go, but wondered why I had been promised more.

Chapter 17

I can live alone, if self-respect and circumstance require me to do so. I need not sell my soul to buy bliss. I have an inward treasure born in me, which can keep me alive if all extraneous delights should be withheld, or offered only at a price I cannot afford to give.

Charlotte Bronte

1878

It was to be three years before Wash had his first look at the bridge again. Train travel was too stressful, so we arranged to take a gentle journey down the Hudson by canal boat. The voluptuous colors of autumn, the iridescence of the sky, flocks of birds pealing past us was thrilling. There was a cacophony of boat horns and whistles as we entered the bay and turned into the East River. The cities I had missed so dearly were swollen with activity and life. The sea spray, the varying smells, from rotting fish to salty sweetness, all revived my senses. Then Wash had his first glance of his life's work.

"It looks precisely as I had imagined it would," Wash said happily, clutching his hands to his heart. "Each day I think about the progress and have tried to make a picture in my head of what it would look like, and here it is, at last!"

"It's spectacular, and will be even more so in the near future," I said, sharing his glory.

"The towers being almost complete is a thrill, isn't it Em? The anchorages are built and the cables set in position! I must meet with the inspectors immediately! Oh, the granite is magnificent, isn't it?"

"Wash, control yourself! Calm down. This excitement will set you into a tailspin!"

"How can I be calm when I am viewing the work of the past eight years!"

"You deserve all the joy you are feeling right now," I said taking his hand in mine.

"So do you, my dear. This will raise my hopes and spirit immensely."

We moved in temporarily with Gouverneur and his family on West 50th Street while preparing our new house on Columbia Heights. It was a joy to be near my brother again. I could not have been prouder of him. He was a graduate of West Point, had been a general in the Civil War, and was a New York state assemblyman. G. K. was a man of great generosity, and it was because of him that I had a fine education. He always said if he were to have a choice of ways to spend his money, he would rather devote it to advancing his brothers and sisters than anything else. That generosity was surely appreciated after we lost my mother and father at such a young age.

Wash served under G. K., and was a bit intimidated by how formidable a man he was. When we decided to marry and my father was no longer alive to give his blessing, Wash determined that it was my brother whose approval he would seek for my hand in marriage, but he was a bit frightened of the prospect. As I expected, G. K. was wholly in favor of my happiness, and gifted Washington with a fine sword, saying, "Long may he wave!"

G. K. had a distinguished career, with one very sad chapter. A few months after Wash and I were married my brother was still serving in the Civil War. He had grown weary, overworked, and engrossed in details he should have left to subordinates. My brother was commanding the V Corps, one of the most famous infantry units in the Federal Army. Ulysses Grant had put V Corps and my brother under the leadership of Major General Philip Sheridan. Unknown to my brother, Grant told Sheridan to remove Gouverneur if needed because G.K. was having some emotional difficulties.

One day, G.K. received conflicting orders on which route to take. He marched his men all night in the rain, and they arrived late at their destination of Five Forks. Sheridan was enraged and blamed G.K. for delaying the attack that was to have taken place. In his rage, he ordered that G.K. be relieved of his command immediately. All of my brother's subordinates were quick to defend him as an excellent and loyal leader, but to no avail. G.K. resigned his position, and was demoted to the rank of major. It crushed G.K.'s career, as well as his spirit: a humiliating experience for such a distinguished general.

After Five Forks, G.K. was put in command of defenses at Petersburg, and then to Memphis to command the Department of Mississippi. After the war, he stayed in the army as an engineer and on the commission for the Union Pacific Railroad. He also assisted in surveying the Gettysburg battlefield where he had valiantly fought.

Although he had many responsibilities and reasons to be proud, my brother never fully recovered from the incident at Five Forks. It affected his health and his finances, and he became more and more incapacitated in his duties. He obsessed over his desire to have his name cleared and regain good standing in the army once again. But after the war, Grant was a powerful, popular man and no one would cross him. Wash and I supported G.K. in every way possible including financially.

The two most important men in my life had suffered great misfortunes and hardships, which was an ever-present heartbreak for me. It made me constantly question why such awful things had happened to such fine men as my husband and brother.

The school that I attended through my brother's generosity had two mottoes: *Nothing is so strong as gentleness and nothing so gentle as real strength.* And: *Be who you are and be that well.* I gained understanding of both truisms by knowing and loving G.K. Warren and Washington Roebling.

All three Roeblings were happy to be near the bridge again, although my brother's house did not afford Wash a view of the bridge. Wash's emotional state was mostly tranquil although his physical deterioration remained. He had little spare time, but set himself to learning Danish and Swedish to better understand what the Europeans were doing with steel as it might apply to the bridge.

It was a bit crowded and noisy at the Warren house, as John and his three cousins enjoyed playing together. It did my heart good to see John with other children although they were some years older. It was awkward living with my sister-in-law Charlotte, though. We had never been able to forge a close relationship with each other. She seemed to view me as an anomaly. She did not understand how I could involve myself in the interests typically held by men. She raised her children with more stern discipline than Wash and I did with John.

My brother, although a very good, attentive father, seemed to leave the discipline and training of the children to Charlotte. During our time at his home, I recognized the same drive and ambition in him that I saw in myself. I pondered our upbringing and the influence of our parents, yet, of all my siblings, G.K. and I were the only ones born with the need to accomplish so much in our lives. It was still a conundrum to me, and my relationship with Charlotte, or the lack of it, reminded me of the dearth of women friends in my life.

Fortunately, we were only to be there for a short time, as we did not want to take advantage of their kindness and generosity.

Mary and I kept up our friendship from afar. I wrote to her at her cousin's address frequently, and we sent her monthly gifts of money to help her get by, but were not told of her actual whereabouts. She only mentioned the gifts in her letters once. Perhaps it was hard to accept help. Young Bridget had taken a job as a nanny, and that helped the family. I regretted not being in Brooklyn to be a better friend.

On a blustery gray afternoon, Mary O'Connell knocked on the door and was let in by the house maid. John ran to the study to find me and tell me of her visit.

"Mary, my dear, it's wonderful to see you," I opened my arms and attempted to embrace her, but her arms hung limply at her sides, her face wan and devoid of feeling.

"Hello, I heard you had come to live with your brother. I just came to tell you we have returned."

"Where have you been? I have not even been able to extend my condolences over Dennis's untimely passing."

"We've been to the O'Connell farm in Monroesville, where Dennis was buried. His sister has been caring for us since the accident."

"The accident?" I said, "You mean...."

Mary's eyes filled with tears, and I stopped.

"I'm so sorry for your great loss. How are the children?"

"They are fine. We are fine. I only came to tell you of our return. I'm sure you wondered where we'd gone."

"Yes, I had been worried. Is there anything I can do for you? How will you get on now that you are...."

"A widow? I'm a widow! A woman with five children and no husband, and all because of that bridge!" Mary began to wail loudly. I had not any idea how to respond to her grief, and felt powerless. There was no reason to argue about the bridge or Dennis's demise or anything else with this desolate woman. Mary wrapped her thin shawl around her shoulders and moved to the door. She turned.

"I will always be grateful for your help, but we can no longer be associated. Good-bye, Emily. I wish you well."

I did not move to stop her from leaving, but felt numb and strangely unmoved. I had done all I could for the O'Connells, and now I was being dismissed as a friend. All of the letters, monetary gifts, and concern had not changed the divergent circumstances of our lives. If Mary wanted to blame the Roeblings for her husband's death, if that made her grief more bearable, I would not attempt to change her mind.

Contemplating our last encounter made me even more determined to help in the fight for women's rights and equality. Mary suffered at the hands of her husband and there were no laws to help her. Women were considered second-class citizens. In Europe, they, too, were fighting for suffrage and the ability for a woman to own property. Even if Mary went on to be employed and earn money, she would not be allowed to purchase her own home without it being in a man's name.

Knowing Mary O'Connell made me remember that I lived a privileged life; a life within a family and marriage that valued my intelligence and contributions. Mary was seen as nothing but a birther of babies. Her husband had had no respect for her beyond that. My conviction was that women should be allowed to choose how many children they wanted, how many times their bodies would carry a child and struggle through the difficulties and pain of childbirth. Someday this would come to pass.

Victoria Woodhull had done her best in her effort to have the Fourteenth Amendment apply to women to secure the vote as well as the right to practice law. How was it that women, who give birth to all the people of this country, were not considered citizens? What would the outcome of Rev. Beecher's trial would have been if women were lawyers and judges? The state of Iowa was the first to allow women lawyers, and Helen McGill was the first woman to be granted a PhD at The Boston University—a start. I continued to subscribe to the weekly *Women's Journal*, whose mission was "devoted to the interests of woman—to her educational, industrial, legal and political equality, and especially to her right of suffrage."

Suffrage must include property rights for all women, and greater access to professions for women, as well as voting rights. Women should be the executors of their own money, giving to charity while they were able and assured that proper use be made of it.

Julia Ward Howe wrote in the *Women's Journal*: "The strokes of the pen need deliberation as much as the sword needs swiftness." Her glorious "Battle Hymn of the Republic," which we often sang in church, stood as a monumental achievement of a woman's keen mind and heart. Mrs. Howe was an inspiration to me. She fought not only for the right to vote, but for women who were less valued in their marriages. She wrote that her own husband thought nothing of her mind and ideas. Imagine! Even though Wash was sometimes oblivious to certain needs of mine, he treated me with equity. I continued to send my essays to various publications for women and men alike in the hope of also becoming an inspiration someday. Mrs. Howe's "Mother's Day Proclamation" was inspiring:

Arise then...women of this day!
Arise, all women who have hearts!
Whether your baptism be of water or of tears!
Say firmly:
We will not have questions answered by irrelevant agencies,
Our husbands will not come to us, reeking with carnage,
For caresses and applause.
Our sons shall not be taken from us to unlearn
All that we have been able to teach them of charity, mercy and
    patience.
We, the women of one country,
Will be too tender of those of another country
To allow our sons to be trained to injure theirs.

From the bosom of a devastated Earth a voice goes up with
Our own. It says: "Disarm! Disarm!
The sword of murder is not the balance of justice."
Blood does not wipe out dishonor,
Nor violence indicate possession.
As men have often forsaken the plough and the anvil
At the summons of war,
Let women now leave all that may be left of home
For a great and earnest day of counsel.
Let them meet first, as women, to bewail and commemorate the
  dead.
Let them solemnly take counsel with each other as to the means
Whereby the great human family can live in peace...

Each bearing after his own time the sacred impress, not of
  Caesar,
But of God -
In the name of womanhood and humanity, I earnestly ask
That a general congress of women without limit of nationality,
May be appointed and held at someplace deemed most
  convenient
And the earliest period consistent with its objects,
To promote the alliance of the different nationalities,
The amicable settlement of international questions,
The great and general interests of peace.

Chapter 18

My own sex, I hope, will excuse me if I treat them like rational creatures, instead of flattering their fascinating graces, and viewing them as if there were in a state of perpetual childhood, unable to stand alone.

Mary Wollenstonecraft

Our new house at 110 Columbia Heights was closer to the bridge than Hicks Street and sat parallel with the East River. It was a beautiful three-story red brick home built before the war in the Greek Revival style, with a deep garden in back extending out over the top of a carriage house and stable built below the brink of the bluff, fronting on Furman Street beside the wharves. Our neighbors were very fine people: such as the inventor Dr. Edward Squibb, the Pierreponts, and the Lows. Mr. Thomas Shearman, the lawyer who defended Henry Beecher in 1875, lived a few houses down the street. Moses Beach, the publisher and pillar of Plymouth Church, lived next door. Henry Bowen, who had done much to promote the Beecher scandal and whose deceased wife was said to have been another female interest of the famous preacher, lived just up the street in a large white mansion with a two-story portico. Henry Beecher lived in the next block.

Across from us stood a row of three-storied brick houses with brick sidewalks lining the street. Our home was spacious and airy, with arched doorways and large plate-glass windows to let in the sunshine I so craved. We had additional rooms for John to study and play in. The large, light-filled library was my favorite room of the house. The bay window in the back of the house looked out upon a lovely courtyard, and beyond that, the river, harbor, and the city all were in our view—and, of course, the magnificent bridge.

The bay window upstairs was the portal for Wash to see the daily progress of his bridge, and the view was magnificent. He felt fortunate to be able to have such a perch to see the world, but sometimes envied my ability to come and go freely. I could take walks in good weather and visit with our neighbors or follow the river banks until I was too weary to go on. It had always been natural for me to live by water, growing up in the upper Hudson River valley, each river being grand and powerful.

Living close to the river allowed us to view all sorts of weather. All we needed to do was look out the window to see whether the waters were calm or churning. First thing every morning, Wash could determine whether his crews would be safe working that day. I loved hearing the boat horns and whistles day or night. At sunset, the water looked as if diamonds were scattered across its surface. The river constantly changed color, from black as night, to blue as the sky. When aroused by mighty winds, it took on an exotic turquoise hue.

Soon there was an actual path from Brooklyn to New York City. It was a temporary footbridge that hung sixty feet above the river. The public and the newspapers were anxious to investigate the new development. We feared that it might be used unwisely and with great danger, so a sign was placed at the visitor entrance:

> SAFE FOR ONLY 25 MEN AT ONE TIME.
> DO NOT WALK CLOSE TOGETHER NOR RUN,
> JUMP OR TROT. BREAK STEP!
> W. A. Roebling, Engr. in Chief

On the morning of Wash's birthday, a messenger arrived to inform us that two young women were crossing the footbridge alone and with great recklessness, causing quite a fuss. It was reported that they were intent on waving to those below, and seemed unaffected by the height and the wind whipping their scarves and skirts about. That event seemed to set off a flurry of visitors and more than one hundred people also crossed the same day. The consensus was that women should not even attempt to cross such a precarious walkway. Silly, I thought.

"I'm glad that the bridge is finally a place of enjoyment, instead of criticism and ridicule, but we must do something to prevent another tragedy," Wash said.

"I agree, but what?"

"Em, please write a message to Henry Murphy informing him that, henceforth, visitors must apply for a pass. This will ensure that only a reasonable number of people will be on the footbridge at one time."

"That's an excellent idea!"

A few days later, wires started crossing the great divide and my husband was back at his bay window to watch with a pair of strong field glasses. The progress was going exceptionally well, and people were coming from all over the world to see and cross the bridge although its completion was still years away.

Most visitors reported a thrill at being among the first to cross. Some fainted or turned back after looking down, others were bold enough to bring their babies and young children. One reporter commented on how fearless the women were to cross. Rubbish! Why should women be any more fearful than men hanging over the tumultuous East River with nothing below them but death?

"People from as far away as Australia and New Zealand have walked the footbridge," Mr. Murphy reported to us. "My days are filled with giving out passes. Elderly couples, people with babies, preachers, and children have all attempted the walk. Some of them turn back in fear after a few yards, some wave and shout as they cross, hoping to gain attention from loved ones below. One man told me he was a foreigner. When I asked where he was from, he said, New York!"

"There are many people who have never before crossed the river, if you can imagine that," Wash said.

"Have you made the journey, Henry?" I asked.

"Well, ma'am, I started out, but when I looked down, I decided that I was needed here and had better not take the chance!" Wash and I both laughed.

"There have been no accidents, but, several times people have frozen in terror halfway across and had to be rescued. The most interesting thing is the bravery of so many women."

I opened my mouth to say something, looked over at Wash, and closed it.

"The only one I've denied access to was a woman who wanted to ride her horse across!" Murphy said. "Things are going extremely well, Colonel. Never better.

The network of wires going across makes it look like a real bridge, and everyone's spirits are high because of that."

"Good to hear it, Henry. I appreciate your eight years of dedication. There is still much to do, though."

"Oh yes, I know, sir. I wouldn't miss it. Oh, one more thing, Colonel."

"Yes?"

"If it's all right with you, I would like to give permission for two of your Plymouth Church musicians to take their coronets out to the center of the bridge. They have requested to do so, and would like to play 'Rock of Ages', 'Jesus, Lover of My Soul,' and 'Old Hundred.' Sort of a blessing of the bridge."

"That's a wonderful idea," I said, "Wash, isn't that just the thing to appease the public over requesting passes for the footbridge?"

"Yes, maybe if we open the windows and the wind is just right, I will be able to hear them." Wash replied wearily.

Many of our evenings were filled with discussion of the day's false reports and rumors about the activities at the bridge. In September, a man almost fell off and workers caught him. Wash decided that the public's enjoyment in being able to travel the small walkway was not worth any more deaths or injuries, so the footbridge was closed.

In October, Henry Beers, a spokesman for the Council of Political Reform, called for having the bridge construction stopped altogether. He deemed it a waste of public money and hazardous to navigation on the river. There was a big fight between stakeholders and the public reported in the newspapers over those accusations. Then the *Eagle* wasted paper and everyone's time reporting new and imaginative ways one could commit suicide on the bridge!

There were constant reports of Wash's death, or that he was near death. The Brooklyn *Union and Arbus* wrote of the "stupendous enterprise being wholly committed to a single brain, which is extremely liable at any moment to be stilled forever." Poor John came home crying because someone had told him his father was dying. It was a bit of a mystery how a man could be the chief engineer in control of such a massive undertaking from afar, yet it was taking place right before our eyes! True, my husband was in constant physical torment and completely dependent on me for all of his wishes and needs, but reports that I had taken over due to Wash's mental incapacities were false, of course. In reality, I was chief secretary and head nurse to the most brilliant man I had ever known. Yes, I understood the engineering and math, but how could I not, when it had been the center of our lives for so many years! I was blessed with a quick, retentive mind and a particular gift for mathematics, and I was always prepared to learn more. I could calm my husband's mind when worries and anxieties overtook him. Although I was sometimes outraged at his treatment by others, I tried not to let him see it, but used my wiles to keep peace among all those with whom he came in contact.

Shielding Wash from the public was a main concern, but we eventually consented to one reporter in the hope that some of the rumors would cease. I left the reporter and Wash alone to converse. In the paper the next day, Wash was quoted as saying, "At first I thought I would succumb, but I had a strong tower to lean upon, my wife, a woman of infinite tact and wise counsel."

"Emily, come see this," I heard my husband call from his seat in the bay window. The winter of 1878 was turning out to be one of the worst we had ever seen.

"Look at how the wind and snow are throwing the cables about." He pointed in the distance. "It's hard to see through the snow, but are those men down there?"

"Where, dear? Why would the men be out in this storm? Didn't you order them off today?"

"Of course I did, but still I believe I see them. Farrington must have allowed this. It looks as though they are attempting to secure the wires from flailing around in these gales."

"The footbridge is swinging like a pendulum. How will they be safe?"

There was nothing we could do but watch helplessly through the sheets of snow, hoping there would be no more fatalities. Just before Christmas, there had been another loss of life. A crack had developed in one of the arches about 25 feet above the street. The conscientious foreman noticed and ordered all the men off and out of the area, but a man standing below never heard the warning. He was buried in the rubble when it fell. There was great panic among the crowd of observers, and false reports that many men had died. But the loss of one life, of course, was too many.

Diane Vogel Ferri

Chapter 19

Every man seems to feel he's got the duties of two lifetimes to accomplish one, and so rushes, rushes, never has time to be companionable—never has time at his disposal to fool away on matters which do not involve dollars and duty and business.

Mark Twain

The morning after the wire incident, I awoke to the darkest day I had ever witnessed. It was as if the sun had not returned to the eastern sky, or the world had ceased to turn. The wind screamed like a woman giving birth, the trees bent to half their height. The glimmers of that familiar sense of hopelessness returned. What need did I have to arise from bed? Not one that I could think of except caring for Wash and John, and although those were, indeed, worthy, they did not seem like enough for the day. There was nothing for Emily, nothing but living out the role of a woman: to care for others. Why was I cursed with the ambitions of a man? My husband and his father had been driven to complete an enormous feat, and they were freely given all they needed in the world to accomplish it. Women were given minimal expectations and little else.

"Mama, why are you in the dark?" John had opened the door a crack and peered in.

"I am not feeling well. What do you need?"

"I don't need anything. I'm old enough to take care of myself."

"Well, why are you intruding on my rest, then?" As soon as those words left my mouth, I wished they would have gone unsaid. John started to close the door.

"Wait! Please come to your Mama, liebchen." I reached out a weak hand towards him.

"Would you like me to check on Papa today?" he whispered.

"You are such a kind young man. What would I do without you?" I attempted to smile at him as he stood in the light streaming in from the hallway. "If you would look in on Papa, I would be most appreciative."

"Yes, I will do that," he said. "I cannot go to school today. No one is out on the streets, and the snow has risen too high."

"Of course not. Then you must have a day of rest, too."

John quietly closed the door and I felt myself drifting back to sleep although I had slept soundly through the night. I suddenly realized that if the schools were closed and the streets were blocked, that there would be no nurse to visit Wash that day. I pulled myself out of bed as if my limbs weighed a thousand pounds and reached for the lamp. Its light hurt my eyes, and I covered them and bent my head as if to weep, but tears did not come. At times, crying was desirable, with the hope that tears would wash out the sadness, but even tears were elusive. I got to my feet and went to my husband. John was there, tending to his father as if he were a grown man, filling me with shame and pride all at once.

"There you are, dear. What a bleak morning it is!" Wash exclaimed.

"Yes, the bleakness of the sky reflects the dimness of my spirit, as well," I replied.

Neither John nor Wash said anything after that, confused at my mood changes. I left to complete my toilette and returned to sit by my husband and child and keep them company for the rest of the day.

I sometimes wondered if the mind could overcome the body in knowing that it must stay healthy. Women didn't have the privilege of being sick or having a day off from duties in the home or in motherhood. Even during monthly discomfort, we carried on and did not speak of our womanly burdens. Men had no such experience, and had great difficulty showing any compassion for our disabilities. When things were most chaotic and my boys needed me the most, I maintained a robust energy. But when things calmed down, such as after a holiday, I sometimes developed a chest cold or a sudden fatigue. Did my mind overrule my body until it was free to collapse? Was that always the millstone of being a woman?

That night as I lay in bed, I prayed for sleep that would not visit me. My brain felt wound into a spiral of negative thoughts and worries and bereft of anything useful. I attempted to recount the dimensions of the bridge towers that I had recently written down for Wash, or some other inane thing.

Just as my arms and legs began to relax from their tension, I heard the voice again. My body jerked under the sheets and I let out a small gasp. This time it said: *You are more, you are more....* I lay stiff and quiet in anticipation of hearing further or determining whether I had gone mad, but neither materialized. Strangely, the voice and its message soothed me and I fell into a peaceful sleep. In the morning, the sun returned to Brooklyn and so did the remnants of my spirit.

The brevity of life was so distressing to me. I constantly felt the urge to achieve my goals, and yet the years were gone like dreams. In the mirror I saw a face I'd never seen before and wondered how that had happened when I was unaware. It was a waste of time comparing myself with other women. My status in society was certain, and I tried to look my best to reflect the dignity of our family. I enjoyed the new styles of the day, and was lucky to be able to afford most of whatever my heart desired. Washington appreciated seeing me in new dresses and hats. He insisted that a chaperone join me when I took the ferry to New York.

New York continued to flourish and expand in ways good and bad. The poverty in the tenements and slums was appalling, especially in the immigrant neighborhoods like Chinatown, Little Italy, and along Mulberry Street: laundry hanging out of windows every Monday, wagons lining the roads with fruits and vegetables, filthy children playing in the streets. There were beggars everywhere, and I wondered what had become of their dream to make a better life?

Other areas of the city had become places for lewd entertainment in vaudeville and burlesque. One could view "movies" in black tents. I'd heard that one could see moving pictures of anything from Niagara Falls to the royal children in England! At least such entertainment was of some edification.

Then one could travel along Fifth Avenue and see the Vanderbilt mansion in its gaudy indulgence, and rows of the very wealthy homes where parties were the sole pastime. Once Wash and I went into town for the Easter Parade down Fifth Avenue to be among all the women in their enormous flowered hats and the men in their straw ones. It was enjoyable to be a part of it. Afterward, we had a delicious lunch at Delmonico's.

The city was frantic, with boys selling newspapers, trolleys, carriages drawn by neighing horses, and motormen shouting at each other to get out of the way. Street lamps had recently been installed, and large advertisements called billboards were everywhere you looked. We passed a building wall that advertised Heinz 57: *Good Things for the Table! Baked beans, India relish, tomato soup, sweet pickles!* The wall seemed to shout from above us.

The Roebling's lives stood somewhere between the tenements and Fifth Avenue, and that was satisfactory. It was not that I did not have a heart for the poor, but the need was so overwhelming. What could one person do?

Central Park was an oasis from the odious, loud city streets. We took a carriage into the park and allowed John to climb Belvedere Castle and wave from the tower while we watched from below. We made our way to the zoo, where John enjoyed the antics of the monkeys and an enormous black bear. Swans and geese populated the pond, kites flew, and toy boats floated lazily on the water.

Wash was not as enchanted with the excitement and energy of the city as John and me. He abided it for John's sake, but I went much more often to shop. Women were required to have an assistant if traveling alone into the city. The chaperone was left at the door or went to the smoking rooms, and the department stores were full of women in their glory, talking and laughing freely. Because men were scarce, it gave women a sense of independence if they were fortunate enough to have money and permitted to go into town. Ladies were expected to keep a handsome home and person, and stores such as Bloomingdale's and Macy's provided everything needed. These stores were the first place where women had the opportunity to be in charge of their day and their choices.

I always found something that appealed to me, although there were very few places to wear anything formal. Wash's incapacitated state left us unable to attend any formal affairs or symphony concerts. I missed those occasions, but would never leave Wash home alone just to please myself, although he wouldn't have minded.

I never considered myself a beautiful woman, but from our first meeting, my husband looked at me with the eyes of a man in love. As we grew older together, he did not see the gray pouches beneath my eyes, the deepening lines around my mouth, or the sagging under my chin. When we were in our bed, his hands caressed the very places I despised, the folds remaining on my stomach from childbirth, the imperfect curve of my jaw, the shapelessness of my arms. He never saw me as I saw myself. His first letter to me after we met said, *Your lips are like a perfect bow, your large brown eyes reflect a joy for life, the chestnut waves of your hair shine in the sun.* I was always taller than most women, only one inch shorter than my husband, but that allowed our bodies to fit together most wonderfully.

Before we married, we were both curious about the marriage bed and freely shared our thoughts on it. Wash had learned a great deal from a book called *Advice to*

Married People, which he wrote to me about frequently from the war.

My Dearest Em,

When I first kissed you, I knew there would be no end to my desire. I am utterly incapable of resisting your sweet kisses and your touch. My lips have not fully recovered from your attacks, and are in excellent fighting form to receive you. You ask how it was you came to pet me so much? Why, I always pretended it was such a bore to be kissed by you, so that you made it a point to give me twice as many, which was just what I was fishing for. You must not apply that rule, though, after we are married. I shall claim everything then, and bite you if you don't obey willingly.

Affectionately,
Washy

I was not shocked by my fiancée's directness, but a bit insulted that he assumed me to be naive. I had been raised in a home where no topics of discussion were off limits. I knew more about the matters of physical love than most other young unmarried women my age. I was unconcerned about the wedding night, and very much looked forward to it.

Dear Wash,

I see that your taste is perverted past all redemption; a good person gets tired of reading all piquant and racy books of the kind. I am prepared for true experience and intend to enjoy all manner of our relationship, just as I hope you will. I shall, however, constitute myself your purveyor in that line and get you anything you want; I want you to know as much in that line as I do. I am not ignorant in these matters, dear.

However, if you are to have your way after the wedding, then I believe I will have my way in all aspects of our wedding day. The plans are in motion. I know that as a Lieutenant Colonel, your mind is occupied with more important matters, so I assure you it will be a most magnificent day.

Affectionately,
Your Em

Dear Sweet Emily,

I never realized that I could love you so much, and I know after we are married I will love you all the more; it is a feeling that with me increases with the lapse of time. I assure you, it a great happiness to know that you fully possess the heart of another human being. The love we share in our bed will be equal to the love in my heart.

Your Washy

Although Wash and I worked out ways to maintain our intimacies after his illness, there were no more children. While we were in Germany, I had a bad fall right before John's birth. Thank God, our baby was unharmed, but after his birth, I bled terribly for more than a month. Lying in bed nursing John, I would feel a river of blood seeping out of me, through my bedclothes, and onto the linens. The conflation of emotions was tumultuous as I looked down at the fragile beauty in my arms, feeling the very life drain from me at the same time. I prayed that John would not be motherless. We sought out several doctors, and all of them told me I would most likely have no more children.

It was then that I fell into my first dark spell. I was told it was due to the strain of the birth and losing hope for another child, yet I felt a failure at motherhood from the beginning. It is the happiest of occasions and a great miracle from the Lord to create a new life, and I felt nothing for a time. I did not cry or smile, but stared at my son as if he were a little stranger, an alien at my breast. Wash helped with the baby, and hired a nurse to assist us. He said little about my tenebrous demeanor, but sat with me every evening, reading me poetry or my favorite stories from the Bible.

One night he read Proverbs 13:12, *Hope deferred makes the heart sick.* I held that verse in my heart and clung to its message, believing that I would be well enough to mother my son, knowing I was not alone in my misery. Our trip home across the Atlantic was almost unbearable, physically and emotionally, but soon the dark spell relieved itself of me, and I was elated at every sight and coo from my baby.

Chapter 20

His spotless integrity and high sense of humor are unquestionable. His great skill as an engineer is established and his devotion to this work has been attended by the sacrifice of his health.

Daily State Gazette

Many times, I had to be mother and father for our son. Living near the water gave John a curiosity for life in the seas. Much to my dismay I had to pass on my skills in fishing to John. I grew up in a home where girls were encouraged to have a variety of experiences. My parents were of the mind that children should be exposed to many things, and be able to choose which they would prefer to pursue. I learned to fish, but did not enjoy the sight of the poor creatures being tortured. I much preferred riding horses.

Of course, Wash should have been the one to teach John where to dig up worms, how to force them onto the hook, and remove the piercing from the pitiful fish, but that was not to be. Nevertheless, my fondest hope for my son was that he would be like his father in many ways—strong, capable, humble, and kind. Wash wanted him to follow in his footsteps and his father's, and be an engineer.

John had intelligence, but I wanted him to make up his own mind about such things.

Although we had help, I was still the primary one to care for Wash and manage the household. I carried on, dark spells notwithstanding. I learned to arise from bed, whether or not my day held any enjoyment for me. In my youth I was quite the horsewoman, but that went by the wayside after our marriage. There was just no time or opportunity. All women sacrifice their own passions at times for the ones they love, no matter how privileged their lives may be. There was no reason to resent my husband, but one could become distraught over the treatment of women in general in our society. Writing and women's club readings helped me make the choice to be happy in between crises concerning the bridge.

Each morning, I took our six daily newspapers to Wash and read them aloud. His eyesight had been terribly affected by the disease, but he wanted to be constantly informed about the world and what the New York papers were writing about the bridge. When there were articles and quotes about the bridge or about us, I cut them out and pasted them in scrapbooks. Reporters somehow thought they understood our situation, and often commented on what it must be like up here, sitting near this bay window each day for my husband, but they did not even come close to the agony he suffered in his seclusion. There was never any empathy for the torture he would feel watching his own project arise from a window. Fortunately, he had a powerful telescope that enabled him to see great details of the bridge. He carefully watched the activities of every worker, and could even identify them by name. He sent messages when there was something not being done to his standards. Although his vision was poor for reading, it excelled for distance, and he often put the telescope aside and simply watched. Did the reporters imagine that he was just lazy and wanted to stay in bed all day? If he'd had any ability whatsoever to travel to the site and conduct business, he most certainly would have done so, but his nervous system was as fragile as his physical body.

"That is hogwash!" he shouted, as I read aloud about Abraham Miller's suit to stop the bridge.

"After all the years of building and now someone believes he can end it?" Wash started trembling and tried to get out of bed on his own. I had to push him back down which, sadly, was easy to do.

"Stop it, Emily! I must stop them!" He became hysterical, weeping and pulling at his hair.

"You must lie down, dear. They will never succeed, you know that. It says that he waited this long because he never believed it would be completed, but it is, dear. You know it will be finished. He cannot stop us; no one can."

I had to convince him to take a tonic Dr. Smith had given us for nervous anxiety. I had never seen him so distraught and enraged. Before this sickness, my husband had never even raised his voice to anyone; he was never the least bit perturbed at another human being. It was a horrible thing to behold in the man I loved, but he was the same man inside his heart, and what we sacrificed for this bridge could not be changed or helped at that point.

To make things worse, there was news of a bridge collapsing in Scotland, killing dozens of people. When I brought the papers up to Wash that morning, I desperately wanted to keep the news from him, but we were not in the habit of lying to each other. The Tay Bridge was the work of Sir Thomas Bouch. He was blamed for shoddy engineering in using wrought iron, not steel. The train full of passengers had dropped a horrifying ninety feet. This led to more ridiculous speculation on the safety of our bridge, and more distress for my husband.

"Emily, my study of steel has led me to believe that we must make a change in the construction. Iron is not enough for the truss-work. We must incorporate steel, starting immediately!"

"Then the bridge will be made wholly of steel," I said.

"Yes, yes it will. Please call a meeting of the trustees immediately."

The meeting was held in our parlor, and the trustees appeared to agree with Wash on the use of steel. A call for bids were sent out immediately, but Wash had already decided his father's wire business, now in the hands of his own brothers, would be reliable.

A week later, the papers reported that the trustees had met again without informing us. Congressman Henry Slocum was quoted as saying there were some questions about certain transactions of the Roebling company, that Wash's brothers should not be furnishing materials. Mr. Kingsley, the paper reported, regretted to hear such statements about gentlemen who were not present to defend themselves. He added that the John A. Roebling Sons Company had a reputation for honor and integrity.

Just when things looked positive, something would always delay our satisfactions. At times I cursed the day my dear father-in-law had first conceived of his monumental idea. Without the bridge, I would certainly be using my life for learning more than engineering and mathematics, such as literature, art, and music. But none of that was to be, and I was not a woman to often bemoan my circumstances. Life is easier when you accept what you cannot change, and this bridge, this marriage, were immutable. The work for women in general was quite the opposite—something that could and would, indeed, be changed in the future.

I often arose before my family, and before the nanny or cook arrived for the day. The pale light of dawn was calming, sitting in the bay window, looking out on the beauty of God's good earth. The silence was a gift and a time to pray, to read, to contemplate the daily activities. I was just starting to read *Anna Karenina* when there was a furious knocking at the front door and I rushed down the hallway to quiet whomever was about to wake my husband and son. I opened the front door to a young man, a messenger who had been to our door many times before.

"What is it, Jack? Please! You will wake the household!"

"Terrible news, Mrs. Roebling! Terrible!" He looked as if he would burst into tears.

"Come in, dear. Sit down and gather yourself."

"President Garfield has died!"

"Oh, Lord, no!"

"That means Mr. Arthur is now the president."

We knew Chester Arthur. He had been the collector of customs for the Port of New York in the early years of the bridge.

"I will inform the Colonel. Thank you, Jack."

I did inform Wash, and we discussed the situation in our country at length, but how useless the opinions of females were!

"It's not as if I had voted for either of them." I said.

The beloved president had lasted only eleven months after he had been shot at close range by Charles Guiteau, a madman. He contracted an infection that he was not able to overcome. The papers were full of accusations of neglect by his personal physician, Dr. Bliss, who had refused the opinions of other doctors and the recommendations of cleanliness in treating the wound. Alexander Graham Bell had brought his new invention, a metal detector, to locate the bullet, but even that was discouraged and given little consideration. At the end, Garfield wanted to visit his home by the sea, and hundreds of men volunteered to extend the railroad tracks to the door of his home so he could travel there peacefully and die surrounded by sounds of the ocean.

"What a tragedy for this country. I believe he could have been one of our greatest presidents," Wash said. "Our friend Chester will officially be the President of the United States. Imagine that."

"Perhaps he will visit on the opening of the bridge one day."

"Perhaps."

Chapter 21

The name of Mrs. Emily Warren Roebling will thus be inseparably associated with all that is admirable in human nature, and with all that is wonderful in the constructive world of art.

Congressman Abram S. Hewitt

"How I dream of the day we will traverse this great bridge together," I said, gazing out of the window at the spectacular structure stretching from shore to shore.

    I looked over at Wash, and he smiled at me in the way he used to. I went to him, crawled under the covers, and we held each other. My husband's expression was clear and I removed my clothing. I slowly removed his as well, and our skin touched and burned into each other's. He searched for, and found the hairpins that held my abundance of hair, removed them, and let it fall over my shoulders. He kissed me upon the forehead, the eyelids, the cheeks. Wash still had all of his abilities except the ability to move as he wished or to hold up his own body with his arms. I slid my body atop of his, and we merged. We held each other for much of the morning as the snow flew outside the bay window.

    "Sometimes it seems as if our roles are reversed. I am sorry for that, Emily."

"There are no roles for us. We are entwined as one. All we do is equal and just."

"But a wife should not have to...."

"All a wife must do is to love her husband and be loved in return. We have that, do we not?"

That afternoon, Wash announced that I must indeed walk on the bridge and report the experience back to him. I continued to be his eyes and ears, and would allow him that experience through me as soon as the weather permitted.

Washington attended the Rensselaer Polytechnic Institute from 1854 to 1857, and graduated as a civil engineer. In the following years, he assisted his father on the Allegheny Bridge project before returning to Trenton to work in his father's wire mill. In 1861, he enlisted as a private in the New Jersey militia. He rose steadily in rank during the war. In 1864, he was brevetted lieutenant colonel for his gallant service, and eventually made a colonel. Wash's dearest wish for our son, John, was that he also attend Rensselaer.

When Wash received an invitation to attend a gathering of Rensselaer alumni, he immediately sent a response that I would be attending in his place. I was a bit surprised, knowing that I would be the only woman there, but in my role as my husband's eyes and ears, I must do as he wished.

"The bridge will be the main topic of the evening, and I do not want to hear what was said second hand or read it in the paper. You know how that can be. You must take my place and report back to me every word that is said."

"I will do my best, dear. I hope my presence is not intimidating to those speaking."

"Why would it be? If anything, they should be honored to have you. And you must purchase a new dress for the occasion."

"Well, that I can do," I replied, brushing back the hair from his forehead.

The evening's main speaker was Mr. Collingwood, who had been a foreman with us since the beginning. He was a longtime friend of Wash's and had graduated from Rensselaer two years ahead of him. Mr. Collingwood's speech was a bit long, and it seemed as if some of the audience were getting bored. He spoke at length about what had been accomplished and the staggering quantity of brick, stone, steel and iron that had gone into the bridge thus far. When he announced that the bridge was nearly done, thunderous applause erupted.

"The real hero of this bridge is Washington Roebling," he said, "Although incapacitated with illness he never lost his hold on the project. The alumni of Rensselaer are loyal and will see this project through just as our dear friend Washington, and his wife Emily, have. Mrs. Roebling is with us tonight.

I quickly sat up taller in my seat. All eyes were on me.

"There has been much speculation as to what Mrs. Roebling's role has been in the building of this bridge, and I believe it has been an enormous contribution and sacrifice for the entire family." Applause filled the room, and I felt a bit of an unaccustomed blush creep up my cheeks.

"Emily Warren Roebling, we all have the greatest respect for your devotion not only to your husband but to the building of this bridge. Many a time have I visited the Roebling house for a meeting of engineers, and I have witnessed Mrs. Roebling's remarkable ability to keep peace between the opinionated engineers." There was some laughter at this comment, and I smiled, knowing exactly to what he was referring.

"It is clear that Mrs. Roebling has a firm grasp on every detail of this project. I would like to call Mr. Raymond to the podium now." Another engineer, Mr. Rossiter W. Raymond, was widely known as an after-dinner speaker.

"Gentlemen, I know that the name of a woman should not be lightly spoken in a public place, but I believe you will acquit me any lack of delicacy or of reverence when I utter what lies that this moment half-articulate upon all your lips, the name of Mrs. Washington Roebling!" With that, he raised his glass in a toast to me. I was taken aback, and simply bowed my head, just as my husband would have done.

On the carriage ride home I marveled at the honor bestowed upon me that evening and pondered, as never before, how great my role had been in the bridge. It truly was an effort that both my Wash and I had accomplished together although I never expected any recognition. I loved everything about our life and the excitement and sense of accomplishment we felt every day when we looked out our window at one of the wonders of the modern world.

That December, on a mild, but breezy morning, I once again served as my husband's eyes and ears as I was driven directly to the foot of the Brooklyn tower. The steel beams and suspenders Wash had ordered had indeed been strung all the way from tower to tower. I knew he was watching as I climbed the spiral staircase as far as the roadway. A delegation of trustees followed me up the staircase, and we began our stroll across the planks that had been laid only five feet in width across the entire bridge. I had the honor of leading the group that included New York mayor William R. Grace and Brooklyn's Mayor Howell. Reporters and engineers followed us. The views were spectacular, and I waved in the direction of our home, hoping Wash could see me.

At first, it was a bit frightening to look down and see the turbulent green waters of the East River from such a small walkway and such a high elevation! Boats looked like toys, and hundreds of gulls swirled around us, screeching. But I calmed myself, remembering my utmost confidence in the men who had built this walkway. When we arrived in New York after the one-mile walk, champagne bottles were popped open and there was another toast to my health and the success of things in general. It was my great honor to walk the bridge, but, oh, I wished I had walked it arm and arm with Washington.

Chapter 22

Colonel W. A. Roebling, chief engineer of the Brooklyn Bridge, has taken Meyer Cottage for the season, and proposes to remain there, far from the madding crowd.

The *Knickerbocker*

1882

For thirteen years, our lives revolved around the building of the bridge. Washington had loyally and devotedly taken his father's place, and I had taken his place in many ways. Through controversy, mistakes, and deaths, when the bridge was almost completed, Chief Engineer Roebling could retreat without worry. The rumors continued to swirl that I was wholly in charge of the project, and that Washington was completely paralyzed. Although he had not improved much through the years, his doctors believed his nervous irritation would be diminished if he were away from the city.

We rented a cottage in Newport, Rhode Island, in the older, less fashionable section on a street parallel to the bay. It suited Wash's need perfectly: quiet, calm breezes, a large front porch, and bedrooms with views of the water and the Newport Harbor light. It was ten minutes from the steamboat landing, so bringing Wash from the boat was not difficult. Newport was known for its yachting and tennis playing, something we would not participate in. We had not been away from Brooklyn for five years, so it felt like a vacation.

One of the reasons we chose Newport was because my dear brother, G.K. was newly stationed there. He was in charge of the Corps of Engineers, working on the breakwater at Block Island.

"There's Emmy, my free girl!" G.K.'s voice thundered as he jauntily strode up our walkway.

"I am so proud of you, my brother. This work seems to suit you."

"It does, indeed. It is good to be doing important work and serving the country once again," he said cheerfully. "Well, hello there, John. Look at you! A grown man before my very eyes! It's been much too long since we've laid eyes on each other, but your mother has been faithful in keeping me informed of all your successes."

"Hello, Uncle G.K." John reached out his hand to shake my brother's, and it was a wonderful sight for me. "When can we go fishing?"

"As soon as possible. The bay is a remarkable fishing area. So many kinds of the little swimmers!"

"Let's go inside and get caught up," I said. "There are refreshments in the drawing room."

"Fresh lemonade, I hope!" said G.K.

"Of course. I know it's your favorite." It did my heart good to see my brother so hale and hearty. I had prayed for him nightly since his tragedy at Five Forks. His letters were filled with remorse, anger, and the desire to see his name cleared. It's all he ever wrote about, and I worried that he was not able to move forward with his life, but had always looked back. This new assignment and work were blessings, to be sure.

"How is my brother-in-law?" G.K. inquired.

"Washington has not given up any of his hold on the bridge simply because we've moved here to Newport. He prepares directives and instructions for its completion, and there is not a day that he does not spread out his diagrams and papers across the table and attend to the work at hand," I said, laughing. "He will be very glad to see you."

"I have recently read rumors and misinformation questioning whether Wash is even alive!" G.K. laughed robustly.

"I'm afraid my husband doesn't find that as amusing as you do," I said, pouring him some cool lemonade.

"And what is my nephew doing these days?" Gouverneur asked my son.

"I'm occupied with my studies, and hoping to attend Renssaeler one day to study civil engineering," John pronounced.

"Following the family tradition? That's glorious. We will talk about my work on the railroads sometime soon."

"I already know about railroad work. I'd like to hear about your Civil War service, Uncle."

My brother's head bowed slightly, and his face took on a mantle of sadness and pathos.

"Yes, tell us of the Battle at Big Bethel in Virginia!" I asked brightly, trying to dispel his murky mood. "That was when you were promoted to Colonel, was it not, G.K.?"

"Yes, yes, it was," he lifted his head and looked at John. "After that, I led the Peninsula campaign at the siege of Yorktown. Ever heard of that, young man?"

"Of course! We learned about that just this year in school. But how is it that you were able to use your civil engineering skills in the war?" John had heard these stories before, but now seemed old enough to understand their significance.

"I was the chief topological engineer of the Army of the Potomac. We used maps to plan reconnaissance missions and complete routes for the Union army to take in our advances. You can't just lead troops into battle without knowing the geography of the area."

"My brother even planned the routes for the Gettysburg campaign and initiated the defense for Little Round Top," I said, dropping ice into his lemonade. His mood had brightened considerably, but I did not want the conversation to lead us to his disgrace at Five Forks.

"I'm sure Wash is anxious to see you, too, so let's save some of these wonderful stories for later, shall we?"

"Yes, where is my brother-in-law, the one rumored to be dead?" G.K. asked loudly.

"I will take you to him directly," I smiled at my brother, and noticed how much larger he was in girth since the last time we'd been together. It wasn't like him to not attend to his health, and it concerned me a bit. He walked slowly down the hallway and appeared to be in some pain, an ailment I knew all too well.

"General Warren!" Wash moved to get out his chair, but G. K. walked over in time to stop him. I winced a bit, knowing that G.K. did not want to be called General, but Wash had known him as that from the start. It was only natural. G.K. took it in stride.

"Colonel! How good to see you. I see that you are, indeed, alive."

"I believe I am."

"I will leave you two to visit, and will see how our picnic is coming along. You will go with us, won't you, G.K?"

"Of course! I only hope there is some fried chicken on this picnic."

The servants packed enough lunch for a crowd and loaded it onto our largest carriage. When I went to retrieve my two favorite men, my ears filled with their laughter.

Our carriage took us down Bellevue Avenue and all of the lovely wooden mansions from the eighteenth century, the Brick Tower, and Trinity Church. Newport was a social town, with activities on every level: tennis, polo, yachting, and a skating rink recently built. John had asked to participate in the Young Men's Christian Association in town.

"I hear that Newport has installed a city water system," G. K. commented.

"Oh, yes, it's very exciting, all the new inventions we are enjoying. It's a wonderful time to be alive, isn't it?" I said.

"Are you going to take up tennis?" G.K. asked as we drove by the Newport casino.

"I believe I am past my tennis days, but I am keeping very busy with my women's clubs and writing."

"Emily is designing a mansion in Trenton fit for a king."

"Oh, well, yes, it is to be grand. It will be a place for us to retire and be away from the bridge. We found a spot near the harbor where we could watch the sailboats and enjoy the cool breezes."

"Emily, this reminds me of Cold Spring. Such a wonderful place to be a child," G.K. said.

"I have only fond memories of my girlhood, at least when mother and father were with us. You know, sometimes I marvel at the wonders of life, at the things that happen that we could never have imagined. When we were in Cold Spring as children, playing on the banks of the Hudson River, I never dreamed that the boats floating by would one day be able to glide under a magnificent bridge, just down the river from us."

"It's true, life brings unexpected marvels. Remember that, John. Life is almost never what you expect it to be."

"My parents have taught me that well," said John.

"Do you remember Edward Mooney?" G.K. asked.

"Yes, I do."

"He's now working for me at the breakwater."

"Is that right?" I asked. A childhood memory sent a cold wave of prickling needles up the back of my neck.

"Is that all you have to say?" G. K. demanded. "Don't you think it's quite a coincidence that I have come in contact with someone from Cold Spring?"

"I suppose. It's just that Edward Mooney is not someone I want to remember."

"Why is that, Mama?" John piped up.

"He was a mean boy."

"What did he do?" John persisted.

"Oh, let's talk about something more pleasant. I'm sure that whatever he did it is not something you would even think of doing," I smiled at my boy, now almost a man.

That evening, while preparing for bed, Wash asked me about Edward Mooney.

"It was so long ago. I'm sure he's mended his ways since then."

"Yes, but you appeared distressed when G.K. mentioned him. It was, indeed, a long time ago, and only vivid memories stay in the mind that long," Wash persisted.

"He used to touch me. After church, all the children would be free to roam the church grounds and play while the adults were at the Sunday morning socials."

"Touch you? You mean in an intimate way? Why, you were only a child."

"Yes, and he was older. He would capture me behind some bushes or tree and try…. Oh, Wash, let's forget it. I know I have tried to, all of these years."

"Didn't you tell someone? Your mother or father at least?"

"I was ashamed. I didn't think anyone would believe me. Edward had such perfect manners in front of the adults. I had trouble understanding how I could have let it happen more than once. I wondered if it was my fault."

"Don't you think your mother would have defended you? Or your father would have called for his punishment?"

"Maybe, but my mother was ill so much of the time. I didn't want my father to be ashamed of me."

"But you did nothing wrong, Em."

"As true as that is, it is not how a girl feels after it has happened. It's just not."

Wash came to me, attempted to console me, and move me toward the bed.

"Not tonight…not tonight."

Diane Vogel Ferri

Chapter 23

If his intellect had been impaired, I should consider myself a happy man if I had what he lost. He spoke to me with clearness and exhibited a memory which was something astonishing.

Mr. Ludwig Semler

The New York mayor, Seth Low, requested my husband's presence in New York to prove he was alive and capable, which, of course, was impossible. Many of the bridge workers had never laid eyes on Wash, and he and the mayor had never met. Because Wash refused to address the request, it was decided that Mr. Low would come to Newport.

Low traveled by boat, then by carriage, and appeared in our driveway. I ushered the mayor directly into Washington's room.

"It is time for you to step down, Mr. Roebling," the mayor haughtily demanded.

"I will do no such thing," Wash replied.

"I assure you that history will still remember your part in the building of the bridge."

"It certainly will, and I will see it to the end, Mr. Mayor."

"I will consider firing you if you continue to refuse." I gasped, and the mayor glanced over at me briefly.

"Excuse me, Mr. Mayor," I said indignantly, "but what makes you think you have cause for such a demand?"

The mayor stuttered and stammered and clearly had no solid reason, other than the unspoken political gains for himself.

"Mr. Roebling," he said, facing Wash. "I am going to remove you because it pleases me." With that, the mayor walked out of the room and down the stairs.

I followed him, furious, my face reddening.

"Come back here, Mr. Low!" I shouted.

He turned and gave me a dismissive look, then turned around and walked away from me and out the front door.

"How dare you treat Colonel Roebling in that way!"

He stopped, turned towards me, and said, "You are just a woman. You have nothing whatsoever to do with this business."

"I am just a woman? Exactly what does that mean, Mayor? Are you not the mayor of women as well as men in the great city of New York? Have you never apprised yourself of my involvement in the building of the Brooklyn Bridge? If not, then you are not well informed enough to call for any changes!"

"Please quiet yourself, Mrs. Roebling. I do not recall addressing any of my concerns to you."

"You are in my home, sir, and you have disrupted our day with your witless and foolhardy demands!" I stood tall, my hands on my hips.

"This, my dear woman, is the reason women should not be allowed to vote!" He climbed into his carriage and was gone before I could utter another retort. I stomped up the stairs and into Wash's room, where he was peacefully gazing out of the window.

"I have never witnessed anything as uncalled-for in my life!"

"Now, now," Wash began. "Don't be overly concerned. Now that he's seen that I am not mentally impaired, he has no argument for dismissing me. He, no doubt, is acquiescing to someone else's whims for political gain."

"But the nerve!"

"Yes, I understand your outrage, but we have plenty of knowledgeable colleagues who will stand up for me, if needed," Wash said calmly.

"I don't know how you can be so fair-minded about this, Wash. This is your life's work and some arrogant mayor wants to take all your honor from you!"

"Come here, my sweet one. I'm sure he will think twice about tangling with Mrs. Roebling again." Wash put out his arms to me, and I went willingly into them. He had magical ways of calming my fears, and I admired how he possessed his emotions. It was disarming and charming all at once.

We did not hear from the abhorrent Mr. Low again, but read in the papers that he had proposed a resolution that Washington be reduced to consulting engineer. The papers printed the speech of a dissenter, Mr. Ludwig Semler:

I do not think it would be using Mr. Roebling justly to oust him from his position now that he is about to reap the full benefit of his labors. If he had been in any way guilty of delaying the bridge, I should be in favor of retiring him, but there is not a shadow of a charge upon which to base such action. In fact, Mr. Roebling has done much toward pushing the bridge along. Let us not act summarily toward him after his thirteen years of service.

There were other, similar statements defending my husband's honor, just as Wash had predicted. It was decided that the subject be laid over until September. For weeks, every newspaper appeared to have a different opinion about my husband and what was to be done with him. When Wash was having a bad day, it began to cause him great distress, which was terrible for his health. I wrote to Mr. Semler:

I take the liberty of writing to express to you my heartfelt gratitude for your generous defense of Col. Roebling at the last meeting of the Board of Trustees. Your words were a most agreeable surprise to us, as we had understood you were working in full sympathy of the mayors of the two cities and the Comptroller of New York. Colonel Roebling is very anxious for me to go to Brooklyn to convey to you a few messages from him. Can you see me at your office some morning? I will go to Brooklyn any day you can give me a little of your time, and will see you at your own office or house, just as you may prefer.

As you are a stranger to Colonel Roebling, all that you said was doubly appreciated. There are some few old friends in the Board of Trustees who know him well and who have always stood by him in the many attacks that have been made on him in the past ten years, but we never expected such consideration and kindness from those who have never seen him.

Mr. Semler responded by asking if he would be allowed to come and meet Wash in person. He told a reporter: "There is nothing sentimental in my feelings on this matter. The question is simply one of justice."

Mr. Semler and Wash had a brief, but courteous visit, and Mr. Semler immediately returned to his office. He assured us that he would recommend that Wash should have no other position than Chief Engineer. The papers reported the visit thoroughly, and quoted Mr. Semler as saying he found Wash suffering from a severe nervous affliction, but his intellect was perfectly clear and strong.

Before the board meeting in which Mr. Semler would make his recommendations, a reporter from the New York *World a*ppeared at our door in Newport. He insisted on seeing and interviewing Washington. Although we had not allowed this in ten years, I let him in because he promised there would be no direct quotes, that he would print nothing of what had been said. The man won over the trust of my husband, and in his present nervous state, he made some careless comments about his frustrations of the Board of Trustees.

Days later, we read the reporter's great betrayal of our trust when he printed Wash's inadvertent comments. I felt I was to blame for even letting the man into our home. I had let down my guard and good sense in protecting my husband—something I'd never allowed before. All of it only served to harm Wash's case of staying on as Chief Engineer. It was the worst possible time to let him down.

"The papers are always referring to me as a peacemaker, admired by all of the assistant engineers. You yourself call me a woman of infinite tact, but I am not! I am a foolish, foolish woman!" I was devastated by my error in judgement regarding the damned reporter.

"I am as much to blame as you are—more so! I am the one who made the unthinking comments. This debacle is on me, not you."

"But what if the Board actually votes you out? It will have been my fault!" Wash tried to convince me otherwise, but I would not be moved. I was not some irresponsible, absent-minded girl. I had used my brain powers every single day of these thirteen years, and now succumbed to a reporter! That imprudence would haunt me all of that sleepless night.

I immediately wrote an apology to William Marshall, who was one of the non-politicians on the board.

> *There is no doubt of my husband's perfect sanity and ability as an engineer, but he is certainly unfit to be on the work where so many political interests are involved. I thank you very much for your efforts and do not think I shall be greatly disappointed when the bridge controversies are ended, even against us. It has been a long, hard fight since Colonel Roebling first took sick and if this chance reporter's visit changes everything, I shall see in it the hand of God, that all my care could not direct or change.*

In the end, the Trustees voted 10-7 in Wash's favor.

Chapter 24

You left me, sweet, two legacies,
A legacy of love
A Heavenly Father would content,
Had He the offer of;

You left me boundaries of pain
Capacious as the sea,
Between eternity and time,
Your consciousness and me.

Emily Dickinson

A messenger arrived at our door with a telegram on a sweltering August morning. I had just settled Wash at the table with his diagrams and papers.

> *Come immediately. G.K. very ill.*
>
> *Charlotte*

"Oh Lord! My brother!"
What is it?" I heard Wash call from the study.
"Charlotte has sent this note saying G.K. is ill, and I must come at once. Oh, my, there is no one to take me."

"I will take you, Mama," John appeared at the door, his face ashen at seeing my distress.

"Get the carriage, then. I will be out presently." I rushed to my bedroom and grabbed the first dress I saw. I flew out of the house without saying anything to Wash. I heard him call after me, but my anguished heart thought only of my beloved brother.

When John and I arrived, Charlotte was standing at the doorway, weeping so loudly I could hear her from the drive.

"Oh, Charlotte, what happened?"

"He's had some sort of attack. The doctor is with him now, but he does not hold hope for a recovery." Charlotte took my hand and led me to G.K.'s side. "It's very bad, Emily."

"He's only fifty-two years of age. How could this happen?" I turned to my sister-in-law.

"He never recovered from the humiliation of being demoted in the army. It's all he ever talked about. He sought obsessively to clear his name. It affected his health and his spirit. It caused him great nervous distress."

"I understand precisely what nervous distress can do to one's body." I took Charlotte's hand and squeezed it gently, suddenly becoming aware that her loss was greater than my own. She and my brother still had three children at home.

"Dearest brother," I knelt by the bedside but he did not appear to be aware of my presence. His eyes were open, but not focused on anything.

"G.K.! Listen to me. I need you. Charlotte and your children need you. You cannot leave now. I will not allow it!" I felt foolish reprimanding my older sibling, but could not contain my heartache and shock.

G.K. did not move or respond in any way. I went to Charlotte and held her tenderly. The doctor shook his head at us, and we wept together.

Suddenly, G.K. opened his mouth and cried, "The flag! The flag!" Then his eyes closed, and his body went limp. The doctor nodded his head, affirming that my brother, the famous General G.K. Warren's, life had ended. John, who had been standing nearby witnessed the whole event. Of course, he had never seen someone die, had never lost a loved one at his tender age of fifteen. I had to be mindful that I was not the only one who would grieve. But how could I tend to my brother's family, and my own son's grief, as well as my own? All of these thoughts coursed through my mind at that very moment. Then I looked over at the body, the shell of my own flesh and blood, my hero and comforter. My legs collapsed under me, I fell to the floor weeping, and could not find the strength to do anything but cry. I wanted to be strong for those around me, but I could not at that moment.

Could a human being die from a broken heart? Perhaps the strain put on a heart from sadness and despondency? Throughout the years after the war, G.K. had yearned to be exonerated and refused to admit to any blame in the matter. His last words revealed he was still dwelling in the war.

The former Civil War general was buried in Island Cemetery in Newport in his civilian clothes and without military honors by his own request. My grief for my brother was even greater than that for my own parents. G.K. had been a consistent presence in my life. We stayed in constant contact and lived near each other twice in my adulthood. I missed him deeply. He was my champion and defender at all times, and a shining light in my life.

Grief was like a woolen cloak, an encumbrance I could not throw off. I struggled to be free of it, but there was no time limit, no recovery in sight. It awakened me in the night, with phantom voices of our conversations, and burning images of my brother's smile. For a time, my bereavement held me as a hostage, and I felt myself fighting its imprisonment. The sudden beauty and stink of lilies filled the house, and one morning, I could not stand their constant reminder of my brother's funeral. I gathered them into a basket and threw them out of the back door. Then I fell to the floor, wailing in anguish.

I thought my tears would never dry. Questions relentlessly arced in my mind. Where was my brother? He was here just last month, sitting at our table, laughing boisterously, embracing us in his enormous arms. My mourning was so great that waves of pain moved through my body and kept me awake at night. There was no control, no choice but to let each day pass. The world continued on without G.K. Warren, but how would I?

Weeks after G. K.'s death, an unexpected letter arrived informing me that, years before, President Rutherford B. Hayes had convened to hear dozens of witnesses testifying to my brother's honor and devotion to duty. For more than one hundred days, those who knew and served with G. K. at the time of Five Forks attested to his character. It was determined that his dismissal from his post by Major General Sheridan had been unjustified. With no explanation for the delay, they had recently published this report, and although it was heartening to see my brother exonerated, it was devastating to realize that he had not lived to see his name cleared, the very thing I believed contributed to his untimely death.

Chapter 25

Many of life's failures are people who did not realize how close they were to success when they gave up.

Thomas Edison

We left the heartache of Newport behind and moved back to Brooklyn in the spring of 1883. During the fourteen years that the Brooklyn Bridge was being built, we saw other great advances in this country including a population that grew by ten million. Mr. Edison's electric lights were now burning all over New York. Multiple railroads were spanning the continent. The telephone became a wonderful new means of communication.

"Well, my husband, how does it feel to accomplish something that no one else has ever done?"

"I could not have done it without you, my dearest. It feels wonderful, although I regret that it has taken three times as long and cost twice as much as my father had estimated so long ago. I know I will never stop grieving for the many men who lost their lives throughout these years, especially my own father."

"It's just so beautiful, Wash. People are constantly clustered around the bridge, imagining the official opening. They are in awe of what you have achieved. Just imagine standing atop the bridge on a beautiful spring day, watching the boats so tiny below you, swimming down the river, hearing the gulls screech around you, feeling as though you could touch the heavens. It will be a place of retreat from the odious streets of Brooklyn and New York. People will have views of two cities that they had never seen before."

"The boats will enjoy a new perspective, as well. And, of course, getting to New York to shop will be quite easy for you."

"Oh, Wash," We smiled at each other, sensing a moment of contentment that had been rare in the past.

"Our son has grown up since the bridge was started, and is almost ready to attend Rensselaer," Wash said with a tinge of sadness. "How much more I wish I could have done with him...."

"Are you ready to go?" I asked Wash as I brought his coat to him.

"Where are we going?"

"To take a carriage ride," I replied. "You said you the only thing you can't see from here are the two terminal buildings, so we are going to see them. It's a beautiful morning, and it appears you are in a good state of mind and body. Your driver awaits you, dear."

Wash and I rode silently over the short distance to the terminal. The two-story Brooklyn terminal was twice the size of the one in New York. On the upper level, the bridge trains would leave for New York. Commuters would pay their five-cent fare at one of several decorative toll booths, then climb an iron stairway to the waiting platforms. The terminal had elaborate ironwork and moulding, with many large plate glass windows. Hundreds of workmen were installing the seventy electric arc lamps that Wash had ordered from the United States

Illuminating Company at a cost of eighteen thousand dollars. They would be the first electric lights to illuminate a bridge.

Washington gazed out the window of the carriage for a long while, saying nothing. It seemed a sacred moment for him. I could only imagine all the thoughts filling his mind about the past fourteen years of our lives, about whether he would ever cross the bridge, about all that he had sacrificed.

"I'm ready," he whispered after a time, and we returned home.

Once we were back in Brooklyn, I took daily walks to the bridge to inhale the fresh sea breezes and to deliver Wash's messages in person. One day, I happened upon Thomas Edison standing all alone, gazing up at the massive structure.

"Mr. Edison, I'm Emily Roebling. I'm honored to meet you," I put out my hand.

"Mrs. Roebling, the pleasure is mine. I was just getting some air. I have a very nice office around the corner from here, but it's hard to work on such a beautiful day. Nature is kind to us today."

"Yes, God has blessed us with so much beauty if we take the time to look up, to look around us. People are so busy and distracted these days," I said.

"I do see Nature as Creator," he replied watching a seagull glide by above us.

"Certainly with the brilliant mind you've been given, you believe in God, Mr. Edison." I wasn't sure why I had felt the need to challenge one of the great minds of the century, but it just popped out of my mouth.

"I do not believe in the God of the theologians, but that there is a Supreme Intelligence, I do not doubt."

"Oh, well," I stammered as I thought of what to say to that. I had heard that while Mr. Edison was staying in Brooklyn, he did not attend church, which I found most unusual.

"I'm sorry if I've offended you, Mrs. Roebling. It's not that I do not believe in God. I just refer to it as Nature, I suppose. Look at the scandals of Rev. Beecher, of example. Of what good comes hypocrisy and the forcing of humans to all think the same? I believe in mercy, kindness, and love. Call it whatever you want."

"I am a fairly open-minded and informed woman, but I have not thought of such matters in these terms before. You know, when Reverend Beecher was our preacher at Plymouth Church, he used to speak on what he called the Gospel of Love. That, in essence, as Christians, we get too caught up in rules and worrying about who is going to hell instead of simply loving one another, as it tells us to in the Gospels."

"I think that is perfectly logical, Mrs. Roebling," Edison replied smiling warmly at me. A few awkward moments passed, and then I added, "We so enjoy the illumination your amazing invention has added to our lives. Washington and I sometimes sit in the window in the evening and watch the lights of the city come on. It's quite exciting. Oh, if only we'd had the electric light during the building of this bridge."

"I should imagine it would have been of help during those dark winter afternoons."

"Indeed. Mr. Edison, I'm sure my husband would be greatly honored to meet you. We only live over on

Columbia Heights. Could you join us for a drink this evening?"

"That would be fine," he replied, "I should like to meet the genius behind this bridge."

"I'm quite sure he considers you the genius, Mr. Edison. Shall we see you at seven?"

Mr. Edison arrived promptly at 7:00 that evening. I felt great pride and excitement as I led him into the drawing room to introduce him to my husband.

"Colonel Roebling, it is an honor," He reached his hand out to shake Wash's, and Wash did his best to return a firm handshake.

"The honor is mine, sir. I have read much about the Edison Electric Light Company in New York. Please, have a seat," Wash gestured to a comfortable chair.

"Excuse me while I retrieve the housemaid. She will bring us some refreshments presently," I said.

"Our best claret, dear," Wash called after me. When I returned, I heard two geniuses of invention and science having a fine time discussing their respective achievements.

"The distribution of your electricity has been remarkably swift hasn't it?" Wash asked.

"Yes, it appears that the need and desire for electric light has come of age. I see that you have installed electricity here at your lovely home," Mr. Edison looked around the room.

"Oh, yes, we were one of the first in Brooklyn. I can't remember life without it now!" I said. "Imagine our delight when we returned from our time in Newport to see the twinkling of hundreds of lights in the city. It was a thrilling sight! We also intend to procure one of your phonographs as soon as it is perfected. To hear music any time of the day or night!"

"It's true we are still working on that one!" Mr. Edison laughed heartily. "I am surprised you have even heard of it."

"Oh, nothing gets past my Emily, I assure you, Mr. Edison," Wash said.

"I can see that. Quite admirable in a woman."

"In this day and age, Mr. Edison, it is very easy for a woman to be as informed as a man, is it not?"

"Well, I suppose that's true." He took a sip of his claret as he peered over the glass at me somewhat sheepishly.

"Mrs. Roebling is well educated, and I'm sure you've heard of the tremendous help she has been to me in building this bridge during my convalescence," Wash intervened.

"Yes, I've heard about that. I meant no disrespect, Mrs. Roebling. It's just that in my experience, women are not as involved in matters of science."

"Possibly, your experience is limited in that area…," I started.

"Emily, would you see if we might have our claret refreshed?" Wash interrupted.

"Of course," I reluctantly served Mr. Edison, a man who should have been more open-minded, I thought.

"I do have a bone to pick with you, Colonel Roebling," Mr. Edison said.

"I'm sure that you do," Wash replied, smiling. "No hard feelings, I hope?"

"I believe the Edison Company's bid for providing lighting to the bridge was lower than the other company's, was it not?"

"It was, but it was my decision to use the blue-white arc lamps provided by the United States Illuminating Company. I felt they would be superior in lighting the large areas in the terminal buildings. I meant no disrespect to you or to your magnificent invention."

"Business is business," Edison replied raising his glass to my husband.

The two geniuses talked into the night. Wash had not withstood that long an encounter in years. It did my heart good to see him converse with someone on his level of creativity and thought. Both men made an effort to include me in the conversation, but I had the opportunity to discuss matters of engineering and invention all the time, and did not feel the need to prove myself to the inventor. That evening was for Wash, so I left them early and went up to my study to work on the invitations for the bridge opening day party.

Diane Vogel Ferri

Chapter 26

> THE BROOKLYN BRIDGE
> *will be opened to the public*
> *Thursday, May twenty-fourth, at 2 o'clock*
> *Col. & Mrs. Washington A. Roebling*
> *request the honor of your company*
> *after the opening ceremony until seven o'clock*
> *110 Columbia Heights*
> *Brooklyn*
> *R.S.V.P.*

We were so close to the completion of our life's work. I continued to deliver daily messages to the bridge—sometimes two or three times in a day, as Wash asked that I pay particular attention to the finishing details.

"Mr. Finley is not able to comprehend the information you sent him, Wash. I'm going to draw a picture of it for him."

"That's a fine idea. Let me see it when you're done," Wash said.

"You don't want to guide the drawing?"

"I have no need. Only my curiosity makes me want to see it. I'm sure you have all the information in that pretty head, don't you?"

"Well, yes I do. I'm going to include step-by-step directions as well."

"If he has any further questions, I will refer him back to you," Wash smiled at me.

In early May, I had the thrill of my life being the first person to ride over the bridge. Wash wanted someone to test the effects of vibrations on a trotting horse, and I asked to be that someone. I procured a live white rooster to accompany me as a symbol of victory, and rode with a fine coachman in a brand new Victoria carriage with a retractable hood. The shiny vehicle was elegantly appointed, and was pulled by two white horses. The design of the carriage protected one from the elements, but allowed a good view all around for passengers. Fortunately, there was no need for protection from the elements on that crisp May morning.

"Hello, hello!" I waved at the workers putting finishing touches on the bridge.

"Good morning, Mrs. Roebling! What have you got there?" one man shouted.

"Oh, you mean this rooster?" I laughed as the rooster almost escaped my arms. Grasping him more tightly, he let out a mighty crow!

All the men in the area stopped what they were doing and waved and cheered. The mood was joyful as these loyal workers saw the fruition of their labors.

The view was spectacular. I didn't imagine that you would be able to see so far in every direction from the top of the bridge. It was like standing in the sky. It was a most satisfying moment in my life, although I missed the presence of the Chief Engineer by my side.

When I returned home, I was so joyful that I foolishly attempted to talk Wash into attending the opening day ceremonies, but we both knew it would be too much for him. Washington had made great improvements over the last months and my hope was high for a full recovery. His vision had mostly returned and he had gained weight, which gave him a more robust appearance. We had a vigorous talk about the idea of Wash getting out of the house more, but then I saw the weariness in his gray eyes and his demeanor wither, and ended the discussion.

The *Union* reported on my journey and quoted me the next day:

> *"The trotting horse on a bridge makes itself felt very easily, but the result of the observations on the day I drove most satisfactory." When asked if the new bridge could accommodate locomotives, she replied, "I know Colonel Roebling is opposed to using locomotives on the bridge at any time, not because he fears the structure would not sustain the weight, but because they would frighten horses on the roadways and seriously interfere with ordinary traffic across the bridge."*
>
> *Mrs. Roebling was asked whether her husband would retire from the engineering profession, and she said, "This is his last, as well as his greatest work. He will require a long rest after this is over. He needs it, and he has certainly earned it."*

When Wash read the paper the next day, he frowned at me and asked me not to speak for him regarding his personal decisions. I elected not to argue with him for a change.

"At least you will be able to view the wonderful illumination of fireworks on opening day, Wash." I said, attempting to raise his spirits a bit.

"I fear it will be impossible to clear the crowd off the bridge again before night, before the fireworks, and the danger they could bring."

"Of course, there will be great enthusiasm on opening day. Do you really want to quash the happiness of the public after all of these years of opposition to the bridge?" I asked.

"I do not want to ruin the opening day, but I will not be responsible for the consequences if people are allowed to crowd on just as they like. Remember the foot bridge? People had no common sense about it! It would be possible for one hundred thousand people to get on the main span of the bridge and cover every available foot of space, cables, and tops of trusses. This would make a load three times greater than the live load calculated for."

"What could happen?"

"Most likely nothing, but there could be injuries from the fireworks if people don't use their heads about it."

"I cannot quite believe that we are facing yet another dilemma right before opening day, the People's Day. How can we possibly contain the public's enthusiasm after fighting for just that all of these years?" I said, disheartened.

"Would you please call a meeting of the trustees to discuss this matter?"

"Of course, dear." There seemed to be no end to the problems or my duties regarding them. I selfishly wanted to focus on the celebration and party following the opening and be done with controversies and struggles.

Opening day had been deemed "The People's Day." In preparation, I made out the guest list, completed the invitations, and ordered flowers for the house. Extra housemaids were hired to attend to the food and clean up. I commissioned an oil portrait of Washington as well as busts of his head and his father's as well. I did all of this as unobtrusively as possible to keep Washington from worrying about the strain of the reception. Because he could not attend the ceremonies, the celebration would come to him. The trustees, the mayors, the governor and President Arthur would join us at our home, as well as our families and many friends. Mail soon started arriving in large bags of congratulations, good wishes for opening day, and many responses to the party.

Diane Vogel Ferri

Chapter 27

Babylon had her hanging garden, Egypt had her pyramid, Athens her Acropolis,
Rome her Atheneum; so Brooklyn has her Bridge
 —a sign seen on Columbia Heights

May 24, 1883

The weather was perfect, the sky cloudless, the sweet scent of spring filled everyone's head. Red, white, and blue banners covered buildings everywhere in honor of the president's visit. The North Atlantic Squadron of the United States Navy arrived on the river led by the flagship of the fleet.

Thousands of people lined the streets. They came by carriage, train, and boat. School was in session, but thousands of children were not in attendance. Stores were closed. Women dressed in their finest clothes; men in top hats and morning coats, and others in gaudy costumes added to the spectacle. Vendors lined the streets selling photographs of Wash and my father-in-law—still remembered, to my delight. Buttons and medals commemorating the day were being sold on every street corner. Businesses were in their glory selling their wares, especially liquor, but also flags and banners, which were seen moving like great waves across the town. Thousands of handbills, fans, and pamphlets littered the streets as businesses tried to take advantage of the crowds.

The noise woke Wash in the early hours of the morning. John and I were already awake and preparing for the day. I chose a yellow satin dress with gathered sleeves and a floral overskirt. My hat had an upturned brim and was decorated with orange flowers and pink feathers. As we looked out the window, we could see adornments lining the streets of our neighborhood. It seemed as if everyone in Brooklyn, rich or poor, had decorated their home for the great occasion. Our own house was covered with flowers and the coats of arms of New York and Brooklyn. An enormous American flag was suspended across the street, in front of our house, high enough for carriages to ride under it.

The water of the river reflected the bright blue of the sky, and there were more boats floating under and around the bridge than ever seen before. Banners and signs made the boats look as if they had wings and would suddenly lift into the sky.

Wash and I sat cozily at the window in amazement and wonder that we had anything at all to do with this historical celebration. But we did. We had everything to do with it. John sat with us, pride evident on his boyish face.

At nine o'clock, the fence across the Chatham Street entrance to the bridge was torn down and a wall of policemen stood in its place protecting the bridge from the hordes of spectators that filled the streets. For as far as we could see, a mass of humanity pushed and shoved to get closer to the bridge. I wondered whether Wash had been right to fear some sort of disaster that day, but excitement and joy overturned my worry.

"Look down the river!" John pointed. The river was almost as full as the streets. Barges and steamers with hundreds of passengers sailed towards the celebration. Private boats filled the harbor.

"Oh, my goodness, I don't see how there will be room for everyone! It's as if a forest of masts has blossomed beneath the sun into a thousand gorgeous colors. Every boat has a glorious and unique decoration!" I exclaimed.

I truly hated to leave my husband, but he was thrilled to have me experience this once-in-a-lifetime event. After John and I dressed, we went out the front door to our carriage, the same one that had been used to cross the bridge. I waved at Wash, still staring out the window, and he smiled back widely at me. More than twenty carriages lined up behind ours, full of Warrens and Roeblings who had all traveled here for the occasion.

Ahead of us, the Twenty-third Regiment Band marched in red coats, followed by the Twenty-Third Regiment in white helmets and blue coats, as well as marines from the Navy Yard. Behind them were the city officials, bridge trustees, and the mayor. As we traveled down Remsen Street, John pointed upward. Crowds of people lined the rooftops!

The noise was deafening as people shouted and clapped in anticipation of seeing President Chester A. Arthur and Governor Grover Cleveland. Bands played with fervor, people cheered, joined arms, and sang along. The processions halted under the arched roof of the great iron terminal, where thousands of people got their first glimpse of President Arthur. The Seventh Regiment formed two lines at the right of the promenade and presented arms as the president passed by. He moved into the bright sunshine dressed in a black frock coat, white tie, and a flat-brimmed black beaver hat that he continually removed in response to the cheering of the crowd. No one seemed to notice Governor Cleveland until he stood and waved his hat. William Kingsley stepped forward, removed his hat and extended his hand to the president. The band played "Hail to the Chief." All the while, guns were booming from Fort Hamilton and the Navy Yard. I'd never witnessed such commotion!

Seth Low pronounced official greeting for the City of Brooklyn, the marines presented arms, a signal flag was dropped and a gun thundered from a ship below. Then every boat on the river set off whistles, guns, bells, and cannons while the band continued to play "Hail to the Chief!"

My son had his hands over his ears, but was still smiling. I would have done the same if I could. Wash would have no trouble hearing the excitement of the day, even if he could not see everything.

The speeches commenced and it appeared everyone involved in building the bridge had something to say. John sat by my side respectfully throughout the proceedings. At first, the speeches were thrilling, but after two hours, the midday sun was unbearable. The fashionable upturned brim of my hat did nothing to protect my face from the sun.

I was distracted thinking about Wash, sitting alone at home, with his field glasses, until I heard my name. Abram Stevens Hewitt said, "Emily Warren Roebling will forever be inseparably associated with all that is admirable in human nature, and with all that is wonderful in the constructive world of art. So with this bridge will ever be coupled with the thought of one, who through the subtle alembic of whose brain, and by whose facile fingers, communication was maintained between directing power of its construction, and the obedient agencies of its execution. It is thus an everlasting monument to the self-sacrificing devotion of a woman, and of her capacity for that higher education from which she has been too long debarred!"

"Indeed!" I said in a whisper. There was great applause, and I slowly rose to my feet and waved at the crowd. I felt humbled and awed by the whole event, but shortly after that unexpected honor, I suddenly realized the time and took my leave. John and I scurried back to our carriage and returned to the house to prepare for the party I had spent months planning.

I reminded John of the suit hanging in his bedroom, and urged him to dress as quickly as possible. I changed into a heavy black silk dress trimmed with crepe with a knot of violets in my belt. Wash looked handsome and regal in his Prince Albert coat.

The flowers had been delivered, and they were beautiful. Red and white roses, wisteria, lilacs and calla lilies were draped and clustered everywhere around the house and wound up the banister. On the buffet table stood a three-foot-long sugar model of the bridge, which was the centerpiece for a sumptuous feast. On the drawing room mantle were the white marble busts of the Chief Engineer and his father that had been commissioned. A laurel wreath with tiny flags and ribbons circled the bust of Wash. On the ribbon was written:

Chief Engineer, Washington A. Roebling, May 24, 1883. Brooklyn Bridge.
Let him who has won it bear the palm.

A band played from the balcony in the drawing room and my husband and I stood side by side inside the parlor door as President Arthur and Seth Low entered. I had my arm looped through my husband's so I could detect if he was becoming too worn out to stand.

President Arthur greeted us warmly, then moved into the parlor to make room for hundreds of guests waiting to enter our home. After a brief time, Washington could no longer stand, so we moved to the sofa in the parlor and greeted guests from there. John stood next to the sofa and presented his best adult manners. I was so pleased that my son had the opportunity to meet the president. President Arthur enjoyed the party immensely, but left after about an hour to attend a dinner at the mayor's home. Wash had become weakened by the excitement, and a nurse helped him upstairs.

As the sun began to set, the guests gathered at the windows and outside in the streets. When the dark overtook the light, a series of electric lights started to glow like tiny diamonds until there was a chain of light stretching from Brooklyn to New York. The trustees had agreed with Wash, and had found a way to limit the number of people on the bridge that evening, so we were free to enjoy the moment. The crowds cheered, and I ran up the stairs to stand by Wash's side. From the mayor's estate, a solitary rocket jetted into the sky and burst into blue fragments. Then the lights on the bridge went out and after a moment, dozens of rockets exploded into the sky above us. The spectacle lasted for an hour, dozens, hundreds of fireworks at a time. Bands played, crowds cheered, church bells rang, gas balloons floated by.

Then, as announced, at midnight the bridge was opened to the public for the fee of one cent per person.

Massive crowds had gathered at both ends of the bridge. As the crowd grew disorderly, more policemen arrived to ensure a safe crossing for all. We watched from our magnificent viewpoint for as long as we could keep our eyes open. It had been a day we would never forget. At daybreak, there were still people trudging across the bridge.

Diane Vogel Ferri

Chapter 28

The Brooklyn Bridge being completed, and open to travel, the Trustees are no longer in need of my services. I therefore desire to relinquish my connection with the work at the end of the month.

Colonel W. A. Roebling

"The paper calls your bridge 'The Eighth Wonder of the World,' I told Wash as we ate breakfast the next morning. "The report is that 150,300 people crossed yesterday." Wash's face looked exhausted and forlorn. "I wish you had been one of them, my dear."

"Yes," he looked up from his newspaper and tried to smile at me. "I wonder what it will be like on Decoration Day next week. Did you see this in the *Eagle*? Great praise for my wife!"

"What? Let me see."

"Please read to me, Em." He put his magnifying glass on the table.

> *Great emergencies are the opportunities of great minds. Mrs. Emily Warren Roebling met this difficulty as nobody would. She addressed her remarkable intelligence to the acquisition of the higher mathematics; her luminous mind was well-adapted to its profound and*

often desperate labyrinths. She mastered the most bewildering of sciences, applied it to the bridge, was in rapport with her husband, and dazzled and astounded the engineers by her complete and intelligent concept of the chief's theories and plans.

"And here I thought I was just the meek little wife," I smiled at Wash. "They are giving me much too much credit, I fear. You are still the Chief Engineer of the Brooklyn Bridge."

My husband continued smiling at me, "Keep reading, O meek one."

Day after day, when she could be spared from the sickroom in cold and wet, the devoted wife exchanged duties of chief nurse for those of chief engineer of the bridge, explaining knotty points, examining results for herself, and thus she established the most perfect means of communication between the structure and its author. How well she discharged this self-imposed duty the grand and beautiful causeway best tells.

"I think," said Wash, "that we are both given credit for our labors, that's all. Continue, please."

The true woman possesses, above all attributes, that lovely and most womanly characteristic, modesty. Out of deference to Mrs. Roebling's aversion to posing in public and standing apart from her sex, those who have long been aware of her noble devotion and the incalculable services she rendered to the people of the two cities, to the world indeed, have discreetly kept their knowledge to themselves.

"I think that certainly sums it up well," Wash said reaching across the table to take my hand.

"Perhaps you are the more humble of the two of us, Chief." I replied. As we completed reading the morning papers, a small item caught my eye.

"It says here that P.T. Barnum intends to take elephants across the bridge to prove its solidity! How silly," I said. "I'm sure he's just saying that to get more publicity for himself."

"I hope he knows there are tolls for animals as well as people. Five cents for a horse and rider, ten cents for a horse and carriage, five cents per cow."

"I'm sure he can afford the fees. What will they charge for an elephant?" We laughed together at that image.

But one week later, we sat at the upstairs window with John and watched twenty-one elephants cross the Brooklyn Bridge.

"This reminds me of when you took me to the circus years ago, Mama," John commented.

"If Barnum had thought the bridge wouldn't hold, why would he be in the procession? He sure knows how to attract attention to his circus, doesn't he?" Wash said.

"The bridge appears to have many uses for many people," I added.

Decoration Day was another bright, sunny day. Crowds started filing across the bridge early in the morning. Wash sat at the window watching and reading the papers with John at his side. I was in my study when Washington and

John both began shouting. I ran to them. Wash had his telescope to his eyes.

"Something horrible is happening! There are too many people on the bridge! I think.…it looks like some are falling!"

"Oh, Mama, look!" John pointed. At the top of the Brooklyn stairs to the promenade, human beings were piled up like dolls in a toy box. Arms and legs were flailing in all directions. You could see hats, bags, and umbrellas falling from the stairway.

"Oh my Lord, what is happening? Where are the police?" I put my hands on my heart and began to weep. How could something so horrible happen on our beautiful bridge? I wanted to shield John from the horror, but he was much too old to protect from the atrocities of life. We sat there, helplessly watching people pile up like so much firewood in a heap.

"Oh, God, what have we done?" My husband wept. I went to his side.

"We haven't done anything. Something has gone terribly wrong this morning, and we will find out what it is so it never happens again."

There was constant pounding on our front door, and I directed the maid to ignore it and not let anyone in. Reporters were lurking about, arrogantly searching for a failure to report although we had not been on the bridge witnessing the terrible event. It was not a mechanical or building issue; it was foolish human beings, and there was certainly nothing we could do to help.

"This is one time I wish I did not have this bird's eye view of the bridge," Wash said, moving the back of his hand across his eyes.

It wasn't until late in the evening that we let the chief of police in to tell us what had happened.

"I am sorry to report twelve deaths on the bridge today," he started. "We are not sure exactly what happened. There have been various stories." He wiped his handkerchief across his forehead in anguish.

"Chief, please tell us what you've heard. Is any of it plausible?" Wash asked.

"If I hadn't seen it with my own eyes, I wouldn't have thought any of it possible. There were so many people on the stairs at each end of the bridge that when they all got on and started coming toward each other, there was nowhere to go. No one could move, and people started to panic. They were shoving from both directions, and they couldn't back up because the stairways were full of fallen bodies. I heard a woman scream on the stairway, and many others started to scream as well. I'm so sorry Colonel and Mrs. Roebling."

"Please do not apologize or blame yourself. It is a freak occurrence. I'm sure there will be lawsuits, and then maybe we will hear more details," I said.

"I also heard that someone in the middle of the bridge screamed that it was falling, and people tripped over each other to get off. Another story was that a gang of roughs started pushing people. Either way, twelve people were trampled to death. A hell of a way to go."

We spent the evening quietly grieving over the disaster and attempting to explain to our son what folly human beings are capable of.

One month later, Wash asked me to write his letter of resignation. His work was over, and Mr. Low would be pleased to be done with him. I hoped it would be my last duty as chief secretary. So many erroneous reports had been circulated about my husband for the past fourteen years. As I wrote the brief letter, I put them all to rest in hopes that our new life would be without controversy and gossip. No one needed to further concern themselves with the health of the chief engineer except me.

Chapter 29

There were days when she was unhappy, she did not know why—when it did not seem worthwhile to be glad or sorry, to be alive or dead.

Kate Chopin
The Awakening

That winter, there was a great blizzard. The snow fell for days without cessation, and it was noted in the press that the bridge showed particular strength in holding many tons of snow. It was astounding when we could only see a faint shadow of the structure through the blinding whiteness although the bridge was only one-half mile away. The blizzard lasted for days, and we were truly snowed in. It piled up so high around the front and back doors that we could not exit the house. We had enough provisions for the week, but the darkness and isolation set off one of the worst dark spells I had ever experienced. We no longer had a project to work on, none of our daily papers were delivered, and we had so little to distract us from the storm that one morning I simply couldn't arise from my bed.

"Emily, my dear, when are you getting up? Can I bring you a cup of tea?"

"No, nothing."

"I've never seen you like this. It seems it is my turn to nurse you back to yourself, but I fear I do not have any idea of how to do that."

"There is nothing to be done. Please leave me be."

"I will return shortly," he said, and closed the door quietly behind him.

I heard him speaking to John and attempting to reassure our son that I would be fine, but this time I was not sure. What good was I, sitting at my desk writing about issues that never changed? Of what use could I be to my husband, now that his health had improved and his life's work, completed? My son was grown and able to care for himself. But who was I? No one. A nobody in this world. These terrible thoughts traveled through my mind unceasingly, and I was powerless to stop them. I had the ability to look at my life differently, but in those gloomy days, I became completely incapable of changes in my thinking. I felt bruised from the inside, and an aberration to society.

Three days passed. I attempted to read selections from Whitman or Dickinson, but they brought me no joy or relief from my obsessive ruminations. Wash brought me tea and toast, and I would take a few sips or bites, then lie back down, exhausted. Debilitated for no earthly reason. I felt myself falling farther down into a black pit of despair and lifelessness. No one could understand my state of being. No one could come to my aid. The snow flew outside the window, the wind sounded like a child screaming, and I was utterly alone in my tortured mind and vacuous heart.

On the fourth day, I was awakened by a sliver of sun falling across my eyes. I sat up and saw that the snowstorm had ceased and I was still alive. My beautiful son opened the door a crack and peeked in at me. I felt ashamed, mortified that I had been absent from my own life and his for so many days. What a despicable example of a parent, a wife, a human being of faith.

"Mother, someone is here to see you."

"Oh, John, I cannot see anyone today." I didn't wonder who it was or how it was possible for someone to travel the snow-covered streets and enter through the blocked-in doorway.

"But you look better," he said hopefully. "Are you going to come downstairs today?"

"I'm sorry to disappoint you, but I don't think so, dear."

John looked crestfallen, but said, "Mrs. O' Connell is here."

Mary waited for almost an hour as I lethargically bathed and dressed for the first time all week. When I entered the dining room, she was sitting at the table with tea and biscuits she had prepared in my kitchen. I'm sure there was little else. I went to her, and we embraced.

"I'm sorry if this was a bad time, Emily."

"You don't know how much it means to me to see you again, Mary. How are the children?"

"Everyone is well, and so am I."

"What are the children doing now?" I asked out of propriety and expectation, but not with my normal true concern.

"Bridget and Deirdre recently married and live in New York. I'm afraid they don't have any easier life than I gave them. Business owners still don't want to hire the Irish."

"Oh, my goodness, that's awful. Can I do anything to help?" I asked, feeling the strain of the conversation.

"Oh, no, your generosity got us through some terrible times, you know."

"What about the others?"

"I have not seen Timothy for months. I don't know where he's gone. Oh, Emily, he takes to the drink just like his father. I can only pray he is still alive and will return to me one day."

"But he's still a child, isn't he?"

"He is sixteen, but still too young to be on his own," she said tearfully.

"Yes, much too young. We are friends with the chief of police in Brooklyn. I will have him look out for Timothy," I offered.

"Oh, I don't think he's still in Brooklyn. If he were someone would have seen him. The city streets are so dangerous, and New York is so vast…."

"I will pray every night for him. I'm sure you will see him again." I took Mary's hand and patted it, not knowing what else to do. Her heartbreak was unfathomable.

"Are you quite all right? You look unlike the Emily I knew," she asked, genuinely concerned.

"Oh yes, I am fine. Just a bit of a spell…this weather, you know. It gets one down sometimes. I haven't been out of the house, and…," My brain seemed to drift away from me.

"Well, yes, it's been a brutal winter, to be sure. I wonder if I can do anything for you."

"Oh, no, dear, I have Wash and John to watch over me." I hesitated, then, after a time I said, "I am so sorry we lost touch, as I am very fond of you."

"I know you are, but we don't live the same type of lives. It was to be expected. I know you tried to help me when Dennis was...."

"I would have helped much more if I could," I said. "What do you mean, it was to be expected? Am I not a loyal friend?"

"Oh, yes, it's not that. It's just...well, I have employment now in the Browning Garment Factory. It doesn't pay much but...."

"How much are you paid each week, Mary? If you don't mind me asking."

"My wages are 30 cents a day."

"Oh my, the men at the bridge made that much an hour! I'm quite sure you labor as much in your factory job. That's not a living wage. That's less than two dollars a week!" I felt myself begin to feel something. A familiar inkling of concern, even outrage at the injustice Mary was enduring. Being up and about and conversing with another woman was reviving me.

"Yes, I know. We work ten hours a day and six days every week, but we have no choice."

"We? Do you mean you and the children?"

"Yes, me and young Daniel and Siobhan as well."

"Are you telling me children are working in the garment factories?"

"Oh, yes, many children. But Siobhan is almost fourteen now and Daniel is seventeen."

"What kind of working conditions are there?"

"Emily, that does not matter," she interrupted. "We are lucky to have jobs at all, and I just want to take care of myself and my family. If I have the sin of pride, so be it. People like you don't know what it's like to struggle to care for your children, to put food on the table every day. I thought it best that we let our friendship go, although you and your husband were most generous to me and my family."

"It is true that I have never experienced some of the trials you have faced, but that does not mean that I cannot put myself in your place as a sympathetic human being and a woman. I believe things are going to change for women in the future. You and your children should have never been afraid in your own home," I said, taking her hand.

"You don't have to think about money when you have it," she said.

I paused, trying to imagine Mary's life, so many lives, knowing the veracity of her statement full well.

"It is true that I have never wanted for anything," I said, "But does that make me a bad person, an unfeeling person? I did not choose the family I was born into, just as you did not choose yours."

"Be that as it may, I came to you today first to thank you for your kindness and the money you sent me. It truly helped us. But now that we are living back in the area, you may hear things."

"What sorts of things?"

"Well, I've found some happiness in my life," she hesitated. "Something many people will not approve of."

"I cannot imagine not approving of anything that brings you happiness, or the safety and well-being of your children."

"That is because you don't know what I am talking about. You don't even know such a thing exists."

"Whatever could you mean? I am very aware of many things, dear."

"Not this, I'm sure." She looked sad, but at the same time, was trying to tell me about something that made her happy. I was perplexed.

"It's that I have found love," she said with no joy in her voice.

"That's wonderful! Why would I not understand? One never forgets the first feelings of love, do they?"

"'Tis forbidden. A sinful love."

"Do you mean the man is married?" I felt all joy drain from me. There was a long pause, a silence in which my mind was jumbled up with illicit visions that I did not want to see.

"It's not a man. It's a woman."

I said nothing for a moment. I had heard of such things, but knew nothing of what caused such a strange abnormality.

"I know that you will no longer want to associate with me, so I just came to thank you for everything you did to try to help."

"Why would I not associate with you? I will admit that what you have told me is out of my realm of experience, but that means nothing. Mary, your very life was in danger when you lost the baby, and then with a husband who mistreated you. I want nothing but your safety and happiness, I assure you."

"I don't know what to say," she replied, "My family has disowned me for being with Sarah. They could not understand why we would live together, then one night, there was an argument and Sarah told them we were in love. Before that they had thought we were good friends, just two lonely women. There was a horrible scene. They have threatened to take my Siobhan and Daniel away, so unless we can find a way to explain our living arrangements, I may have to leave Brooklyn again."

"What do the other children think of all of this?"

"They don't ask much. Sarah and I must hide our affection for each other at all times. I'm sure my older children understand, but I am unable to speak to them about it. All Siobhan and Daniel know is that there is food at every meal and that Sarah is kind to them. We have been so happy, so safe, so hopeful."

"Then that is all that matters. They have no father, after all. Another person to love them is a blessing. It matters not to children who the people are in their lives, as long as they are loved and cared for. But I am concerned about your family's intentions and what I can do to help."

"If someday we are gone again, you will know why," she said. "I will not let anyone take my children. I am not done raising them. I have already lost my Timothy."

"I'm afraid it is we who might be leaving. John has been admitted into Rensselaer Polytechnic Institute, following in his father's footsteps. Now that Washington's health is improving a bit and his work here is done, I intend to convince Wash to move to Troy to be near our only child while we can. When he graduates from Rensselaer, who knows where he will go?"

My insides clenched at what I had just said. My son was healthy and strong. My marriage secure. We could live wherever we chose. And Mary was correct when she said I had never had to think about money. I felt worthless at that moment in my own good fortune.

"Then we will do a much better job of staying in touch this time, won't we?" Mary said cheerily.

"Yes, I will write to you weekly. Will you do the same, Mary? I do want to hear of your continued happiness and good health."

"Thank you, my friend. You are the only person in my life who has not abandoned me. First Dennis, and now my family."

"I promise you, I only want the best for you. And you will write to me immediately when Timothy returns home, as I'm sure he will."

Diane Vogel Ferri

Book 2
Away from the Bridge

Diane Vogel Ferri

Chapter 30

We too often bind ourselves by authorities rather than by truth.
                                                    Lucretia Mott

The bridge represented victory as well as tragedy for our family. A place of joys and sorrows, of beauty and progress and endless controversies. We never tired of its majestic sight, but once my husband's life's work was done, it was time for him to retire and be away from the work that had encompassed his attention for so many years.

"Now that we are free to have our own lives, I would like to move to Troy while John is attending Rensselaer," I announced, trying to sound confident.

"Do you really think that is necessary? John is almost an adult. Does he really want his mother hovering about?"

"Hovering? Is that what you think I would do? We have only one child, and my role as mother is far from complete. Do you intend to just abandon our son to the world? To not care what happens to him, just because he is of college age?" This matter was so heavy on my heart that tears flooded my eyes, something neither of us was accustomed to.

"My goodness, don't cry."

"I can cry if I wish! I've been the strong one for so long."

We were silent for a few moments, not looking at each other, as if what had been uttered was an unspoken wound in our marriage.

"I'm sorry. I didn't mean that."

"Yes, yes you did," Wash reassured me. "And you are correct. You have had no choice but to be strong and brave and unrelenting in your care for John and me. You have been calm when my nervous disease got the best of me. You intervened with contractors when I was unable to communicate well. You've given up much for my dreams and ambition, and those of hundreds of other workers. Now, I suppose, it's your turn."

"Thank you," I said, still feeling an inner sting. "You know, you missed a great deal of John's life while you were working. Maybe you can make it up to him now, guide him into engineering as your father did for you."

"If that's what he wants."

"My dear, that is all the boy has ever wanted—to be just like you. Don't you know that?"

"No, I'm not sure I knew that," he paused. "A father should be aware of his son's dreams, shouldn't he? My own father, while an accomplished and admired man, was often too busy in his work to care for his family. I did not allow myself to be eaten up inside over that, but followed in his ways and tried to understand his ambitions. Perhaps I have done exactly the same thing to my own son. Does he truly want to be an engineer, or does he feel he has no choice?"

"That is something you can discover simply by talking with him, I think."

"I shall do so," Wash said hanging his head.

"It's not too late. If we move to Troy."
"Yes, let's do that."

1885 Troy, New York

In Troy I finally had the time to begin working on my first book. I did a genealogical research on my paternal ancestors and discovered many important relatives in history including a French nobleman and his Huguenot descendants. Another relative, Claude de Maitre, settled in New York and Anglicized his name to Delameter. I also learned of distinguished ancestors such as Richard Warren, Duke of Normandy, and great-grandfather of William the Conqueror.

Most exciting was another Richard Warren who came to America on the Mayflower and was the twelfth signer of the Mayflower Compact. I found renewed purpose in visiting cemeteries and compiling my family tree. It was just the sort of project I needed to ward off the dark spells.

Our home remained peaceful so Wash could continue his recovery. I also worked diligently on plans for our new home in Trenton, where we planned to live after John graduated with his civil engineering degree. Washington's strength and virility continued to improve in the stress free environment, but he became somewhat restless as well.

"I believe I will involve myself in a new project soon," he said.

"Oh, Wash, are you sure? Your health is paramount."

"Of course, but I have been summoned to consult on the Niagara Falls suspension bridge."

I held him close and said, "Once again, the world needs you, but not more than I. Must we be apart again?"

"Yes, but not for too long. You have our son to keep track of." He winked at me.

"Yes, I know he is practically a grown man, but he is my only child. Don't make fun of my devotion to him. Who will I be when I am no longer a mother?"

"You will always be a mother. That doesn't fade with time, does it? Maybe even a grandmother someday. I intend to continue in my role as father," he smiled contentedly at me.

"I am trying to prepare myself for when John has his own life by participating in new ventures like my genealogical research and my book, but…."

"That's my Emily. I believe in you and your future. Your devotion to both of us has been admirable. Do something for yourself now. You won't have to look after me for a while. I will take the nurse with me. I will be fine, and so will you."

I tried several other times to talk Wash out of traveling, but was unsuccessful. Shortly after he left for Niagara Falls, I had a message from Rensselaer to come immediately. John was ill. I rushed to his side, bringing his doctor with me. John had been stricken with symptoms of his weak heart. My own heart was failing as well at the sight of my handsome young son lying on a bed, gasping for breath. He had experienced several bouts of weakness growing up, but it had been years since it had happened. I had dreaded these days since his childhood doctor had informed me of the possibility of heart troubles. Wash had never been told about John's condition for fear it would exacerbate his nervous problems. John and I had agreed to keep it a secret. Now I debated within myself whether to tell him.

"Please do not tell Papa about this episode," John implored.

"I feel that I've been dishonest with him for so long already. We both have." I brushed his light brown hair back from his face. It is not right to see your child in physical distress when you are the adult, when he should be enjoying his college days and his youth.

"I don't think I could stand to see Father decline again," John objected. "We know that worry can bring that on. That's why we have kept this from him during his illness."

"Yes, but he is so much better."

"Mother, it's my life now. Please. I want my father to gain strength from me, not give him another burden."

"You could never be a burden to either of us. All you have been is a joy all of your life." I blinked back tears. I knew I must honor my son's wishes, yet, protect my husband in the process.

"It will be as you wish, John. But if you take a turn for the worse, I might have to contact your father after all."

I stayed awake that night. The secret I had kept from Wash was unfair to him. I imagined our positions reversed, and how hurt I would feel. I decided to write to Wash and explain the situation in the gentlest way so as not to upset him. John was close to graduation, and Wash would return for the event. If John did not recover from this episode by then, how would it be explained?

John did recover splendidly, and was given advice from the college physicians on how to proceed carefully with his condition which they continued to diagnose as a weak heart. I told John that I had written his father, and although he was somewhat annoyed, he conceded the need for honesty within the family.

The following week, a letter arrived from Wash. He was shocked at John's condition and appalled at my deception. Nevertheless, he wrote: *Your letter makes me feel ashamed of having shown any discontent with my lot when I think of the fortitude and courage with which you have born your cares and anxieties.* No matter what the circumstances, my husband had always been forgiving and easily saw the best in people, especially me. It was more than I deserved.

To John, he wrote:

I was wholly unaware of the fact that you were not in the best of health, strong and robust, until I received your mother's letter. You yourself have never made mention of it in writing to me, and to learn thus of your ill health has made me forget and sink my own little grievances in my solicitude for and constant thought of you.

Happily married couples tell themselves that they have no secrets from each other, but even the most truthful people carry thoughts and burdens that are never shared aloud. How many times after intimacies did I look into my husband's searching gray eyes and convince him of my satisfaction when there had been very little? How many times had John come in from playing short of breath, and I kept him from his father until he recovered? In truth, there had been so many days when I would have been happy to have finished the Brooklyn Bridge project myself and return to normalcy, but I never said so. It took all of my strength not to shout it to the world, to spit out my grievances to a reporter. There had been days when I yearned to yell at Wash, asking why on earth he had assumed his father's dreams, why he hadn't been able to predict more accurately how many years of our lives would be consumed with his ambitions? I repeatedly refrained from explanations about my dark spells, terrified that Wash would see them as weakness.

Married people never speak their fantasies about other lives, other loves. Once there was an attractive, young nurse who attended to Wash several days a week. I never said how uncomfortable I was with her presence. I struggled through each day in discomfort while she was there, hiding in other rooms in my own home. I felt the privacy of our bedroom had been invaded, yet there was nothing I could do about it. I lay awake at night wondering whether my husband would prefer a prettier sight each morning across the breakfast table, but I never asked him because I did not want to seem petty or lacking in confidence.

We hide many things from our loved ones and from the world. We make great efforts to only reveal our strengths, and never our failures. As women, we are not given allowances for emotions that are unappealing to men. Mayor Low suggested that my anger at him should make me unqualified to vote, yet how many men gathered in our parlor on many evenings, shouting and arguing for what they wanted? They felt free to insult each other, curse, and raise their voices without inhibition. The next day, it seemed to be forgotten.

Men also enjoyed daily comforts that were not afforded women. Their very clothing is of their choosing and for their luxury. Women are expected to crush their ribs and waistlines into the smallest possible dimension with torturous corsets. On sweltering summer days, we are covered from head to toe in layers of petticoats and crinolines and men wonder why we sometimes faint! It is not from emotional distress—it is from the heat! I have witnessed men at the bridge stripping off their clothing to their undergarments and leaping into the river after work. What does a woman have but a tiny fan to ease her perspiration?

When I was a girl in school, we read *The Scarlet Letter*, by Nathaniel Hawthorne. I had raised my hand and asked why Hester Prynne was being punished for her sins, but not the pastor who impregnated her. My teacher sputtered and stammered and clearly had no answer to my innocent observation. I still thought about our friend Henry Beecher. Although glad he went on to a successful life, I wondered about the women he had preyed upon and the effect on the family when only the man's desires were fulfilled.

I often thought about a childhood friend named Elizabeth who lived with her father. Her mother died while giving birth to Elizabeth, and she had no siblings. She was often absent from school, and I could not understand why. One day, I decided to visit her and bring some schoolwork she had missed. As I approached the house, I heard cries and shouting. I hesitantly walked up the front steps and peered in the window to see Elizabeth's father lifting her dress. I was horrified, but did not understand what I was witnessing. I had never experienced abuse of any kind, except for the meanness of my own brother, and in my fright, I ran away weeping. I never told anyone what I had seen. Eventually, we were told that Elizabeth had moved to another town. That scene never left my mind, and I wondered why a man would overtake a young girl like that. Was it because men were larger in physical stature and strength that made them believe they were more powerful, more entitled to have what they wanted at all times?

I tired of the fact that men found my mathematical skills wondrous. Why would my brain be less capable than theirs in that line? Most girls were not exposed to such subjects, and did not have the opportunities to apply those skills, even if they had them. I prayed that someday that would change; perhaps, one day, we would have a granddaughter who would be able to fulfill her own desires and talents freely.

My friend Mary never left my mind, either. A long-awaited letter arrived, but she did not inform me of anything pertinent.

Dear Emily,

We miss you and your family and hope you are well.

You cannot imagine how many people cross the bridge each day in carriages and on foot. Visitors from all over the world are in Brooklyn every day of the week. I don't know what it would be like to have accomplished something so great in life as you and your husband have. Sometimes I tell people that I know you and they think me daft or a prevaricator!

The children are well. Both me and my Bridget earned a raise of 2 cents an hour and we are fine. Please do not send any more money. You have done too much for us already. Just accepting my life as you have is all I could ask for in a friend. You must be so proud of young John in college like he is.

Please be well my friend. I hope we see each other soon.

Affectionately,
Mary O'Connell

I had a sense of helplessness whenever I thought of Mary and her children. I did not understand her relationship with Sarah, but I did wish for her happiness. I put the letter down and found myself wondering how a woman could ever manage in life without a husband. It seemed a silly thing to wonder, given all my blabbering about the strength of women. It was terribly wrong that women were still dependent on men in so many ways. Susan B. Anthony had begun her fight for working women sixteen years ago, and so little progress had been made. The strictly patriarchal society in which we lived allowed men to not only control all the wealth and political power, but the upbringing of children as well. That was certainly a sphere where women were superior. How my friend Mary was surviving I did not understand at all.

Chapter 31

Greatness lies, not in being strong, but in the right using of strength; and strength is not used rightly when it serves only to carry a man above his fellows for his own solitary glory.

Henry Ward Beecher

In Troy, I'd often wake in the morning thinking I was in my bed in Columbia Heights, that I would pull the drapes back and see a massive structure just outside the window. Some days, I could not fathom that we were no longer working on the Brooklyn Bridge or how we had done it all those years. When Wash was home, he and I still sat at the breakfast table reading the morning.

"I see our former pastor Henry Ward Beecher is in the news again," I said.

"Oh, is that right? What is it now?"

"It seems he is endorsing Grover Cleveland for president in his run for another term."

"I was just reading about Cleveland. There is sufficient evidence to suggest that he has fathered an illegitimate child. Is that the sort of man we want running our country?" Wash commented.

"This article says that, although Cleveland has evidently fathered an illegitimate child, our dear Henry believes he should be forgiven that indiscretion." I looked up for Wash's reaction. "Of course, Henry would like to see a man forgiven such sins!"

"What is Henry doing these days, besides forgiving other men their sinful ways?"

"He is continuing to lecture around the country. His *gospel of love,* no doubt." Wash and I sniggered quietly.

My husband often inspired me with his versatile interests. Although unpretentious, he was a classical scholar, a fine linguist, and a mineralogist. He took time each day to bird-watch and listen to music. It was time for me to expand my interests as well.

Troy was filled with the grandeur of the past. We lived on the corner of Washington Park, one of only two privately owned urban ornamental parks in the country. I decided to become involved in the society life of Troy with the time I had while planning for our grand new house in Trenton.

We opened our home to John's fellow students. The well-known musicians Dudley Buck and banjo player Reuben Brooks were hired to entertain us, and we encouraged everyone to dance. Wonderful refreshments were provided to keep the students happy and well fed.

One lively night, the dancing lasted into the wee hours. John was having a wonderful time and dancing with a lovely young girl. I watched with delight until I saw him falter and droop into her frail arms. She looked up in fright, and I ran to John's side. Some of his schoolmates helped him to a sofa, and he was revived in minutes, but I was relieved that the episode was no longer a secret to Wash.

Wash walked over to John, slapped him gently on the back, and made light of the whole thing. "Too much excitement dancing with this pretty girl, son?"

"I guess so, Father. Maybe I haven't eaten enough this evening."

They kept John's dignity intact in front of his friends. I smiled at Wash, knowing he understood the humiliation that physical weakness could bring about. It ended up bonding my husband and son.

Shortly after that, the news arrived that Henry Ward Beecher had gone to the loving arms of his Lord. Whether he was what he purported to be or not was now in the hands of God. Brooklyn had declared a day of mourning, and the state legislature recessed in his honor.

"We must go back to attend the funeral, Wash."

"Oh, I don't know, my days are….what I mean to say is that my health…."

"I do not see any reason that you cannot make it back to Brooklyn. You traveled to Niagara Falls."

"John might need me."

"Really? That's your excuse now? What is it truly? Why can you not travel to Brooklyn for the funeral of a friend?"

"I don't want to see the bridge right now. I have been having too many memories of all that it cost us, all the physical pain, the time lost, the deaths."

"I didn't know you were experiencing such regrets."

"Not regrets, just memories, and not the good ones. You were the one to cross the walkway. You were the one to hear the speeches on Opening Day, not I. I do not have those victories to celebrate."

"I'm sorry," I said, "I never thought of it that way. Perhaps I will go myself. We should have someone represent the Roeblings after all the years of Henry as our pastor. And, of course, for Eunice."

"Yes, you should attend. Maybe you can tell me how the bridge is faring now, how people are using it for the good of mankind, the benefit of the cities."

Crowds of people in mourning clothes were streaming down the streets surrounding Plymouth Church. The lines to enter the church were five across, and extended for as far as one could see. I was not sure I would be admitted, but one of the Beecher children ushered me in to greet Eunice.

Inside the church, Henry's body lay in state, the casket adorned with roses and an enormous cross of flowers behind it. Even the organ had been decorated and the balcony strewn with greenery. Henry's sisters, Harriet, Isabella, and Catherine, were sitting in the front pew, comforting Eunice. I nodded and joined the line to pay my respects at the casket. Eunice looked away from me. Harriet rose and ushered me past the crowd to the front of the line. We stood quietly gazing at the man who had lived such an abundant, influential life. Although I had not always believed in his virtues, he had done his best to give himself to all he encountered, including the Roeblings.

"He was just a man, was he not?" Harriet asked quietly.

"Yes, we are all human. That is why we need forgiveness. I am sure the Lord is rejoicing to welcome Henry home today," I said, taking Harriet's hand. "He is saying, 'Well done, my child.'"

"Thank you, Emily. Thank you for always being present, for your forgiving ways."

"It took me some time to remember Henry's virtues, not his foibles in later years, but I do remember. I do not believe it is up to us to judge others when we all have our failings. Henry brought comfort and strength to us when Wash was sick, and he visited often to offer prayer, and support. He even visited the bridge to encourage our workers."

"Yes." Harriet took my gloved hand.

"Do you think Eunice will accept my condolences?"

"Why wouldn't she?"

"I was not always the friend she needed, I'm afraid."

"You are much too hard on yourself, Emily."

After the funeral, I asked to be taken to the bridge. I sat quietly in the carriage and watched multitudes of people climbing the stairway, despite the March winds whipping their coats and dresses about, as they crossed into New York. Dozens of carriages flowed beneath them like a parade. All was well. I would tell Wash that his legacy was secure, his effort being enjoyed and appreciated every day of every year. He could be at peace. But as his wife, I would try to be more understanding of the reality that the Brooklyn Bridge had not always been a joyful memory for the chief engineer.

Diane Vogel Ferri

Chapter 32

Your children distant will become,
and wide the gulf will grow;
The lips of loving will be dumb,
The trust you used to know
Will in another's heart repose,
Another's voice will cheer
And you will fondle baby clothes
and brush away a tear.

          Robert William Service

The years flew by, as they always do. When you think back to the years gone by, it is hard to recall what you spent all your precious days doing. Life is fleeting at best, all the more reason to accomplish something on every day God gives you. Most of my days were filled with meetings with contractors and decorators for our impending move to our home in Trenton. My greatest wish was that it would be our final move in a marriage full of moving from place to place and endless upheavals. I continued to research my ancestor Richard Warren and spent many days in my study. We spent as much time as we could with John when he was free from studying and his own social obligations.

  Then on June 13, 1888, we gathered as a family to see our only child graduate with a degree in civil engineering, as the third generation of Roeblings to do so. I reflected on so many things as I sat in the Music Hall for the ceremony. Commodore B. F. Isherwood of the United States Navy told the graduates that the present age of history should be called the "age of engineering."

"Better for them that art were dead, poetry forgotten, and eloquence forever dumb, rather than be deprived of the mighty gifts which engineering bestows on the present and promises to vastly increase in a magnificent future!" the Commodore bellowed.

It was only five years ago that we opened the Brooklyn Bridge to the world. I nodded my head in agreement with the Commodore's statement, and looked next to me to see Wash smiling and nodding, too.

"You did a wonderful job raising our son, Em. I was preoccupied or ill so much of his childhood," he said, taking my hand.

After the ceremony, John walked toward us with a lovely young woman at his side, the girl he had danced with at our home the night he collapsed over a year ago. With all the confusion, we'd not been properly introduced.

"Mother, Father, I would like you to meet Margaret McIlvaine. She likes to be called Reta." He smiled at her in the way of a young man in love.

"What a surprise, John. We had no idea that you had found someone special. How do you do, Miss McIlvaine?" I extended my hand, and she took it warmly. I felt a bit betrayed by not knowing that Reta and John had been involved, but reminded myself that it was John's life, not mine.

"Colonel and Mrs. Roebling, I have heard so much about you. John speaks only fondly of you both."

No Life But This

"All of this is cause for celebration!" Wash remarked. "Let us return to the house to get to know each other better. Would that suit you, Miss McIlvaine?"

"I'd be honored," she smiled demurely, and although I immediately found her charming, it was a bittersweet moment for me as a mother. I knew my role as the most important woman in my son's life would soon end.

Reta was the daughter of Edward and Anne Hunt McIlvaine of Trenton, and only twenty-one years old, but she and my son clearly were taken with each other. I told Wash I predicted an approaching wedding, and I was correct. I was not only thrilled at my son's happiness, but also at the prospect of grandchildren. My dearest hope was that my son would be blessed with more children than Wash and me.

I still worried about John's health, although he was carrying on without any hindrance to his goals. Reta also suffered from occasional breathing problems, but appeared to be strong. I knew John would have great sympathy for any health issues his new wife might have after growing up with an impaired father and his own battles with a weak heart.

"Mama, look at what is in the paper today," John said. "Mr. Edison has filed for a patent on a new invention. He calls it the Optical Phonograph."

"How does that man continue to come up with new ideas?"

"It's a system that combines sound and images concurrently. Edison says it will do for the eye what the phonograph does for the ear."

"That's a wonder."

"The phonograph has recorded sound vibration on tracks around the edges of a cylinder and Edison says pictures will be recorded in the same way."

"I will look forward to that. Is there a photograph of such a device?" I walked to my son's side and looked over his shoulder. My eyes spotted another article.

"Oh, no, look at that. Louisa May Alcott has passed. What a loss. *Little Women* shall forever be my favorite book. I wish I could write something as influential as that." I felt true sadness whenever someone of Alcott's stature passed away. It was as if their gifts, their singular talents died with them, never to be reborn.

"John, are you all right?" He suddenly looked pale and wan.

"Yes, Mama. I'm fine. Will you please stop worrying about me?"

"I'm afraid that is a promise a mother never can make. Now that you are working at the Roebling mill, you must be careful not to overexert yourself."

"I hardly think that sitting at a table with drawings and diagrams will exhaust me."

"Nevertheless, you have Reta now, and I hope your family will grow."

"Mama! We are not yet married!"

I stopped. I did not intend to be one of those mothers who treated a grown son as a child. There was nothing worse, in my opinion. My hopes and dreams for my son and his future family would remain in my heart only from that point forward. I promised.

Being away from the bridge and New York sometimes created a sense of isolation for me. Wash didn't care a whit about city life, but I missed being present for all the news of the day. I missed having messengers constantly knocking on our front door, as they had in Brooklyn. The vitality of the cities, the traffic, the noise, was something that maintained my energy. Troy was a lovely town, and it had been my idea to move there, but I worked to keep boredom at bay. It was my enemy.

Our newspapers were lifelines to the rest of the world, and Wash and I never failed to discuss the most interesting articles. I was glad we had kept that habit intact.

"I'm surprised I haven't heard you speak of the Congress for Women's Rights." Wash was holding his magnifying glass close to an article, squinting at the small type.

"Yes, I read about it."

"Susan B. Anthony organized it. Isn't she of interest to you?"

"Yes, of course, but I made a fuss about moving to Troy to enjoy the rest of my son's time with us, so I didn't think it proper to go running off to Washington, DC."

"I see."

"Besides, when the event was taking place, I was not feeling myself."

Wash did not respond to that, but I was sure he understood my reference.

I was of the mind that one could reinvent herself if the opportunity presented itself. A woman of my age, a woman whose son was grown, could become a new creature. Instead of bemoaning all that was lost, my reinvention could and would be whatever I wanted it to be. If I'd had a daughter, I would have told her that this is what women do throughout their lives. I was a girl, a young bride, a mother, a field engineer—by opportunity, not choice—now I was to take on the mantle of a mother-in-law and, I hoped, a grandmother. What other good I could do in the world remained to be seen.

Chapter 33

But Mary treasured up all these things and pondered them in her heart.

Luke 2:19

There were no words to describe my emotions on my son's wedding day. Now my son would always have the shelter of someone's love to come home to; they would weave themselves into a bountiful basket of safety and protection, just as Wash and I had.

The years of wiping a runny nose, rocking in a chair all night, listening for his breathing sounds as I knelt by his bed to pray were in the past. I could feel his little arms wrapped around my legs as I tried to leave the house. I could hear his small voice, now the sonorous voice of a man. I felt like a disassembled puzzle that could not be put back together. Where had the years gone? They were snow under the sun.

The warm spring day of the wedding was the harbinger of all to come. It was the fruition of a lifetime of love, and that very same love would now be passed on to someone else. My heart held a confluence of joy and fear. Joy for my son and his lovely new wife, but fear for myself. Would I find my new place in the world? Would I be the kind of mother-in-law a young woman needed, and not overstep the boundaries? Most of all, would I find something to replace the void in my life, the cavern in my heart?

Dressing for the wedding was a most difficult task, as my eyes would not stop tearing and burning. Once I was ready, I would have to leave the shelter of my room, walk down the stairs, and witness the beginning of a new chapter in all of our lives. I was not normally given to tears, but that day was unique. Workers had been at the house all week, preparing for the event, and that prevented me from truly reckoning what was about to happen. The ceremony would take place in the parlor, then everyone would move into the dining room for a reception.

I opened the door and peered out. There was no one in the hallway, so I walked slowly toward the top of the staircase. Reta was in another room, dressing. Wash quietly walked up behind me and took my arm. As we slowly descended the stairs, he handed me a lovely embroidered handkerchief with the date sewn into it.

"This is your day too, Mama," Wash said. "You look beautiful, as you always have to me. As lovely as the day we married so long ago."

With that, my emotions overflowed and I stopped and put the clean white handkerchief over my face until I could compose myself. I took a deep breath and we slowly completed our descent down the stairs. It seemed as if the last step did not exist. It was then that I saw John standing near the doorway, greeting guests. I went to his side and, for some reason, I could think of nothing to say. He looked at me queerly, as if my muteness was an anomaly, which it truly was.

"Mama, you look lovely. Thank you for being my mother." He took my arm in his and we moved towards the parlor.

The day went as planned, and had the quality of a dream. By nightfall, I did not think I could shake another hand or smile another smile. I was relieved when the last guest left. John and Reta changed out of their wedding clothes and stood by the door to leave on their wedding trip. Reta's parents, Wash, and I gathered in a sort of huddle, basking in the wonderful day. I took Mrs. McIlvaine's hand, and could see that she, too, had been overwhelmed with the event.

"We cannot thank you enough, Mama, Papa," John said.

"It was our pleasure, son. Now go and have a wonderful life," Wash said, shaking John's hand.

I felt a keen sense of loss in the months after the wedding. The wedding signified the true end of motherhood for me. My son belonged to someone else, and my job was completed. That there were no more children to usher into the world left a great gap in my soul. I fell into a short dark spell, although it was summer and sunlight flowed through the windows.

Once again, I spent too much time in bed, the drapes drawn, my appetite and rest evanescent. Wash climbed the stairs several times a day to check on me and bring me food and drink. I thought about how bad it was for him to strain himself for me, but could not seem to do anything about it.

One night, I spent restless hours tossing about. When sleep finally came to me, I dreamed of the bridge. I had the very real sensation of the first crossing, the joy, the acute pride and satisfaction, but then the dream turned grotesque. I saw John falling from the bridge, and in the dream, he was a child. I awoke with a startled gasp, sat up in bed, and felt my pulse throbbing my limbs. My mind replayed my little boy falling through the air, helpless, calling for me. I took several deep breaths and felt a turning, a sense of fate. I was not given to nightmares, and believed this one to be significant. "I must pull myself back together," I said aloud.

With that, Wash woke beside me and mumbled something incoherent.

"Go back to sleep, dear." I rose, donned my dressing gown, and left the room in the light of the moon.

In the deep glow of moonlight, I thought deeply about how I had spent the days since John's wedding. I was the embodiment of selfishness. I recalled the voice I had heard in times like this. The words *there is more, you are more* settled in my heart permanently. If there were more, then I was the one to ensure that it came to pass. No one else would rescue me from my pitiful spells; only I had the power to do that. The *more* would remain to be seen, but it was clear that Washington had not sat around, moping about lost time in his life. He had taken the reins and begun new projects, and I would do the same.

So much of life lay in the ability to make decisions that are final, binding, and cause change. Nothing could be achieved until one decided to first welcome it into one's life, then to follow through without doubt or imagined obstacles. I did not go into the work of the Brooklyn Bridge with my husband reluctantly. I made the decision that it would be my work as well as his. I rarely stopped to regret or question that decision, and we reveled together in its success. In this present spell nothing tangible pulled me into the darkness. I was a healthy woman of forty-six years of age, and life held no impediments. I would discover the meaning of *more* if it was the last thing I did!

Diane Vogel Ferri

Chapter 34

A gentleman opposed to their enfranchisement once said to me, 'Women have never produced anything of any value in the world.' I told him the chief product of women had been men and left him to decide whether the product was of any value.

Anna Howard Shaw

I threw myself into the design of the new home we planned to build in Trenton, New Jersey. We chose a large parcel of property on the banks of the Delaware River. An old homestead from the 1700s was demolished to make way for our commodious mansion, which would be constructed with cream-colored sandstone in the Tudor style. It was to have huge gables and towering chimneys. My knowledge of construction and engineering helped in designing the home to our specifications. Sometimes I consulted with Wash, but he plainly trusted me to do the job correctly.

The raindrops that had drummed on the roof through the night had turned to mist, and there was a gauze of fog over everything. There were no meetings planned with builders or decorators, and the day was unwelcoming. My brain felt like tumbleweeds. I walked down the same stairway to the same man sitting at the same table reading the same newspapers, and said to myself, "It's not his fault you are bored, Emily Roebling."

"Good morning, dearest," Wash said warmly.

"Yes, I suppose." I noted his crestfallen face. Was he anticipating my foul mood? Was he weary of dealing with it? For a moment, I felt pity for him, but then the years in which I had attended to his needs, his nervous conditions, his fears shot through my mind. It might be a woman's nature to care for others, but, at times, she craves the same nurturing. I had no choice but to sit at the table and lift a newspaper before me as I did every other morning. I glanced out the window and could plainly see that the weather held no improvement. The haze was so intense, I could barely see past the street.

I disappointed myself. My convictions had lasted for so little time. What was wrong with me? Then I opened the paper to something that quickened my pulse.

"It says here that The National Women's Suffrage Association and the American Woman Suffrage Association are merging." I put the newspaper down and looked over at Wash. He seemed disinterested.

"Wash, did you hear me?"

"Yes, dear. What's the difference?" He peered at me over his magnifying glass.

"Do you really want to know, or are you just placating me?"

"Well, I asked, didn't I?" He looked back at his paper and started humming almost imperceptibly.

I glared at him until the humming stopped and he returned my glare.

"The difference is that the National Women's Suffrage Association has been trying to secure women's enfranchisement through a federal constitutional amendment, and the American Woman Suffrage Association wants to do it through state-by-state campaigns."

"I'm inclined to think that an amendment is necessary to provide any long-lasting effect," Wash commented.

"Long-lasting? Do you mean this is just a temporary occurrence?"

"No, I didn't mean that."

"Do you realize how little progress has been made ever since the word 'male' was added to the Constitution? It completely eliminates half of the population! After the war, there was more discussion on opportunity for former slaves. It has taken three years of negotiations by these two organizations so they can merge."

"Hm, hmm."

"Wash! I am intent on voting for president before my life is over, yet I feel so helpless to help make that happen. Elizabeth Cady Stanton is president of the merged groups now. She has done so much, but she is only one woman."

"You are only one woman as well."

There was no use in trying to impress Wash with the importance of these issues, so I took myself into the study, and read for the rest of the morning, making notes of my thoughts, trying to find something, anything, to inspire me to action.

Commotion at the door made me look up to see John and Reta standing with Wash.

"What a wonderful surprise! You are bringing sunshine to this gloomy day. Come, sit."

"Mama, we have news," said John.

"Yes, what is it, dear?"

"You are going to be a grandmother!" Reta blurted.

"Oh my, already? Oh, I didn't mean that. This news is right on time, I would say. I am overjoyed, as you knew I would be." I got up to embrace Reta. Wash was shaking John's hand and beaming. I was ashamed of my sad demeanor and remembered that life always brought something unexpected that changed everything.

This wonderful blessing arrived sooner than expected, and I was thoroughly delighted. Wash didn't say much about the news, but I was certain he was happy as well. We immediately decided that our gift to the new little Roebling would be a complete nursery in John and Reta's new home, with all the accoutrements. The very next week, I traveled to New York to purchase the most beautiful bassinet, crib, rocking chair, and chiffarobe. We hired painters to make the walls a sunny yellow, and commissioned a mural on one side of the little one's room. On one wall, adorable baby animals marched across; on another, small sailboats cruised beneath a small image of the Brooklyn Bridge. Wash thought it a little silly, but Reta was overjoyed with the artwork.

Several months later, in the early morning on a glowing, crisp fall day a messenger arrived at the door. A little boy had been born to the John A. Roebling II family. He and his mother were doing splendidly. I immediately made arrangements for a carriage to take us to them, although we had not been invited. Wash argued that we should wait a day or two, but I was not about to miss a moment of my grandson's life. I certainly would not have the patience to wait a day or two!

When our carriage arrived at the house, John was waiting by the door looking happier than I had ever seen him. Wash handed him a bottle of our finest champagne, and we all embraced. The new father's eyes sparkled as he ushered us into the bedroom.

Reta looked like a child holding a child, and I wondered how it was possible that she had given birth only that morning. The nurse-midwife hovered nearby looking disapproving at our arrival. I went to Reta and she gently handed the beautiful baby to me. He had a shock of hazel hair and was tenderly sleeping as an angel.

When I held my first grandchild, Siegfried, for a solitary moment I believed him to be mine. The love was so intense, so genuine, that I never wanted to give him back to his mother. My body immediately began to sway in the familiar movement of one holding a baby. How this child was Siegfried, and not John, I could not grasp at that moment. But when he lustily began screaming, it broke my reverie and I realized I had nothing to offer him—nothing but my devotion and love. How blessed I was to know a child again, to give unblemished affection, to live to see the future of the Roebling family.

Diane Vogel Ferri

Chapter 35

West State Street, Trenton, New Jersey, 1893

The view of the Delaware River in Trenton was as breathtaking as the one of the East River in Brooklyn, but no city, no people, nothing man-made could be seen from our enormous windows except the rushing waters and the green hills that lined its banks. From the back of the house were views of Stacy Park, and Raritan Canal. There were elegant rooms for entertaining and more intimate chambers for the family. We commissioned a large stained-glass rendering of the Brooklyn Bridge that hung majestically above the main staircase facing the front of the house. In a certain light, it glowed as if it were three-dimensional, as if we were back in Brooklyn. In the evening, when the house was lit from within with Mr. Edison's wonderful lighting, people stopped in front of the house to view the window. They sat motionless in their carriages on the street, gazing at the glass rendition of our life's work. I wondered if they knew that the Chief Engineer lived in the home behind the stained glass.

The house had a lovely curled staircase, vaulted ceilings, and plenty of tall windows to let in the light I so craved. It was decorated with elegant china cabinets, wicker furniture, lovely flower-patterned drapery, and tiger and polar bear skin rugs on the floors, lush potted plants and beautiful artwork filled the house. Wash's conservatory held his orchids, and a special section for his mineralogy collection: beryls, aquamarines, topaz of varying hues. His prizes were a black diamond, and a large opal that he found in Nevada.

I had loved dogs as a girl, and at last we had the perfect playground for one. We inquired throughout Trenton, and found a large yellow mixed breed stray with great energy and vitality. His hair was scruffy and unruly, his bark wild and vibrant. We named him Ponto, which means "bridge" in Esperanto. He enjoyed chasing squirrels and digging up my flower beds daily, but I adored him. He was wonderful company on a dreary day. He must have viewed himself as a much smaller dog because he attempted to climb onto my lap every evening after dinner.

It didn't take long before Ponto found his way to the river. He would return hours later, adorned with mud from head to paws. Nevertheless, Wash and I enjoyed his enthusiasm for life. He made us laugh together, something we needed very much.

Whenever a small crowd gathered in the street to view the stained glass, Ponto would bark enthusiastically in an attempt to chase them away, simply doing his job as watchdog. There were reports of robberies in the area and we had many fine possessions, so we appreciated his vigilance.

Eventually, we had a complete staff of servants, and I was pleased with all of them. It was not always easy to find loyal employees, especially with the amount of precious and expensive objects in our home. Each one had to contend with our energetic beast as well, and they all seemed to fall in love with the boisterous animal.

One of the new housemaids screamed the first time she saw the white rooster I had had stuffed and mounted above the mantel. It was the one I'd carried on my first crossing of the bridge, and it reminded me of that wonderful victory. It always inspired a conversation when we entertained.

In the country, there was freedom from the propriety of the city. We owned the most exquisite carriages, and I enjoyed driving them myself. In the city, the sight would have been scandalous, but in Trenton, our coachman was happy to sit behind me and let me have my way. I resumed riding some of the many horses we owned when my joints were not too painful.

The house held a bowling alley and a billiards table. The bowling alley was a bone of contention between Wash and me. At first, I found it a frivolous waste of time, but I came to enjoy bowling, especially when we had guests. We entertained often, and had comfortable quarters for those who wished to stay overnight. Our late nights included card games and billiards.

We furnished a playroom for Siegfried, and silently wished for more little ones to fill it with fun. Wash had a wonderful time assembling a large train set for our grandson that we had purchased before we knew he was a boy. After meeting our little one, I took a two-day trip into New York to shop for toys at FAO Schwarz and arrived home with building blocks, a miniature farm and a rocking horse. I unpacked some of John's toys that I had saved, and Wash and I had a good time creating a playroom fit for a prince. John and Reta believed it too indulgent, but we did not concern ourselves with their disapproval. We were having too much fun being grandparents.

Joining several of Trenton's women's groups allowed us to make many new friends and acquaintances. We hosted many enjoyable parties, but I sometimes made the mistake of inviting new people I did not know very well. I always believed the more, the merrier, and was often overly anxious to have these neighbors get to know us. Most of them were well-to-do, but none of the men as accomplished as my unassuming husband.

"I understand that you were your husband's helper in building the bridge," Mrs. Jenkins remarked during the first course of our dinner.

"Well, yes, I wouldn't use the word 'helper.'" I started, but Wash interjected.

"Yes, Emily was of great assistance when I was unable to be present at the work site. She wrote out all of my correspondence with the workers and kept…"

"That must have been tough understanding what he was talking about, huh?" Mr. Jenkins interrupted.

"No, I had no trouble understanding the concepts of the engineering. I was usually able to answer any questions that the contractors had," I replied.

"Oh, come now. Aren't you exaggerating a bit?" Mr. Jenkins asked. "Women don't have a mind for such things."

"I'll have you know that I am an educated woman."

"What my wife is trying to say is that…."

"I can speak for myself, Washington." I turned to Mr. Jenkins. "Being a woman does not reduce our brains to idiocy. Please ask me anything you like about the building of the bridge, and I assure you I can answer it handily," I smiled at my husband expecting his support, but he was not smiling back.

"I…I wouldn't know what to ask," said Mr. Jenkins.

"Precisely," I said. "Now, if you'll excuse me, I will check on the rest of our dinner."

Talk of the bridge ended for the night.

As we prepared for bed later that evening, the discussion resumed. "And Elizabeth just sat there like a big dummy. She doesn't appear reticent at our women's meetings. Imagine kowtowing to her husband like that. Speak up, woman!" I said.

"Maybe she keeps a peaceful home by not speaking up so much," Wash suggested.

"Really? You'd prefer a mousy little woman to me?"

"Of course not. You were fiery from the day I met you. I wouldn't have had it any other way."

"Sometimes I wonder, Wash. I really do."

He did not respond. As I lowered myself into bed, a groan escaped my mouth. A great deal of swelling had accumulated in my joints, especially my knees, and now that we had made a life with so many enjoyable activities, there were days when I could do little but sit at my desk, writing.

"Are you all right, Em?" Wash asked.

"The pain is acute today, I'm afraid. I seem to tire much more easily, and some days, I disappoint myself by accomplishing so little."

"Don't put so much pressure on yourself," he commented.

"It is simply my nature to want to be vital, and there is nothing I can do to change that fact. You know that." I said, annoyed at his nonchalance.

"I am more worried about your eyesight," Wash said. "After all of the years you spent being my eyes, now I must be yours."

"Yes, well, it seems to be failing rapidly. I will make an appointment in town soon."

It was frightening to know that there were certain things I would not see any more. I had spectacles for reading, but they didn't always aid me through the entire day, and I often retired to my bed to close my eyes, even if I was not tired.

Nevertheless, I spent much of my time writing essays on the issues of equality for women, and a good number of them were published. In addition to writing a book about my ancestor Richard Warren, I joined the Daughters of the American Revolution, which required completion of a detailed family tree from which I wrote the book, "Richard Warren of the Mayflower and Some of His Descendants." It was published by The Boston Press of David Clapp and Son. It began thus:

Richard Warren, the first of the Warren name in America, sailed from Plymouth, England in the historic Mayflower, 6 September, 1620. He was not of the Leydon Company, but joined the Pilgrims from London and he was one of the signers of the Compact framed in the cabin of the Mayflower while in Cape Cod Harbor, which was the first platform of civil government in the new world, and which converted the band of unknown adventurers into an immortal Commonwealth.

I was a proud descendent of such prestigious ancestors and in having my book published. I was anxious for John to read it because I primarily wrote it for him and my grandchildren. Young people do not always appreciate the roots of their family, but I believed in time he would be thankful for my efforts to document our family tree.

The tranquility of our home allowed much more time for reading. I made myself comfortable in the library and reread my favorites, *Little Women* and *Leaves of Grass*. I also craved new writings and ideas, and frequently took a carriage into Trenton where there was a small, but up-to-date bookstore. There were new, exciting books like *Dracula*, *The Picture of Dorian Gray*, and *The Awakening*. Wash enjoyed *The Adventures of Sherlock Holmes* and *Around the World in Eighty Days*.

Discussing the books we were reading at the dinner table was often more agreeable than the disturbing accounts in the daily newspapers. The United States economy was on the brink of disaster. There had been a panic in the stock market, and the papers called it a depression. Wash wrote many letters on our behalf to our stock brokers, hoping to be assured that our investments were protected, but the letters we received were not always encouraging. We had to count our blessings for our investments, but also face the fact that no one was left unscathed, including the Roeblings or the Roebling Wire Company.

"Did you read the story about a Jacob Coxey in today's *New York Times*?" Wash asked at breakfast.

"No, I haven't read the *Times* yet today. Who is Jacob Coxey?"

"He is an Ohio businessman who is leading a march from Massillon, Ohio, all the way to Washington, D.C., to protest the unemployment problem. They are walking all the way! They're calling it Coxey's Army."

"They're walking? Why, that must be six hundred miles or more! What do they hope to achieve?"

"It's seven hundred miles. He started with one hundred unemployed men. They have just entered Beaver Falls, Pennsylvania and this report says that six thousand people came to greet them, feed them, and cheer them on."

"It's hard to imagine that many people out of work."

"The protesters, as the paper calls them, intend to ask President Cleveland to have the government hire these unemployed men to fix the roads and other public works," Wash reported.

"That is certainly necessary. Just look at the terrible roads we take into Trenton."

Chapter 36

He could plainly see that she was not herself. That is, he could not see that she was becoming herself and daily casting aside that fictitious self which we assume like a garment with which to appear before the world.

Kate Chopin
The Awakening

Then one day, with no forethought, I suddenly felt a great urge to leave. It's not that I wanted to be away from Wash, but I began to despise Trenton and became filled with wanderlust. It took too much effort to interest myself in anything in Trenton. I felt buried alive, and feared that if I did not heed my feelings, I might fall into another dark spell. Although I loved our new house, I continually yearned for New York and the excitement of the city, the shopping, the energy. Strangely, now that Wash was feeling better, we were not near the cultural events and social engagements in New York that I had missed for so many years.

Wash developed many interests that he could manage from home, such as his mineral collection, bird watching, and astronomy. He had a greenhouse built so he could nurture orchids. He did not experience wanderlust as I did, but spent his time writing a biography of his father, and staying involved in the family wire business in which he was still a stockholder and the vice president. Although he took no salary from the business, he traveled to the office on his good days and had lunch with the workers. He enjoyed when they asked his advice, and liked to reminisce about the old days at the mill when his father was still alive.

"What are you working on now?" Washington stood in the doorway of my study one morning.

"Oh, my, you frightened me! What are doing here?"

"Well, I live here, don't I?"

"Yes, but, dear, where is your nurse?"

"I told her to go enjoy the sunshine. I had a hunch I could manage on my own for a bit today."

"I see that. Are you sure?" I rose from my desk, but my husband motioned for me to sit back down. All of this was most unusual, as my study was on the second floor.

"Well, at least come and sit by me," I said.

"I'd like to see what *you* are working on for a change," he said, lowering himself carefully into the armchair near my desk.

"I am writing articles for two women's clubs: the Federation of Women and Sorosis."

"I see," he said, leafing through my *Women's Journal,* then picking up *Sorosis.*

"The women's suffrage movement seems to be enjoying a revival and I intend to be a part of it. I became a member of Sorosis when we lived in Brooklyn, if you remember, and I was so close to so many exciting events for women, but between my work on the bridge, raising John, and managing the house, it left little time for being involved. I feel as if I were extraneous to the world of women until now. Now I'm now awakened to so many issues and causes. My life in the male world of engineering has ended, and now I can immerse myself in the interests of women."

I looked up to see my husband smiling more widely than I'd seen in a long time.

"What?" I asked.

"That's my Emily. You were meant for great things, my dear."

"Wash, I was just thinking, as part of the Federation of Women's Clubs, I would like to travel with the others to Chicago for the World's Columbian Exposition. It is being held in commemoration of the four hundredth anniversary of Columbus's arrival in the New World. I've been working on the materials promoting women's suffrage to be distributed at the event. Do you think you could accompany me, now that you are doing so much better?"

"I would be proud to accompany my illustrious wife on such a trip. I'm afraid I will still be in need of the nurse, so it might not be the romantic venture you're dreaming of," he laughed.

I smiled at him. "Maybe one day we can make our way back to Brooklyn now that your health has improved. No one would believe that Washington Roebling still has not walked across the Brooklyn Bridge."

"I will leave you to your writing, then," he said after a quiet moment, humming as he walked slowly down the hallway.

The women's club meeting at our house was lively with anticipation over our trip to Chicago.

I tapped lightly on the table to bring the meeting to order.

"Welcome all! As Secretary-Treasurer of the New Jersey Board of Lady Managers for the World's Columbian Exposition of 1893, I would like to begin the meeting," I announced.

"Mrs. Ford, would you apprise us of the details of the coming event?" I sat down and gave the floor to Wilhelmina Ford.

"Ladies, the Exposition in Chicago has a particular significance, and it is the perfect place for us to promote our efforts," Mrs. Ford, the president of the club, announced. "With the fragmentation of our society due to race and class, the fair organizers have a mission to counter the spread of political radicalism. This economic depression, as they are calling it, has further divided the classes into rich and poor. Un-American, I say! There should be economic equality as well as equality of the sexes! Although the fair in Philadelphia was a failure, there is great support for this one. The exhibitions in Europe have been successful in bringing together societies previously divided along class lines. The Civil War was not so very long ago, and an event of this magnitude might bring some healing and hope for the future of America—and the Lady Managers will be in the midst of it all."

"What other information do you have about the event, Wilhelmina?" someone asked.

"It is said to be grander than all previous Expositions—more than six hundred acres of buildings of all types designed by the most prominent architects. The fair will open to the public on May 1st, and I suggest that we travel there as close to that date as possible. I have read that more than $15 million has been pledged by the Vanderbilts, the Morgans and the Astors, among others."

The ladies present clapped politely.

"Yes," I said somewhat impatiently, "but what will our role be? How will we be allowed to promote our cause?"

"Women's groups from all over the country have been invited, but there has been great controversy as to how they will be represented. Originally, we were to be in the major exhibition palaces, but now it seems that we will have our very own building very near the main exhibition grounds!" Mrs. Ford replied.

"Is it true that Miss Anthony and Mrs. Stanton will attend?"

"Yes, and we must hear every one of their speeches."

We then passed motions on the materials we would distribute at the Exposition, and the meeting was adjourned.

My husband and I enjoyed traveling together. Seeing new places expanded our minds. As humans, we tend to think and understand only what we see each day in our own lives, but there are the lives of others to consider. Traveling brought my attention to the fact that everyone did not live as we did. People who travel were more tolerant and open-minded about so many things, seeing the truths of the world. There were never any dark spells on the road. There was so much to ponder and so much of the world to see and understand.

"I was thinking about a conversation I had with Mary O'Connell."

"Yes," said Wash, "What was it about?"

"She said that I could never understand the life she has. She inferred that the privilege of wealth makes one unable to commiserate with those who have less. I don't think that's true. There is sympathy in one's heart for those who struggle. If we try to put ourselves in their place, we can at least have compassion—and that is the only path to change. If we who have more do not help those with less, who will?"

"You certainly demonstrate that with your charity work with the Home for Consumptives and your efforts towards the infants in the New York tenements, and, now with your enthusiasm for women's rights," said Wash. "You also helped Mary as much as she allowed at the time."

"Yes, but her pride prevented her from accepting the additional help we could have provided. She tried to cut herself off from our relationship because she was ashamed."

"You did what you could, Em."

"I regret that we do not have a daughter who will enjoy the equality I am fighting for now. I don't need equality. I have all I need, a husband who supports my interests and a fulfilling life. But, somehow, I cannot tolerate the injustice of it all. Whenever I see something wrong in the world, I feel a responsibility to change it, to speak out, to bring awareness to it."

"That's my Emily," he recited his familiar mantra.

"When I become upset about an injustice, I don't know where to put the frustration except into writing, but does that really do any good? How many people would even bother reading it? Women's voices have been silenced for far too long. As women, we have completely different lives and perspectives than men. Sometimes I'm not even sure you understand, Wash."

"I have always tried to understand."

"I know you have tried, and you have always been supportive of me, but as a man, do you really know what it feels like to be treated as less, to have your ideas derided and ignored, to have it assumed that you cannot do the things of which you are actually capable?"

Washington was silent for quite a while, and I feared I had hurt his feelings.

"It's not specifically you that I say this about—it's every man. No man in this society truly knows what it feels like to be second best, sometimes invisible, to not have certain choices." I felt I'd said too much, as I often did. I did not want to upset my husband. Lord knows, it was not his fault that I was frustrated.

Diane Vogel Ferri

Chapter 37

Men, their rights and nothing more; women, their rights and nothing less.

Susan B. Anthony

The World's Columbian Exposition of 1893 was thrilling and well attended. We were among 27 million visitors during its six-month run. People came from all over the world, and I was enthralled by their styles and traditions and the mingling of languages.

Wash and I walked the midway when we were both feeling up to it. There were carnival rides and sideshows that made me wish I could have brought Siegfried with us. One day we stopped and watched a magnificent Ferris wheel rotate endlessly. We looked at each other and shook our heads after hearing screams coming from the top of the dangerous ride.

One of the most popular exhibits was the reproduction of the Nina, the Pinta and the Santa Maria. They had been constructed in Spain and sailed to America for the event. We were able to climb aboard and imagine the treacherous trip Columbus had made five hundred years before.

Everywhere we looked, there were dancers, musicians, and games to spend your money on. I was particularly enchanted by a chapel designed and built by Louis Comfort Tiffany for the event.

"Oh, Wash, aren't the windows beautiful!" I exclaimed.

"I believe we are already in possession of a spectacular window," he replied, reading my mind. He shook his head, unimpressed.

We frequently had to stop and rest at one of the benches along the midway. There was a moving walkway along the banks of the lake, and we took great advantage of it. It ran in a loop to the pier and back to the casino. Travelers could sit or stand, and we were happy to sit and ride, taking in the sights as we went.

One afternoon, there was some confusion ahead of us. A woman rushed by, and I asked her what was happening.

"Oh, it's Helen Keller with her teacher Anne Sullivan! Everyone wants to say hello to her. Alexander Graham Bell is with them, too!"

It was pleasing to know that a blind and deaf woman could experience the fair as we were, but I was distracted by the Electricity Building ahead.

"I wonder if our friend Mr. Edison is here?" I asked, pointing to the exhibit.

"I wouldn't call him a friend, but let's find out."

Inside the building were interior and exterior lights, Mr. Edison's kinetoscope, search lights, electric incubators for chicken eggs, and a telegraph, but no famous inventor in sight.

"I cannot imagine what human beings will come up with next, can you?" I asked.

"It appears we have thought of everything, haven't we?" Wash replied.

No Life But This

Two men nearby were talking. I stopped to listen.

"Did you hear about Westinghouse underbidding Edison for this fair?"

"Edison's initial bid was outrageous, then he re-bid, but Westinghouse underbid him by seventy cents per lamp to get the contract. Then they couldn't use the Edison incandescent lamps because the patent belongs to Edison General Electric!"

"Ha! Yes, but I read that Westinghouse found a way around that by changing them slightly. The lamps don't last long, though, and they keep having to replace them. Been a hell of a problem here."

"Now Edison is considering a lawsuit. Serves the old man right!" They laughed loudly. "His prices are always out of line!" Wash looked tired, and I was as well, so I didn't try to discuss what I had heard with him.

While I passed out flyers and information twice each day, Wash often stayed in the hotel room to rest so we could explore some of Chicago later in the day if we were both able. People were generally receptive to the information we were passing along—men, as well as women. One man took the flyer and I was pleased to see him sit on a nearby bench to read it. A little while later, he appeared next to me, dragging his unwilling wife, and told me our ideas were rubbish and that a woman's place was in the home, caring for her husband and family.

"What makes you say that, sir?" I asked, standing as tall as I could. The man's wife seemed to shrink into the background as she stood behind him.

"Women don't have the intelligence of men. Why should they be able to make important decisions like voting?"

"I'll have you know, sir, that I have more brains, common sense, and know-how than any two men you might know. You might have heard of the Brooklyn Bridge? Well, I was instrumental in the building of that structure. I am educated and thoroughly capable of voting or achieving any other intellectual pursuit that a man does!"

"Let's go, Harry," the wife said as she tugged on his sleeve.

"The Brooklyn Bridge, huh? The only thing women like you are good at is lying." He turned and walked away, angrily taking out his misgivings on his poor wife.

My colleague and I just laughed as he walked away. Ignorance is bliss, Thomas Gray would say.

But of all the exciting things at the Exposition, I was most thrilled by hearing Susan B. Anthony speak. Wash chose to rest at the hotel and I took a carriage to the Art Memorial Building. The famous Miss Anthony was there on behalf of the World's Congress of Representative Women. Several other speakers expressed their concerns from their own vantage points. I estimated three thousand people were in attendance on that first night.

Miss Anthony expressed her concerns over the fact that other organizations had memberships well above the Women's Suffrage Association of the United States, which only numbered seven thousand.

"Now, friends," she bellowed, "I can tell you a great deal about what the lack of organization means, and what a hindrance this lack has been in the great movement with which I have been associated. If we could have gone to our state legislatures saying that we numbered in our association the vast masses of the women—five millions of women in these United States who sympathize with us in spirit, and who wish we might gain the end; if we could have demonstrated to the Congress of the United States, and to the legislatures of the respective States, that we had a thorough organization back of our demand, we should have had all our demands granted long ago, and each one of the organizations which have come here to talk at this great congress of women would not have been compelled to climax its report with the statement that they are without the ballot, and with the assertion that they need only the ballot to help them carry their work to greater success!"

With that, the audience stood and cheered, women and men alike.

"I want every single woman of every single organization of the Old World and the New that has thus reported, and that does feel that enfranchisement, that political equality is the underlying need to carry forward all the great enterprises of the world—I want each one to register herself, so that I can report them all at Washington next winter, and we will carry every demand that you want!"

Again, cheers and applause rose from the massive crowd, my heart was thrilled and my mind swirled with inspiration at her words. I waited in a long line to sign the petition on the way out, as almost everyone in attendance did that night. I couldn't wait to get to the hotel to tell Wash everything I had seen and heard, but when I arrived, he was sound asleep and I had to contain my enthusiasms to writing it down in my journal.

The next morning, I headed to the Women's Building to see paintings by women artists and browse the Library Exhibit, which held seven thousand books written by women.

Chicago was a wonderful place to visit. Wash and I took carriage rides along the lakefront and enjoyed wonderful meals. One morning, we had pancakes that came from a mix in a box for breakfast and I tried Juicy Fruit chewing gum for the first time. We took in beautiful artwork, we heard John Phillip Sousa's band and the Mormon Tabernacle Choir, and attended a concert where Anton Dvorak himself conducted.

Wash found many of the exhibits foolish, like the eleven-ton "Mammoth Cheese" from Canada. He called them exponents of silly, competitive vanity, and claimed the food was vile and could kill a shark, but I thought most of it delicious and unusual.

All in all, the Exposition was a tremendous success. We read later that Helen Keller had been there because of a new device that could print books in Braille. Sadly, Carter Harrison, the mayor of Chicago, was assassinated right before the closing ceremonies, which cast a pall on the entire city after worldwide success. Then immediately after the Exposition closed, the fairgrounds caught on fire and most everything was lost. The city also struggled with an outbreak of smallpox later that summer, and I was grateful that Wash had not been exposed to the disease.

On the way home we read that Jacob Coxey, the man who led hundreds of men on the walk to Washington D.C. to protest unemployment, had been arrested and jailed for walking on the lawn of the Capitol.

"All his efforts were in vain! Does the government of the United States not have the responsibility to listen to its citizens? Is that not why they are there? What is this country coming to, I ask?"

"Not everyone has as an attentive audience as you, dear," Wash said, patting my arm.

"I'm well aware of that, but the government should be an audience for the people, if it is nothing else."

Wash started his incessant humming, and I ended my rant.

Diane Vogel Ferri

Chapter 38

Sweet is the swamp with its secrets,
Until we meet a snake;
'Tis then we sigh for houses,
and our departure take.

Emily Dickinson

A few days after the wonderful, exhilarating trip to Chicago, I felt myself slipping into a blueness. Anticipation of the trip was over, and I was unsure of what my next steps would be toward my goals. Although we had passed out hundreds of flyers and had spoken to many women who agreed with our cause, our work had not been received as well as we'd hoped. We had heard many derogatory comments about our efforts, and although Susan B. Anthony was inspiring, I wondered what effect her words would have in the real world. The struggle for women's rights had been a long one, with very little progress over the years.

Instead of moping about the house, I decided to take the dog for a short walk around the grounds. He was overjoyed at seeing the leash in my hands. Ponto often brightened my spirits, as animals tend to do. Their unconditional love and pure joy are their gifts to us. Ponto's rambunctious nature did not always provide a peaceful walk, but being outside never failed to clear my head. It was much easier to say my prayers while strolling the grounds than sitting in a chair with distractions all around.

Ponto was funny and greeted us affectionately whenever we arrived at home. He was so happy to see us that he tore around the house at top speed when we walked in the door. We laughed as he slid across the wooden floor and banged into the stairway, popped back up, and kept running.

The nation's poor economy had caused robberies to increase, especially in affluent neighborhoods such as ours. There had been some thieves in the neighborhood before we left, so I appreciated Ponto's boisterous barking whenever strangers neared our house. It sometimes took two people to hold and calm him down, but it was worth it to have a guardian for our property.

In our absence, our coachman Mr. Somers stayed in the guest quarters to watch the house and care for Ponto and the horses. One night, a prowler approached the house. Ponto barked robustly and would not be soothed. Mr. Somers awoke, looked out the window, and saw the prowler running through the garden. Ponto had done his duty, and the story of our brave beast quickly made its way around the neighborhood.

Then about a week after our return, our neighbors the Oliphants were shocked to find that a burglar had entered their second-floor window and had taken some of Mrs. Oliphant's jewelry. Richard Oliphant sent for Ponto, the neighborhood hero. Ponto sniffed along the fence at the rear of their property, but instead of locating the burglar, he came upon policemen carrying lanterns. He barked ferociously and tore at one of the policemen's pant legs until Mr. Somers arrived to call him off. The policemen were unhurt and understood the dog's enthusiasm. With that, Ponto ran off into the darkness. When we found him, he had pinned the burglar up against a fence, and was growling fiercely. Mrs. Oliphant's jewelry was retrieved from the burglar's pocket. After that incident, I stored our valuables in a safe-deposit box at the Trenton Trust Company, in spite of having such a wonderful watchdog.

Trenton offered many entertainments. Wash and I enjoyed going to the theater and the opera. I had studied both in school, and had a firm grasp on the positives and negatives of the performances. It seemed that Wash and I had less and less to converse about, so these shows gave us something to discuss, although we didn't always agree.

We went to a play called *The Contented Woman* in which both a man and a woman were running for the mayor's office in their town. In the end, the woman won. At the conclusion of the play, I applauded enthusiastically, but Wash looked detached and hardly clapped.

"You know, Colonel, in Arizona, women can vote. Maybe we should move there and I can run for governor." Wash was unamused.

My favorite operas were by Wagner. Wash preferred those of Verdi and Rossini. Nevertheless, it was wonderful to have the time to attend these performances and to have him by my side once again. I took trips into New York several times a year to buy new dresses for such occasions.

We attended lectures, and there was nothing that did not interest me. I went, whether Wash wanted to go or not. I also frequented the bookstores and library, and often gave John books after I had finished reading them. I sent children's books for Siegfried.

Wash continued to pursue his love of the natural world, mineralogy, and botany. He came home one day with a new pet—a snake! I was not happy about having such a creature in the house. "I hope this is not something you are intending to start a collection of!" I said upon seeing the ugly thing.

"Well, Ponto seems to have taken a shine to you, so why shouldn't I have a companion as well?"

"What kind of pet can a snake be?"

"I find the reptile world fascinating. Now I can view it up close," Wash said, running his fingers over the snake's scales.

"Just make sure Mr. Snake stays in his own living quarters!"

But only days later, the snake, whom Wash had named Trent, was missing from his chambers. Wash and the servants frantically searched the house. Of course, the snake could slither, climb, or hide just about anywhere. In the end, it was found in a vase, thus informing the Roeblings that it was a water snake.

Wash treated it like a baby, even giving it a Christmas tree that year. Trent the snake divided its time between stretching across the top branches and lying among the roots in the pot.

When John came for a visit he asked if we had learned the snake's gender.

"I don't know, but it might be a female because it likes to look at its reflection in the looking glass!" Wash replied. Indeed, the snake enjoyed slithering onto the dressing table and admiring its reflection in the mirror.

One afternoon, I was feeling unwell, and my joints and muscles ached deeply. I was scheduled to meet with some ladies of the local women's group. I didn't want to disappoint them, so they were ushered to my bedroom. While we were planning our next meeting, Wash appeared at the door and told the ladies they must leave because my health was too fragile for their visit. They left immediately.

"I was in the middle of a meeting!" I snapped.

"I had to get them out of the house. The snake! It bit me! I might be poisoned. I could die!"

"I doubt that, dear. John told us that Trent was not poisonous."

Wash plopped into a chair, appearing too weak to go on.

"I guess I will be the one to get out of bed and tend to you as usual," I sighed, "I'm quite sure you aren't dying, however." I brought him a glass of whiskey and some ammonia for his injured finger, which had only turned pale pink. Wash had taken to being a bit of a hypochondriac who could only be soothed by me. After that incident, Trent was relegated to the greenhouse in the care of the gardener.

Diane Vogel Ferri

Chapter 39

I measure every grief I meet
With analytic eyes;
I wonder if it weights like mine,
or has an easier size.

I wonder if they bore it long,
Or did it just begin?
I could not tell the date of mine,
It feels so old a pain.

Emily Dickinson

In researching my book about Richard Warren, I sought out cemeteries near our home. Strangely, they brought perspective and comfort. I imagined my ancestors' achievements and tried to comprehend how their lives were over, simply gone; life being evanescent. Soon no one would remember them if I did not ensure their memory. I imagined what it must have been like when they lived.

    Ashamed of my melancholy after our exhilarating journey to Chicago, I enlisted a carriage and rode to the Riverview Cemetery to visit my father-in-law's grave without Wash's knowledge. I thought about all he had fought to do in his active years, how he had had no idea he would not live past sixty-three years of age, to die in the middle of a massive engineering project, to never know that he would leave it all to his son, Washington. I thought about my own mother, who did not live to see some of her children grow to adulthood, and my father, who likely died of a broken heart. He was never the same after she died. He cared a little less about living each day without my mother. Would Wash and I suffer as much when we departed from each other? I enjoyed so much more independence than my mother ever experienced in her short life. Was it bearing twelve children that had shortened her life? If so, what right did I have to bemoan having only one child?

    I knelt at Mr. Roebling's grave and said a silent prayer in his honor, talking to him as if he were present. Many people never visit a grave. They believe it is too sad, and do not wish to relive their grief. But they are missing a precious time of communion with their loved one. Whether you can be heard matters not, it is the closeness you sense, the memories that clarify in your mind, the time to concentrate only on the one you loved and miss so dearly. Nothing else in the world matters when you kneel before a gravesite.

    "Mr. Roebling, I want you to know that your bridge is a monument to your brilliance. Your son did well, very well, and you would be proud of him. I did my best to be his loyal assistant—but you knew that, didn't you?" I asked aloud staring at his name elegantly carved into the headstone.

    In that fleeting moment, I questioned whether life was worth all the struggle. We live, we die, and then what? Was linking two cities worth the lives that were lost? Did it matter at all? My faith taught me that there was something better, a place without pain and tears, and it

No Life But This

was only faith that could take us on the journey there. How did unbelievers survive the loss of a loved one? How did they view their own brief moments on this earth and find purpose in our struggles here? I did not know, but I had faith that there was a glorious reason.

I fell across the gravesite, awash in tears and frustration—a grown woman—still hungering for answers, cursed with the need to know everything, as my mother had claimed. I constantly frustrated my husband with my need to understand and experience everything. "Let it all rest, Emily. Let it be," I said aloud.

Returning home, Wash met me at the door, which was unusual. He looked serious, even sad.

"What is it?"

"Em, I'm sorry to tell you this, but Mr. Somers found Ponto behind the greenhouse."

"Yes, is he all right?"

"No, dear, I'm afraid he is dead."

My aching knees failed me, and I dropped to the floor. Ponto had been with us only a year, and now my companion was gone! I thought my tears had dried up, but they came all through that evening and into the next day. I had not had a dog since I was a girl, and was not prepared for the grief I would feel for an animal. I had owned horses that had died, but a horse did not lie at my feet while I read, or jump for joy on my arrival home. Ponto had made me laugh, and now cry. We did not know what had caused his death, and I could not bear to see his lifeless body. Mr. Somers buried him behind the greenhouse, and Wash erected a cross for his grave. Just one more gravesite to visit, one more loss to count among the others.

I was desolate for weeks after the loss of Ponto, and although Wash attempted to cheer me and offered to take me on outings, nothing helped.

"Em, I have an idea," Wash whispered as he crawled into bed next to me.

"What is it?"

"Let's go to Brooklyn. It's high time I walked across that bridge, as so many thousands of others have. You can visit with Mary while we're there. I'd like to try to travel the bridge walkway. We can take a carriage back."

With great effort, I pulled myself to a sitting position.

"Walk? You cannot possibly walk the entire mile, more than a mile, and back. How do you propose to do that?"

"I was thinking of a wheelchair. I know that in the past I said it was out of the question. But now that we have been away for so long, I think we can cross the bridge without anyone recognizing us. We can wear disguises."

I laughed for the first time in a week and felt a sliver of hope in my heart, thanks to the wonderful man next to me.

"I hope you will share the wheelchair with me, since it will be a long walk for my weary legs as well. Maybe someday we will be blessed with a granddaughter who will look up to you and be proud of all you will achieve for women's equality. Your work is not done," he continued as he brought me my bed jacket. "Now, sit up, put this on, and let's make some travel plans."

"I would dearly love to see Mary again, and our home on Columbia Heights, and Hicks Street, where John grew up." I said wistfully.

"Then that is what we shall do."

Chapter 40

What a queer medley of women's rights meetings at present! Women in breeches, men in petticoats—white, black, cream-colored—atheists and free-lovers, vegetarians and Heaven knows what—all mixed together, thick and slab until the mixture gets a little too strong, we should think, even for metropolitan stomachs.

Walt Whitman

As our carriage came into view of the bridge, we gasped at its beauty once again.

"Oh my, it could not be a clearer sky today; not a single cloud. It looks as if we could reach out our arms and touch it from here!" I turned to Wash and saw tears in his eyes. Of course, the sight of the bridge, the monument to our family's life, would always be emotional, joyful, and sentimental.

"So many memories, my dear. The thrill of the progress as well as the sorrow of those lost in the effort."

"Yes, that will never leave us, I fear." I took his hand in mine as we gazed upwards.

"I still think of my father and that he did not live to do what we are doing today."

The driver, Mr. Garrison, stopped at the foot of the Brooklyn tower and took the wooden wheelchair out of the back of the carriage. A young lad named Joseph was along to help us across the bridge. We did not attempt to disguise ourselves, but still hoped we would not be recognized and the journey would be peaceful and contemplative.

"I will take the carriage to the other side and meet you there, Colonel Roebling," Mr. Garrison assured us.

Mr. Garrison helped Wash into the chair and Joseph pushed him up the ramp to the bridge. When we got to the top, Wash asked him to stop and turn him around.

"I must look back at my window. The place where I lived for so many years, where I built the bridge," he said.

"Our old house," I murmured. "Where our son grew up, where so much...." I was overcome with emotion. How does time go by so rapidly? I felt a strong urge to walk back down the ramp and directly in the front door of that house, the place I knew so well, every corner and cranny, the dwelling of so many hopes and dreams—but it belonged to someone else now.

"All right then, Joseph, let us travel to New York," Wash said after a few moments, smiling up at me.

There were hundreds of people on the pedestrian walkway moving in both directions. We often had to dodge oncoming groups of walkers. Below, carriages moved between the cities with ease—all because of the man in the wheelchair.

"Please stop," Wash requested as we approached the middle of the bridge. We took in the 360 degree view of Brooklyn, of New York, of the East River, and of the many boats floating down the river beneath the largest bridge in the world. The bridge held a view unseen to humans before its construction. It was a marvelous moment for us both, one I shall never forget.

"Oh, look, Wash! The Statue of Liberty! You can see it clearly from here!" I pointed toward the New York harbor. "Even at a distance, it is majestic, isn't it? We must visit that as well."

"Yes, beautiful," Wash echoed, without enthusiasm. "So much has changed since we left, and yet many things remain the same. The traffic in the harbor is something, isn't it?"

"Immigrants arrive daily to this great country. Everyone in the world wants to live here," I said, "How lucky we are that our ancestors from England and Germany chose to come here so that we could live this American experience."

"Yes, we have lived fortunate lives, dear," he agreed quietly.

I was beside myself with the thrill of the bridge and the massive activity on the river, but as always, my husband was pensive and reserved.

"Here, sit for a respite, dear." Wash pushed himself out of the chair and I sat for a while.

"We must tell John and Margaret to come here soon. Siegfried must see his heritage as soon as possible," I said.

"Yes, we will urge them to do just that. This place is as important to our son's life as it has been to ours."

When we reached the New York side of the bridge, some sort of parade was approaching the City Hall, which was very near the base of the bridge. It appeared to be composed only of women, and my heart missed a beat.

"Do you mind if we stop to see what is going on?" I asked. Wash looked weary, but agreed.

"Of course. Joseph and I will locate Mr. Garrison, and perhaps we shall take a rest over there in the shade of the trees while you see what's happening."

"Thank you!"

The parade had stopped near the New York City Hall, and I hurried over. A woman on a platform was preparing to make a speech as a crowd gathered. My knees ached terribly, and I found a bench behind the crowds.

"As a part of the Federation of Women's Clubs, we are here today to show our support and fervor for women's equality!" A loud roar rose from the crowd of women. I was thrilled at having the good fortune to have arrived at precisely the right time.

"Who is the speaker?" I asked the person next to me.

"Why, that's Jane Cunningham Croly, the founder of Sorosis!" The woman looked at me as if I were daft. I contemplated defending myself but let it go in favor of hearing the speech.

"The object of Sorosis, as set forth in its constitution, is to bring together women engaged in literary, artistic, scientific, and philanthropic pursuits with the view of rendering them helpful to each other and to society," Mrs. Croly shouted over the crowd.

"We have committees on drama, education, house and home, business, and entertainment. Our meetings consist of lunch and musical selections and recitations. We raise money for philanthropy. The question of a club site has been discussed, but no steps have been taken toward procuring one. Sorosis, after more than twenty-five years of active life, stands as the representative women's club of the world. Its principles are purely democratic. It is of women, by women, for women."

With that, the throng of women cheered in victory and mutual agreement. I was wildly inspired; thoughts spilled through my brain as never before about what my contributions could be. Right then and there, I vowed that I would never allow a dark spell to again consume me. There was much too much work to be done.

As I made my way back to the carriage, my joints and muscles smarted madly. Upon returning to our hotel, I soaked in a warm bath for quite a while before feeling restored. I put on a clean dress and called for another carriage to take me to Mary's house while Mr. Garrison took Wash to visit an old friend. Mary and I had continued our correspondence faithfully, as we had promised, and she seemed happy to see me. Her two rented rooms a few blocks from our old neighborhood, although a bit shabby, seemed sufficient for her and Sarah. All of the children had left home and were married except the youngest, Siobhan, a lovely young lady.

"Emily, this is Sarah." I reached out to shake the hand of the woman who had made my friend so happy. She seemed reticent and looked down at the floor.

"There's no need to feel strange around me, Sarah. I do not disapprove of your life with my friend, Mary. You've made a lovely home here."

Sarah seemed quite a bit younger than Mary, but that, too, was irrelevant.

"And look at you, Siobhan! You have grown into a beautiful young lady!"

"I remember you, Mrs. Roebling."

"Please call me Emily. Now I'd very much like to hear about your brothers and sisters."

We sat down to cups of tea and had a wonderful afternoon recalling good times and catching up until Siobhan left us.

"I want to tell you how happy I am that you have made this life together. Your devotion through these years and seeing you together today confirms that what you feel for each other is real," I said earnestly.

The two women stared at me, "Am I out of place to say so?"

"No, no. It's just that all we have faced is opposition and being treated as outcasts in this neighborhood. No one understands how two women can love each other in such a way," Mary explained.

"We've received hateful letters, and been called mentally unfit," added Sarah. "We've had things thrown at us, and the children would come home crying over what they heard at school."

"That's horrible. All you've done is to make a family. The O'Connell children only had one parent, and you helped raise them, Sarah."

"'Tis true, Sarah, what would I have done without you?" Mary asked, turning towards her. "There was no help for a widow with five children, but with you and the help of the Roeblings, we made due as best we could. My children never had much, but they were loved."

"So your family eventually left you alone?" I asked, remembering their threats to take Mary's children.

"Yes, we have no communication with each other, which is sad, but they finally understood that disowning me wasn't going to change my feelings for Sarah."

"That's a high price to pay for intolerance on both sides. What does it accomplish? All of the injustices in the world could be healed if people accepted those unlike themselves. People can only be what they are," I offered.

"There's not many who feel the way you do, Emily."

"How can any type of love be wrong? When I read my Bible, I only see the message that we are to love one another, even our enemies," I added.

"We are told this isn't love, though. It's a sin and an abomination. That it says so in the Bible," said Mary. "We are not welcome in the church now."

"What? How can you not be welcome in a church? What kind of love does that demonstrate? How hypocritical. And although I believe the Bible is what God has given us to know Him better, there are many ways in which our lives are different from when it was written. Many arguments can be made for whether it has been translated correctly and whether certain words meant then what they mean now. When I was a girl, I attended the Georgetown Visitation Convent for my education. Although it was based on the spirituality of St. Francis our motto was 'inspired common sense.' It seems that the world could use some of that, doesn't it? We were simply taught the virtues of kindness, gentleness, and perseverance."

"We are doing fine. Please don't worry about us, Emily," said Mary. "Maybe someday things will be different for people like us."

The next day there was one more thing to do in our beloved hometown and that was to visit a statue that honored my brother G.K. It had been erected in the Grand Army Plaza in Brooklyn, and it had been dedicated on July 4. We located the statue near Union Street, and, at first, it took my breath away. The bronze statue stood atop three steps of granite. G.K.'s image was life-sized and portrayed him as proud and fearless.

"Oh, it's beautiful. It looks just like him, so handsome, so brave. If only he could have seen himself at the end of his days as this sculptor did," I said, brushing tears from my cheeks. "If only he could have known that his greatest wish had been granted, and that he had been exonerated of any wrongdoing in the war."

"He served his country well. That will never be forgotten now," Wash said, taking my hand.

"A statue does the dead no earthly good." I mumbled.

Chapter 41

Oh, if I could but live another century and see the fruition of all the work for women! There is so much yet to be done.
Susan B. Anthony

When we arrived home from that propitious trip, we invited John, Margaret, and Siegfried to dinner to tell them about our visit to the bridge and urge them to do the same.

"I don't think that will happen soon, Mother," John grinned.

"Why is that? Margaret should see the legacy of the Roeblings, now that she is one. You certainly can take time off, and Siegfried is old enough," I reasoned.

"It's not possible, when your second grandchild is on the way," Margaret said.

We rejoiced at the wonderful news, and I immediately imagined a little girl. Being a grandmother is so unlike being a mother. It is an indescribable love. As your children grow, your responsibilities are as plentiful as your love for them. It consumes your waking moments, and sometimes your sleep, as well. Each year of their lives goes by with gratitude. But with grandchildren, the love supersedes the responsibility, mainly because there is not much responsibility other than to love them! It was a pure joy such as I had never known. There was grace, too, in the knowledge that new joys replaced ones long gone.

That evening, Washington retired early, complaining, as he usually did, about his aches and pains. His fussing had increased as his ailments decreased in recent years. Because we saw so little of John and his family, I thought he would not succumb to his nightly grievances while the children were here.

"Your father has been married 30 years, and I, twice that time," I said to my son. He laughed but I doubted his understanding of what I had been through with his father through all the years of caisson disease. "He has taken to one of his cantankerous spells again, but still manages to eat and sleep well." I continued, "To be frank, I am getting weary of this life. The doctors find nothing wrong with him except nervous conditions. Why does he not make an effort to overcome his anxieties more?" I looked at John but he seemed preoccupied.

"Mother, I would like to speak to you while Papa is not here. Reta and I are struggling to live on the meager allowance we are given."

"I cannot believe what I am hearing. Possibly you have not learned to think beforehand about how to spend your money to the best advantage if you cannot subsist on the funds allotted to you from your grandfather's inheritance!"

"You chose to break ties with the family business and move your family farther away and now I hear this!" I felt wounded. I had done everything to keep John close and prepare him for a responsible life.

"Move away from you? Mama, I am a grown man with a family of my own. Reta and I must live where we wish. Another child will arrive soon. We cannot live in poverty," he said arrogantly.

"You cannot be entirely independent if you are dependent on me for all your needs." I looked straight into his eyes, but he turned his head away. "I have always tried to impress that upon you, but you chose to leave the family business."

John was silent.

"Your expenses are likely to increase each year, and will again each time you have another child, of course. However, your income, will not. This country is in hard economic times. Where is your gratitude for what you have been given, John?"

We sat in silence for a few moments, as my heart softened. "Dear, I understand your dilemma. I am in the same one. I have spent my life dependent on your father for all I have, for all I need. It goes against the grain of my character to be dependent in any way. But you are a man; you have other choices before you. Women do not."

"I will work it out for the sake of my family, Mama," John said softly, "I am sorry I have upset you. I have always believed that you were pleased with this arrangement, that I needed to continue to receive your help, just as when I was a boy."

"Are you saying your dependence is to appease me? Have I been so overbearing? So possessive of you?" My eyes begin to tear, but I did not want my son to see them.

"It has sometimes been difficult being your only child," he looked away from me.

My hands rose to my face as though I'd been slapped. I did not have the emotional strength to continue the conversation. To imagine that I had been a failure as a mother pierced my heart and soul. Recently, Wash seemed to have little patience for my ambitions, and my son was disappointed in me. At a loss to say anything further, I walked out of the room and retired to my bedroom to think, but I could do nothing but grieve for the life I'd believed in. Was it gone? Had it never been what I'd imagined? In reality, I had nothing but my relationship with Wash and John—nothing. Now I learned that it was an illusion.

Our grandson Paul was born a healthy little chap and brought great happiness to our family. He was not a granddaughter, but I immediately fell in love with his cheerful disposition and tiny, wrinkled face. Siegfried immediately took to being a big brother, and tried to help with the baby, which was charming.

After Paul was born, Reta became ill and needed my help. John had taken a job in town, and I was often called upon to take Siegfried to our home in Trenton so she could rest. She had terrible fever and pain. The doctors determined that there were several infections involved, one in her breasts. Reta had to continue to nurse Paul despite the tremendous pain. Some days, she could barely lift her head from the pillow, because of blinding headaches and vertigo. Once that infection was cleared, the fever fell slightly but persisted. The doctors were unsure of its location.

Because I missed my own mother after John was born, and I had no close friends to offer advice on childbirth or infancy, I resolved to be the best grandmother the children could ever have. I had made plans to travel and speak at various women's clubs, but those plans had been delayed in deference to my duties as a grandmother.

"Distant travel is out of the question for the time being, so I have accepted invitations to be on the board of the Women's Hospital in New York, and also on the board of directors for Evelyn College in Princeton," I announced to Wash.

"You've been busy, haven't you?" Wash said sarcastically. "How do you get so involved in these things when you've been tending to Reta and the children so much?"

"Through simple communication with some of the trustees. I can do much of the work through letters, and when meetings are required, they are only a day trip away—two days at the most. The nurse can take over when I am not present."

"What about your own health, Em? I see how long it takes you to get moving in the morning. And what about your eyes."

"I can manage. I have the opium drops the doctor gave me for pain, and I will stay only at hotels that provide warm baths. Yes, things take longer than they used to, but that's no reason to crawl into a hole and die, is it?"

Washington chuckled, "Not for my Emily, certainly."

"It's miraculous that a woman was even asked to take these positions. It shows how we are being taken more seriously. Are not the whole world of women progressing?"

"Yes, I can see that, but I did not know that Princeton admitted women to the university," he said.

"No, they don't—yet. Evelyn College is for women, and it's about time, isn't it? If we have a granddaughter someday, educational opportunities will be open to her."

"Grandmamma!" I heard little footsteps coming up the stairway.

"Is that my big boy Siegfried?" He ran into my arms and all thoughts of women's plights and traveling vanished.

"Where are my blocks, Grandmamma?"

"Well, they're right where we left them in the playroom! Let's go find them, now." I looked up to see Siegfried's handsome father, "Well, hello John. How is my son?"

"I'm fine, Mama, but Reta is not doing well."

"Oh no. More pain?"

"Yes, she tried to rise this morning and fainted. It was only for a brief moment, but it frightened me. She had been so much better this week, attending to the household and the boys. Can you keep Siegfried here for a few days?"

"Of course we can," Wash said, quickly. "If your mother is not too in demand for other important things." I looked over, not sure if he was being playful or if he was angry with my earlier news.

"Let's go, Grandmamma," Siegfried pulled on my sleeve. We descended the staircase and he ran ahead into the playroom.

"Let's build a very big tower, shall we?" I knelt down to join him on the floor, but wondered whether I would rise again on my own. The swelling in my joints had steadily worsened. The very thing I loved the most—playing with my grandson—had become the most painful venture for me. Little children belonged on the floor, climbing on furniture, or throwing stones into the river, and I wanted to be a part of all of that, just as I had with John. It was becoming more and more difficult to keep up with my little grandsons, and it broke my heart.

"I'm going to knock it down now!" Siegfried exclaimed.

"You are? Oh my, well, all right, that's the fun of it, isn't it?" Siegfried knocked over our tower and screamed with laughter. My hands went to my head, and I shouted, "Oh no!" Then he laughed at me as well.

As expected, I needed assistance getting off the floor when our playtime ended. The beautiful little boy was out the door and on to his next adventure before I could catch him. I called Wash, who had the nurse help me up. He frowned.

"I can't give up yet, I just can't. Our little grandsons mean everything to me," I said smoothing my dress.

"If they mean everything to you, why must you always find other ways to occupy yourself?"

"What do you mean by that? That I should not use the brains God gave me? Didn't you continue, despite your infirmities? Did you choose to let your physical weaknesses stop you from achieving your dreams?" I was so irritated, that I began to cry.

"Your weeping is unbecoming, wife, and it does not make me pity you," he said coldly.

"It is not meant to evoke pity. Tears are merely frustrations making their way out of the body. What would you have me do instead? Scream? Throw something? Just because it is not a man's way to weep does not mean it is wrong or unnatural," I countered.

He walked out of the room humming, leaving me to gather myself together for Siegfried's sake. I had never shown my son weakness, and did not intend to allow my grandsons to see it either.

Although it was not beneficial for Siegfried to be away from his mother, I was overjoyed to have him so close and all to myself. Wash and I employed a nanny to help with the many physical necessities such as bath times. Unfortunately I was past being able to attend to the bodily needs of little ones. I comforted myself in the day to day delights of my grandson and my opportunity to be such an important part of his life. No matter what the future brought I wanted Siegfried to remember me.

That night I asked the housemaid to lift Siegfried onto my lap and place a blanket over us both. He was almost too big to stay there, but settled easily against my body.

"I don't want to go to bed, Grandmamma."

"No, I will let you stay up tonight, but I want to read to you. I read this book to your Papa and he liked it very much. It's a silly book. Do you like silly stories?"

"I do! Why did you read this to Papa?"

"Because he was my own little boy…"

"That's silly. Papa is a big man."

"Yes, he is, and I have dearly missed having a little boy to read to. Can you listen to the silly story?"

"Yes, Grandmamma."

"Alice was beginning to get very tired of sitting by her sister on the bank, and of having nothing to do; once or twice she had peered into the book her sister was reading, but it had no pictures or conversations in it, 'and what it the use of a book,' thought Alice without pictures or conversations?' So she was considering in her own mind (as well as she could, for the hot day made her feel very sleepy and stupid.)"

"Stupid is a bad word, isn't it? Mama says not to call someone stupid," Siegfried interrupted sleepily.

"Your Mama is right. It is not nice to call names, but…," Siegfried's eyes were already closed, his body relaxed, and although he had heard little of the story, I cherished holding him. We stayed there in the quiet of the evening until the housemaid came and carried my little sweet one to bed.

My relationship with my son had been strained since our uncomfortable discussion about money. John had secured new employment and appeared to be proud of himself. His claim that I found satisfaction in his dependence on me was unsettling, and I worked hard internally to release him from it.

Diane Vogel Ferri

Chapter 42

I do not wish them (women) to have power over men; but over themselves.

Charlotte Bronte

Women's clubs came to be a great joy and satisfaction in my life. They provided female friends and gave me purpose and worthy causes to pursue. Sorosis was a valuable, formidable organization, and I was glad to be a part of it. The group was growing every year, and I had gone through a rigorous process to be admitted. Whenever possible, I traveled to New York to attend the meetings.

The New York Times reported on what they called "the best meeting of the year" that December. Papers presented were on "Travel as a Means of Education," "Kindergarten," "College Preparation," "Physical Education," and "University Centers in America." Four hundred women turned out for a Sorosis gathering at the Waldorf-Astoria. The controversial topic was "Do business pursuits improve women mentally, morally, socially, and physically?"

One speaker pointed out that not many years before, it had been difficult to convince people that business pursuits did, indeed, develop a woman. "The businesswoman has come to remain. Not a jot of grace, charm of manner, or dignity has she lost or need she lose. Some of our strongest and loveliest women in and out of Sorosis are, and have been, businesswomen. Business pursuits are the builder of character, depending on the quality of the pursuits and the enthusiasm of the woman."

I was elected chairman of the philanthropy committee for "Philanthropy Day." I was interested in becoming president, but had not been a member long enough. My committee spent that summer raising money for the Brooklyn Home for Consumptives. It had recently moved into the large hospital building on Kingston Avenue, and provided long-term and short-term care to patients with the "white plague," as it was called, and other chronic lung ailments, that were common among the poor. Before I could involve others in this effort, I believed we should travel to Brooklyn to visit the facility and see what was needed.

The Sorosis board of directors and a few other patrons accompanied me on the visit. The building was clean, but sparse, and members of our group were deeply disturbed at the patient's suffering. We were not allowed to go near them, but their coughing and gagging could be heard throughout the sanatorium.

"What causes this disease?" I asked one young doctor as we stood in the hallway horrified at what we were witnessing.

"We have only recently proven that it is an infectious agent, and that is why we cannot let you come in contact with the patients."

I looked through an interior window to a ward full of living skeletons. All were coughing or sleeping, their handkerchiefs full of blood.

"It is essential that we continue to build these hospitals to keep the patients from infecting the rest of the population, you see," the doctor explained. "But they are all very poor people and cannot contribute to their care."

"How does it spread so viciously?" someone asked.

"The residents of tenements in Brooklyn and New York have been repeatedly warned to take precautions, but few have obeyed our directives. When someone is sick and coughs in another person's presence, or when one spits in the street or in a tenement hallway, the disease can be spread to those nearby. Overcrowded tenements just contribute to the spread. Patients must be quarantined immediately, but we are helpless to reach all those who need to be separated from their families. Often, they refuse to leave their homes, and soon the whole family is infected."

"Why is there blood?" one woman asked, shrinking away from the window.

"It is an infection of the lungs. There is fever, night sweats, weight loss, and terrible suffering before death," the doctor replied.

"What can we do?" I asked.

"You can pray for them. You can help us raise money and find ways to teach people to come here when the first symptoms occur so they do not spread it to their families. By the time most patients reach us, it is too late."

We left determined to publicize this plight as much as we could. We held several fundraising events, and despite Wash's miserly tendencies, I donated a generous amount of money. At home, I scheduled as many speeches as I could to inform the public about this terrible disease and precautions to be taken, but in reality it was not the disease that caused all the suffering: it was the overwhelming poverty that infiltrated every part of New York City and Brooklyn, and the expanding division of the classes.

From then on, every cough by a member of my family unnerved me.

Sorosis was part of the Federation of Women's Clubs. I gave the welcoming address when the Federation met in the Senate chambers of the New Jersey state house. Three hundred women attended, and although no men were invited nor seats provided for them, more than one hundred men showed up and stood for more than an hour, listening to the speeches. Sorosis served as a haven from the world of politics and religion. Neither were permitted at meetings. The organization was strictly for women helping women through art, music, philanthropy and science.

"I have been reading about the Sorosis chapter in Cleveland, Ohio," I began. "Although it started with just 17 members, their accomplishments are admirable. They have formed the Women's Employment Society, which hires ladies to sew garments for sale. They have, to date, sewed five hundred pairs of blue jeans and three hundred gray flannel shirts for the U.S. Department of the Interior. These garments are destined for Indian reservations. The chapter has also formed the Health Protection Association to provide better sanitation for children's play areas around the city."

It was at that meeting that I invited some women to be trained in the parliamentary process. I convinced them that to succeed, we needed to run our affairs as the men did. There would be classes in everything from public speaking to toasts.

Culmination of the training sessions was a festive luncheon at my home on a warm spring day in May. I ordered dozens of roses and the dining table was adorned with a miniature maypole decorated with purple and yellow pansies. After the meal, each guest was required to respond to a toast by saying something witty and original.

We took a group photograph, which was published in the newspaper. Later in the week, while I was at the bookstore, a man was looking at the picture in that morning's paper, and he said, "They are all so ugly, each one worse than the other. Just one look at this picture spoiled my appetite for luncheon." Luckily, neither I nor the members of the Women's Clubs were interested in his petty evaluations of us, nor his appetite.

One of my first assignments was to travel to Washington, D.C. for William McKinley's inauguration on March 4, 1897, to report my impressions to the Women's Clubs upon my return.

It was a cold, windy day, and the swearing-in was brief, but the new President's speech was long. I was glad I had brought my rabbit fur coat and hat. Although many attendees were glancing around as if bored, the new president ended with words that inspired me deeply:

"In conclusion, I congratulate the country upon the fraternal spirit of the people and the manifestations of good will everywhere so apparent. The recent election not only most fortunately demonstrated the obliteration of sectional or geographical lines, but to some extent also the prejudices which for years have distracted our councils and marred our true greatness as a nation. The triumph of the people, whose verdict is carried into effect today, is not the triumph of one section, nor wholly of one party, but of all sections and all the people. The North and South no longer divide on the old lines, but upon principles and policies; and in this fact, surely every lover of the country can find cause for true felicitation.

"Let us rejoice in and cultivate this spirit; it is ennobling and will be both a gain and a blessing to our beloved country. It will be my constant aim to do nothing, and permit nothing to be done, that will arrest or disturb this growing sentiment of unity and cooperation, this revival of esteem and affiliation which now animates so many thousands in both the old antagonistic sections, but I shall cheerfully do everything possible to promote and increase it."

With that, there was much cheering and hat throwing and people immediately leaving their seats to get indoors as soon as possible.

The attendees were invited to a luncheon following the ceremony. I was fortunate to be seated next to Mr. Marcus Hanna who was credited with the electoral success of President McKinley, and a charming and engaging dinner partner.

"If women were ever named to the National Committee of the Republican Party, you would be the first one appointed, Mrs. Roebling."

"I would certainly take you up on that offer, Mr. Hanna."

"I have no doubt that you would."

"But why is that such an unimaginable thought? Are not women progressing in so many ways?"

Mr. Hanna looked at me blankly for a moment.

"Do you think it impossible that one day women will hold places in the government?"

"Women do not even have the right to vote," he replied weakly, looking past me as if he wished the conversation concluded.

"Precisely. But when that happens—and it will happen—I assure you Mr. Hanna, you will see women in all areas of society, including the United States government!"

With that, I turned to the person sitting on my other side. Mr. Hanna, although charming and entertaining, had been left speechless.

I reveled in my little victory over Mr. Hanna, but had to leave the luncheon shortly after that conversation because I felt ill. I returned to my hotel and soaked in a hot bath before packing my things and calling a carriage to take me to the train station.

Sitting on the hard seats of the train hurt my back, and the jogging movement of the railroad tracks wearied me. Although exhilarated by the inauguration, I felt too tired to write down my thoughts, or even read. I spent most of the trip staring out of the window and trying not to see the reflection of an old woman in the glass. When had my jawline begun to sag, and my eyelids to droop? My hair looked dull and my lips pale. I finally closed my eyes to block out the image staring back at me.

Once home I arranged a lovely dinner to share my adventure with my family. Although it was only March, I contacted a florist to bring in some early flowers. The table was set with our finest china, and we had roast veal and oyster soup. Siegfried did not appreciate the soup, but he was well behaved and played quietly while the adults talked. Upon arriving home, I found a letter offering another exciting opportunity. Wash was not thrilled about it, but even he admitted it was too good to pass up. I tried to get him to come with me, but he insisted his health was too fragile.

"I have the opportunity to travel again, and this time, it is to Europe," I announced to my family. "It seems that my work with the Relief Society, Daughters of the American Revolution, the Huguenot Society, and Sorosis have brought me some notoriety. An invitation arrived in the mail from Emmeline Pankhurst, the founder of the Women's Franchise League in England. They have invited me to meet with Queen Victoria at the Court of St. James and to make some speeches on women's equality in London."

"That's wonderful, Mother. Will you be gone long?" Reta asked, bouncing Paul on her knee. I wondered whether she was concerned about not having my help day to day.

"I will be away for several weeks. You can manage without me, can't you?"

"Paul and Siegfried will miss each other's, but I so admire you," she replied.

"Right now, these little boys are your life, but one day, they'll be grown up and you will pursue anything you like, my dear."

"That seems very far away," she said.

"It's much sooner than you can imagine right now."

I saw Reta's smile fade, and knew I had once again said too much. Why did I always need to express every thought passing through my mind? No mother wants to hear that time with her children will be fleeting. It was a worn-out prophecy.

"All you can do is enjoy all of the years of their childhood, and you are doing that wonderfully well, Reta. I see it every time we are together."

"Thank you for that, Mother," Reta smiled serenely at me.

"Anyway, there is great interest in both of our countries on progress in women's rights," I continued, "Queen Victoria, despite being a female leader, is not a supporter of women's equality in the United Kingdom. She views her role as exceptional, not one that should be typical. She was quoted as saying that if women were to unsex themselves by claiming equality with men, they would become the most hateful, heathen, and disgusting beings and would surely perish without male protection. Can you imagine?" I looked at Wash. "I think of Mary and Sarah who have made a life together without the protection of men." I was a bit relieved when he nodded.

"Thank goodness the Queen's daughters are of a new generation and are much more progressive in their thoughts and actions," I continued, "Princess Alice established the Home for Pregnant Women. Princess Helena became President of the British Nurses' Association. Princess Louise has supported women's education and opportunities for female artists, as she is one herself. Unfortunately, although their efforts have been successful they are not able to speak out for women's equality in England due to the Queen's opposition."

"Perhaps you can speak for them, Mama," said John.

"Perhaps. From Great Britain, I will have the honor of traveling to Russia. I am to report my findings upon my return to the DAR in several American cities where the women's movement is burgeoning. My traveling companion will be Mrs. Pamela Palmer of Chicago."

"Will you be joining her, Papa?" John asked.

"I'm afraid that will be impossible right now. But your mother doesn't need the protection of men, does she?" We all laughed but Wash only smiled weakly.

"Would you listen to the beginning of the speech I'm preparing for Europe?" I asked Wash.

"Of course, go ahead." Wash put his paper down and put his attention on me.

"Ladies of Europe, The General Federation of Women's Clubs welcomes you today. Our motto is: 'We look for unity, but unity in diversity!' I come in the name of diversity and the unity of our great countries. I am here today to inform you about the progress of the women's movement in America and to learn about yours. I will take that knowledge back to America and report it to your sisters there."

"Ours has been a long, hard fight since its beginning in the early years of this century. To my mind, the progress has been slow, yet we have made steady headway. One important factor in our progress has been the advent of women's clubs. I am a member of a number of vital, active women's groups. These clubs provide support for women interested in pursuits beyond their marriage, such as owning their own property and money, temperance, and voting rights. Our clubs are a way to have our voices heard and taken seriously. We have recently been permitted to meet with state officials to discuss important issues.

"The first women's rights convention happened more than forty years ago in my own state of New York, but as I'm sure you know, we are still fighting for suffrage. This battle was interrupted by the unfortunate events of the Civil War—a stain on our glorious history. However, we persevere!

"Susan B. Anthony attempted to vote in 1872, and was arrested. Six years later, a Women's Suffrage Amendment was introduced to the United States Congress, but was not adopted. There are varied publications by and for women that are popular. Just this year, the famed former slave Harriet Tubman and several others traveled to Washington, D. C., to form the National Association of Colored Women."

Wash appeared to be trying very hard not to close his eyes. "Go on, dear."

"No, I'll let you rest. I have so much work to do to prepare for my trip."

"I'm sure it will be a wonderful speech, as always."

"Thank you for your confidence in me." I heard him humming as he walked away.

Chapter 43

I am every day convinced that we women, if we are to be good women, feminine and amiable and domestic, are not fitted to reign.

Queen Victoria

The trip was a whirlwind of ships, trains, and carriage rides. It was thrilling to be back in Europe, although things had not changed. I always marveled at how differently they lived than we did in the United States. Their towns were laid out so quaintly, which promoted the townspeople's friendships and acquaintances. In America, we were already spreading out far and wide with cities much larger and more populous than in Europe.

I made three speeches that Mrs. Pankhurst had arranged and promoted. They were well attended, and the women responded enthusiastically to my ideas. Although I had happily anticipated meeting the Queen, I was worried that when I met her, my curtsey would be hampered by my bad knees. I feared I would bend at the knees and not be able to stand again!

Wash was happy not to attend. He said, "Had I been in London, I would have been obliged to dress in knee breeches with a small sword and cocked hat." I, on the other hand, spent weeks planning my wardrobe and packing. For the presentation to the Queen, I wore a dress of the finest golden silk with a matching hat. The bodice was close-fitting with a deep lace flounce and puffy, multilayered sleeves. I brought three strings of pearls of various sizes and my best white kid gloves.

My moments with Queen Victoria were fleeting and, thankfully, my shallow curtsey was acceptable to my knees. The Queen was very stout and serious and did not look at me directly, but at the next person in the long line. It was as if she were waiting for someone more important than me. Although it was an honor to meet her, I did not have the gumption to say anything to her about women's rights. After all, it was her country, not mine. The best way to initiate change, I found, was to motivate and inspire ordinary people to do the work, and eventually it happened.

The joys of visiting England were tempered by the ride to Moscow, which was endless and uncomfortable. For four days my aching body toggled back and forth to the rhythm of the train. It made many stops, and I was convinced we would never get there. My joints stiffened and my efforts to walk about the train were precarious.

I sat down in the dining car for a moment to rest. One mid-morning, two men were speaking English at the next table. Their accents sounded as if they were from the American south. They were discussing engineering, and apparently were traveling through Europe to study bridges and architecture.

"Gentlemen, yes, hello, my name is Emily Warren Roebling."

They glanced at me, then at each other as if I were a great intrusion. "I apologize for overhearing your conversation, but it could not be helped. You might be interested to know that I was instrumental in the building of the Brooklyn Bridge in New York. I trust you are familiar with the structure?"

"Of course, but I am quite sure you were not instrumental, as you say. How could that be possible?" One man asked.

"My husband was the chief engineer and…."

"Yes, your husband, not you. Why are you trying to take credit for something you did not do?" He began laughing and his companion joined in. I was astonished by their rudeness and lack of information.

"Are you saying you have never heard of me?"

"Women are not engineers." The men returned to their conversation as if I were not there. I felt invisible and mortified. I took a deep breath and decided not to allow myself further humiliation. Who were these men, anyway? Nobodies! I daydreamed of a day when they would learn the truth and feel as foolish as I did at that moment.

When I returned to my seat, an excruciating pain sliced through my abdomen. I had not felt anything like it before. I was angry to think that the impolite men had caused me such anguish, yet, when it subsided in a few moments, I knew such pain could not be emotional. I dismissed it as a strange momentary ailment, but it happened repeatedly on the train ride, and I fretted about how I would manage if it were to occur during a speech.

That night as we pulled into a godforsaken station in Warsaw, the screeching of the rails awakened me. Wash and I had visited Warsaw once, and I remembered it vividly. As I peered out the window, I saw the same filthy place.

During the rest of the trip, lovely greening trees and strange little towns with ill-dressed people and ragged children were in view. I rarely saw the working classes in our country, and began to understand my lack of awareness about poverty. I resolved to repair that lack of understanding. Europe had helped me see that.

The berth I was given emitted a stench I could not become accustomed to. The sleeping quarters were much too small for my weight and girth, and sleep was elusive. That night, the third on the train, my mind would not rest, and for the first time, I understood that the men in the dining car had been right. I was not an engineer. I had not built the Brooklyn Bridge. My husband had. It belonged to him. It was his work, his life, his ingenuity—not mine.

Chapter 44

A little kingdom I possess, where thoughts and feelings dwell; and very hard I find the task of governing it well.

Louisa May Alcott

My visit to Moscow occurred during the events surrounding the coronation of Tsar Nicholas II. Our hostess, Mrs. Androva, met Pamela Palmer, my traveling companion, and I at the train station and informed us that we would be attending the coronation with her. I had made this journey mostly for my own edification and enjoyment, so this was a special treat.

Mrs. Androva, Mrs. Palmer, and I joined an immense crowd of onlookers on Coronation Day. The aching in my knees threatened to ruin the occasion but I would not allow it. I remembered my father-in-law and how he simply decided not to be ill. Mind over matter, I thought.

It was a lovely, but chilly day. As we waited I did my utmost to take in the magnificent structures, elegant golden domes, and colorful pillars. I wanted to commit every detail to memory. The crowd cheered as their new ruler processed on horseback into the city, followed by a cavalry. Thousands of church bells pealed in celebration. It reminded me of the opening day of our bridge in

Brooklyn so long ago. The joy and excitement of the crowd was contagious. In navigating the city, we discovered that no one spoke English, so I quickly mastered some essential Russian words.

There was great spiritual significance to the anointing of the tsar. He was considered a holy figure to the Russian people. The ceremony occurred at the Cathedral of the Dormition. We were led into the vast church and seated in a place where it was difficult to see all that was taking place, but it was still thrilling. Most of the church was gilded in gold, with deep red adornments. An enormous chandelier with red drapery hung above us, and the carpets were a deep crimson. Tapestries and frescoes decorated the pillars, and the sun shone through a window in the dome.

The crowd fell silent as Tsar Nicholas II entered.

"I feel rather sorry for him," I whispered to Mrs. Palmer. "He's pale as marble and looks very sad, not at all victorious, as I supposed he would be."

"Yes, but look at the tsarina!" exclaimed my companion. Tsar Nicholas's consort wore a Prussian white court costume with a silver mantle. She was fair and young, but not very impressive. Mrs. Palmer seemed oblivious to anything but the opulence of the ceremony. While everyone else was raving about the tsarina's beauty, the frail forlorn presence of the tsar captured my heart. He looked as though the weight of his responsibilities were more than he could bear. However, the people appeared to love him deeply.

He was handed the Imperial Crown of Russia, which he placed on his own head, as the prelate invoked the Holy Trinity. Next the tsar received the scepter and orb, and was seated upon the throne as his wife knelt on a crimson cushion before him. The new tsar then briefly placed the crown on her head, then returned it to his own head.

When I inquired about the significance of this gesture, I was told that the tsarina had entered into a symbolic marriage with Russia itself, a lifelong commitment.

After the royal couple received communion, the ceremony was concluded and the church bells pealed again. The coronation was followed by a banquet, but after a brief time, Mrs. Palmer chose to retire to her hotel room. This was agreeable to me, as the ceremony had lasted several hours and I was thoroughly exhausted. Witnessing so much royalty and so many European customs and traditions gave me much to write about. That night I tried to stay awake to write while it was fresh in my mind, but found my head bobbing soon after I had settled in my room for the night.

Stabbing pain through my torso woke me abruptly. I could not imagine what it was. I had not eaten anything unusual that day. Perhaps, I thought, it was the exertion of the trip and my stubbornness in extending my strength. I curled into a ball and tried to breathe steadily as if I were in the midst of childbirth. I could not remember as bad a pain since I'd had John in Germany. After a few moments, it subsided and, completely exhausted, I fell quickly asleep.

The journey home on the ship was agony as, in addition to my other troubles, I was seasick most days. I stayed in my room, feeling weak and sick to my stomach. However, the stabbing pain did not return, and I was grateful for that.

Upon disembarking, I was greeted by my coachman, Alfred Pagden, and was surprised to see Wash practically leap from the carriage, grinning. It seemed that he had missed me terribly.

"I did not expect to see you here," I said, delighted.

"I wanted to surprise you. Are you not happy to see me, Emily?"

"Of course I'm happy to see you! How are the boys?"

"The boys are well, as am I. You, however do not look well, dear."

"It was a very difficult trip. I suffered seasickness and some other problems."

"What other problems? You look terribly pale."

"Oh they were nothing. I'm sure being back in America will revive me."

"I hope that you will be content to be among us commoners for a time."

At home I unwrapped all the souvenirs I had purchased. For Reta, a wrapper, dressing sacque, and silk petticoat from Paris. For my two grandsons, pictures of the tsar and tsarina and a few European toys that had nothing whatsoever to do with engineering or construction. For John, I brought a dagger similar to those worn by the Cossack soldiers. And for Wash a Russian evening robe of red silk. I had been gone for three months and although Wash was overjoyed to have me back, it wasn't long before I began dreaming about another journey.

Chapter 45

I only wish I could work to some purpose. I have no right to these easy comfortable days and our poor men, suffering, dying thirsty...my lot is too easy and I am sorry for that.

Clara Barton

I required a few days of rest before I began composing speeches. I was in demand as a speaker in several cities. Over the next few months, I made trips to Nashville, Cincinnati, St. Louis, Kansas City, and Denver. My first speech, however, was to my ladies' group in Trenton.

"I went to the English court first. There is just about as great a difference in state and splendor between the English court and the Russian court as between my own house and St. James palace! When we were wandering through the Kremlin, looking at and admiring all the furniture, nobles, and jewels, it made me think of the way Trentonians stray around the second floor of my home when I have a reception!" Some of those present were guilty of the envy and snooping I referred to.

"The American ladies were, by far, the best-dressed women in the palace. At the reception, the tsar wore his crown and an ermine-trimmed cloth gold mantle. My companion, Mrs. Palmer, was not feeling well, but I left the room by myself in the evening for a magnificent fireworks display. You all know that my curiosity is a curse!" There was laughter at that. "The illumination far surpassed anything I have ever witnessed—even the opening day of the Brooklyn Bridge! Speaking of the bridge, which is never far from my life, the large picture of the bridge that formerly hung in the Eden Museum is now at the National Museum in LeHavre. It was bought by the state and has the post of honor there."

The ladies applauded enthusiastically.

"Are there any other issues to address tonight?" I paused. "As you well know, ladies, there is the possibility of a war brewing. I have read that President McKinley is not in favor of going to war with Spain. However, if that should occur, we must be prepared to aid in the effort in any way possible."

"Oh, dear! I'm so frightened that my Lewis will go to war," Mrs. Roberts whimpered.

"Mrs. Roberts, it is a great honor to serve our country. I'm sure that you know my own husband is a decorated colonel and my dear departed brother Gouverneur was a general in the Civil War. If our young men are called to serve, then they must go. They must!"

"You have a son, Emily. Are you not concerned about his welfare?"

"Unfortunately, John is not well enough to be a soldier. He has a condition." I replied. "The meeting is now adjourned. Will anyone second the motion?"

A mere two weeks later, war with Spain was, indeed, declared. I was shocked to receive a letter from John informing me that he intended to volunteer.

Dear Mama,

I am transferring my stocks in the John A. Roebling Sons Company to father, as I intend to volunteer in the war effort. Please do not try to stop me. I have made up my mind and Reta is reluctantly in agreement with me. The Roeblings have a revered tradition of serving, and this is my chance to be a humble servant of my country, as well. I will take part in the First Regiment, U.S. Volunteer Engineers. You will be pleased to know that I am giving Reta my full power of attorney in my absence. She has been tutored in business transactions, and I have great faith in her abilities just as Papa has always had in yours. I hope you will agree that good-byes are to be avoided on general principles.

Your affectionate son,
John

As I read the letter to Wash, I could see plainly that he had already been informed of this travesty by our son.

"Please do not waste this family's time arguing our son's decision, Em. In addition to his abilities as an engineer, he has a general knowledge of machinery and the art of naval war. He is a grown man, and has made himself clear," Wash said, patting my shoulder patronizingly.

"I understand his right to make his own decisions, but his health, Wash, his heart."

"Roeblings do not allow physical disabilities to stand in the way of their intentions, do they, dear?"

I said nothing further. Wash was correct. Neither he nor I had discontinued pursuing our goals because of health concerns, and this is what we had taught our son. I would be proud of John and would say nothing more on the matter. All I could do was pray for his safe return, as so many mothers had before me.

My prayers were answered when the conflict ended before John could be sent to the front. The Spanish-American War lasted a mere ten weeks, and I was grateful for its brevity. Reta wrote to me after John's return home, telling me of his disappointment and feelings of failure about the whole ordeal. Of course, I wrote to him of my great pride in his efforts and gratitude for his safe return to his family.

The next monthly meeting of the Trenton Women's Club had only one item on the evening's agenda.

"It has come to my attention that we are needed at Camp Wikoff on Montauk. Now that the Spanish-American War has ended, Camp Wikoff is in need of volunteers to assist soldiers with their recovery. This is, of course, where Mr. Roosevelt and his Rough Riders were quarantined upon returning from the war. It is the least we can do for those who served. How many would like to help?"

Many hands were raised and there was great commotion over the new volunteer opportunity.

"Camp Wikoff was created in great haste by our government out of need for the six hundred men recovering there. There are certainly many more sick and wounded soldiers who will arrive in the coming weeks, now that the war has ended. I have heard it is in great need of organization. This is something I can facilitate, of course."

"We aren't nurses, Emily. What are the specific requirements?" Cassandra Horton asked.

"We will not be needed for patient care as much as to aid the doctors and nurses in their duties. Female nurses will not be allowed to enter into the camp, instead the government is asking for male nurses. I have communicated with the secretary of the Women's National War Relief Association, and she tells me they are in need of night clothing, bedding, and wholesome food. We will be able to collect much of what is needed and take it to them. Volunteers will be needed to sort and distribute these necessities."

"I don't know about this. Aren't there quarantines in place for yellow fever? How can we go and bring disease back to our families?" Louisa Barratt asked.

"Oh, rubbish. I visited the military camps of my brother and husband during the Civil War, and I took care not to expose myself to disease. You can do the same, Louisa. Do you intend to help, or not?"

"Well… if you think so," Louisa murmured.

"Oh, for heaven's sake. You go on and on about volunteering. What could be more noble than assisting in the healing and recovery of our military?" I looked down to find that I had crumpled a piece of paper in my hands in frustration. If there was one thing I could not tolerate, it was a weak and indecisive mind.

"Let's adjourn for tonight, and you can all think about what part you would like to play in this effort. There are refreshments in the parlor."

That night, while preparing for bed, I told Wash about the women who could not seem to make up their minds about things that they had previously appeared favor.

"Not everyone is as sure-minded as you, you know. I am not certain myself that this is something you are capable of," Wash said.

"What are you talking about? Although John was only able to serve for a brief time don't you think we should show our appreciation for his safe return?"

"That has nothing to do with it. It's your own health. Who will take care of you?"

"I will not even answer such a preposterous question. Good night."

My husband's fears were not unfounded. I wondered about my stamina and how I would deal with the pain that plagued me daily, but I was determined to do my part. My eyes continued to betray me, as well.

Chapter 46

Though it is little one woman can do, still I crave the privilege of doing it.

Clara Barton

Montauk, Long Island, New York, 1898

The camp was set up on a vast plain with little but white tents dotting the landscape. The work was slow, and rife with problems before we arrived. Warehouses and fences had to be built. Four wells had been dug out of the earth. A small area of the camp was set off for the men quarantined with yellow fever and malaria and other contagious diseases. The other, larger portion was for soldiers weakened by the rough service and poor diet they had received in Cuba and Puerto Rico. Each area had its own hospital.

Striking workers had delayed shipments of equipment and supplies, and the camp was barely usable before the more than 3,500 men began arriving. Tents had no floors, the hospitals were understaffed, and the rations were meagre. Complaints of mismanagement abounded, but the officials and staff were doing the best they could. There was no time to waste.

"We must make life more bearable for these repatriated soldiers as soon as possible," I addressed the assembly of women standing before me at the camp. "I am ordering 800 bottles of beef extract, 50 pounds of cocoa, 3 cases of jam, 75 pairs of socks, 24 pairs of shoes, 50 pillowcases, and 30 nightshirts."

"Mrs. Roebling, some of the men are sleeping on the damp, dirty ground."

"So I have been informed. Tents, sheets, and blankets have been ordered, to be delivered immediately. Will you see to it that the men have comfortable sleeping accommodations, then?"

"Yes, Ma'am."

"Who would like to help me reorganize the kitchen and unload supplies?" Several hands went up. I assigned less significant duties to those present and went to talk to Dr. Roger Whitley, the only surgeon in Camp Wikoff.

"What can I do to help, doctor?" I asked.

"Mrs. Roebling. All you have done in such a short time in nothing less than miraculous. We don't want to wear you out!"

"I am willing to continue to be of assistance. Please tell me what you are in need of."

"My ability to complete surgery is hampered by the lack of surgical nurses, but we have not been given sufficient funds to hire more."

"Well, I will take care of their salaries for as long as needed, Dr. Whitely. Shall I send for two more nurses, then?"

"Yes, you are a savior," he shook my hand warmly. "How is it that you know precisely what is essential here?"

"I have visited many a military camp in my time, doctor. My own husband and brother served in the Civil War. You may have heard of General G.K. Warren?"

"Indeed, I have."

"That was my brother, now deceased. In addition I was a supervisor in the building of the Brooklyn Bridge."

"Really," Doctor Whitley raised a skeptical eyebrow, but I let it go. There was too much to accomplish and too little time.

Some of the soldiers were emaciated and suffering from yellow fever. I left the doctor and arranged for more wholesome food for the patients. I was gloriously busy and feeling very productive when the sharp pain returned to my middle section, so I mentioned to some of the women that I was going to lie down for a bit in my tent. But Mrs. Roberts stuck her nose into the tent and saw the grimace on my face. She went directly to one of the doctors, who rushed to my side.

"Mrs. Roebling, what is it?"

"Oh, it's nothing, doctor. It will pass. Please go back to the men who need you much more than I. Mrs. Roberts should not have sent you here."

"You seem to be in a great deal of pain. Where is it?"

Just then, the sharpness of the cramp cause me to cry out, although I tried mightily to suppress it.

"Mrs. Roebling, I'm afraid I must recommend that you take your leave. We are doing well here, thanks to your organization and planning."

"I will do no such thing, doctor. This ache will pass. It always does."

"I can offer some opium drops to relieve some of the affliction, if you wish."

"That would be appreciated. Now I would like to rest."

"I will return later to check on you."

"That is not necessary. I will be back to my post shortly." When the distress passed ten minutes later, I went out to join the others and informed Mrs. Roberts that she was to mind her own business from that point forward.

The next day, feeling much better, I walked the grounds. Much of the work was already in place, and things were running smoothly. I peered into one tent and saw a young man who looked much like my John, so I quietly entered and he turned toward me, tears streaming down his face.

"What is it, young man? What can I do for you?" He was not quarantined, so I sat beside him and took his hand.

"Oh, you look like my mama. I miss her so."

It was then that I could see he was just a boy. "What are you doing here, dear?"

"My father…well, he beats my poor mother and…."

"Go on."

"One day I ran out of the house. I meant to get help, but no one would come. I was afraid and hungry. Someone took me in, and before I knew it, I was in the war."

"Oh, my, you're much too young aren't you? I cannot imagine what your eyes have seen. Can I get you anything?"

"Would you help me write a letter to my mother? She doesn't know what happened to me." At that, he began to sob. As I tried to take him in my arms, I saw the wound on the other side of his body, blood seeping through the bandages on to the bed. Peeling back the dressing I saw what looked like a mass of raw meat. After replacing the dressing and the blanket, I rose to my feet promising, "I will return shortly to write that letter. I am very good at letter writing. But first I must find a doctor for you." I left to find someone to change the dressings on his wound, but when I returned with Dr. Whitley, the boy was ashen and still. My visit had been too late.

Once again, I was overwhelmed with the futility of war, of human beings fighting each other, of losing our young men. Even when they survived, their brains contained nightmarish memories of all they had witnessed. There were no camps or hospitals for the ruination of their minds and hearts. For years after Wash and I married, he would awake at night, sweating profusely, breathing heavily, reliving some horror he had witnessed during the war. He never told me of his memories or the dreams, and it was a mystery to me what he had experienced.

Dear Wash,

I hope you are doing well, my dear. Conditions here were awful, as I'm sure you can imagine. I'm afraid you will have to admit I was right to come to this camp. So much has been accomplished in such a short time. Over 20,000 men are expected to flow through this camp, so our services were desperately needed. All of the women volunteers have been dedicated and hard-working folks, and deserve our country's gratitude.

I met President McKinley this morning. He visited the camp and could not say enough wonderful things about the women under my supervision. I have been in my glory, as it reminded me of my days as field engineer of the Brooklyn Bridge, a perfectly natural position for me to be in. I will be traveling home at the end of this week and will be required to write a detailed report of our work here for immediate distribution.

I have missed you Washington, whether you have missed me or not.

Affectionately,
Em

Chapter 47

Genuine learning has ever been said to give polish to a man; why then should it not bestow added charm on women?

Emma Willard

"I hear there are plans to build a bridge across the Hudson River," Mrs. Wilton remarked at the next women's meeting.

"I do not see any pressing need for such a bridge, do you?" I replied.

"Are you afraid your husband might take an interest in such a project, Emily?"

"I'm sure he has no such interest, but my son John would be an excellent choice as chief engineer should such an opportunity arise," I replied.

The next day I discovered that Washington had, in fact, visited the site of the proposal in my absence.

"What were you thinking, Wash? I am afraid you might be persuaded to take an active part in one of these proposals for new bridges."

"The cities of New York and Brooklyn continue to flourish. More bridges may be needed to handle the amount of traffic each day," he said, apparently disinterested in my feelings about the matter.

"I have no overriding concern about the needs of the cities any longer. That part of our life is over."

"We shall see, dear," he said blandly. "You have chosen your path to volunteer and travel and speak to groups. I believe I am free to choose mine as well. Caisson disease never affected my mind, and it is as sharp as ever. Why shouldn't I use it for the good of the future?"

"Why don't you leave the future to your son? He is perfectly capable of handling any bridges that are needed in New York."

"The John A. Roebling Company already has the contract for the cables."

"I do not approve of your involvement and connection to the family business. I ask that you not speak to me about it again. Your business plans just further separate our worlds."

"I am not dead, Emily."

"Well, neither am I, and I do not intend to be your secretary ever again."

With that, Wash walked slowly out of the room and I felt bereft of the joy that once flourished in our marriage. After many years, we had no project to work on together. Our son had his own life, and Washington and I had grown apart. I had been so busy filling my mind so that it would not fall into darkness that I had hardly noticed. I thought my husband supportive, but in reality, he just did not need me any longer. Either that, or he resented my travels without him.

That night I laid awake pondering how to continue my pursuits without him. Should I not care about his health and what was clearly best for him? Why couldn't he leave these opportunities to our son? But, Wash's father would not have done that for him. John A. Roebling's ambitions had been too huge and too self-centered. We were thrown into the building of the bridge involuntarily. We each had sacrificed other choices we might have had, were not for the responsibility of fulfilling what my father-in-law had started. I was expecting my husband to continue sacrificing for what I believed about him, and what I so desperately needed to be a vital woman in this life—to not give up on living.

At breakfast, Wash was silent, trying to read the paper with his magnifying glass.

"I received a notification yesterday." I said to capture his interest.

He peered over the paper nonchalantly. "Yes?"

"The New Jersey legislature passed a resolution commending me on my work at Camp Wikoff."

"Is that right?"

"Yes, I believe the commendation will be delivered presently."

"Another feather in your cap, I suppose," he said.

I did not know how to respond to such a bewildering statement, so I said nothing and finished my breakfast.

"I have made a decision," I said quietly.

"Yes? Another one?"

"What do you mean by that?"

"Go ahead, what is your new endeavor?"

"I am enrolling in New York University to study law. I have been thinking about it for a long time." I sat up straighter in an effort to keep my confidence at the sight of my husband's apathy.

"Is that right? Well, good for you," he said, and went back to his newspaper.

We sat in silence for some time and then I said, "I understand that when I make decisions about my life and what I want to do, you have the same privilege."

"Yes, I know that." Wash began humming out his annoyance behind his newspaper.

I felt ashamed of my attitude in front of my husband, of not trusting his judgment in matters of his own health. I had always been bossy, but it was my way of showing my love and concern.

"The Woman's Law Class is a one-semester course designed for businesswomen whose careers would benefit from knowledge of the law and for those interested in learning about the legal system."

Wash looked up from the newspaper and nodded for me to continue.

"It was founded by Dr. Emily Kempin, a Swiss attorney, and is backed by the Woman's Legal Education Society. Dr. Kempin earned a law degree in Switzerland but was barred from practicing."

"I'm sure wealthy women like you are potential donors to the university as well," Wash said rather coldly. I chose to ignore that statement.

"I'm interested in studying contracts, real property, and domestic relations. A full two-year course program is not offered, but I would like to attend for the one semester, after which I would graduate. Women are starting to be admitted to the bar in New York, and well-educated women are gaining more interest in the law."

"What brought on this sudden interest?" he asked.

"I never stopped thinking about Mary O'Connell in Brooklyn and the dilemma she faced when Dennis was so abusive to her. She had no legal rights or options. She had all those children to care for. It has bothered me all of these years. Also, the debates you and John have over the Roebling business make me wonder about some of the legal ramifications. I want to understand, especially for the sake of our son."

"Yes, that's my Emily," he finally smiled at me. "It is I that am worried about your health now, though. Do you think you can manage with the pain you experience on so many days? And what about your eyes?"

"I will simply do the best I can. I cannot let weak eyesight stop me from living, can I?"

"I have never known anything to stop you from getting what you want, whether it be obstruction by men, pain, your husband's infirmities, motherhood, or age."

"Age! I am only fifty-five! If I do not continue learning, what will I do with myself for the next twenty years?"

"Many of your friends appear content going to socials and teas."

"That is one reason I have so few friends. They can be so frivolous! I spent so many years learning to communicate with men about the bridge that I neglected to learn how to relate to my own gender. It's a weakness, I believe—friendship, that is. I try very hard to discuss things with other women, but they usually have puzzled looks on their faces. I find it difficult to speak about the mundane everyday things, and am only comfortable when in charge of something."

"I think you might find more of your own kind in this law school, women whose minds are as bright as yours. It's really a wonderful idea, Em."

"Well, thank you. It's not that I was looking for your approval necessarily." I paused to see Wash's reaction.

"I know. I believe we've come to an understanding about each other's lives at this point in our marriage, haven't we?"

"Yes, I believe we have."

Although I claimed I was not old, I did not feel that way. On many days my multitude of ailments made me feel decrepit and weak. I fought through painful, swollen joints, especially my knees. I struggled to climb stairs and strengthen my muscles, which seemed to grow weaker, so now most days I was unable to walk outside. My eyes continued to deceive and disappoint me. It would be a battle to do schoolwork once again, and I would have to use a magnifying glass or allow someone to read to me. Wash's eyes had inexplicably improved somewhat over the years and I knew he would help me, but the sin of pride kept me from asking most of the time.

I simply refused to see myself as old. I was a grandmother, but that did not mean I was useless. Just as Wash had experienced; my mind was more vital than my body, and it was to be used at all costs.

Chapter 48

It was not despair, but it seems as if life were passing by, leaving its promises broken and unfulfilled.

Kate Chopin
The Awakening

Despite our continuing differences, Wash was kind enough to move to the Waldorf Astoria Hotel with me in New York while I attended classes. While there, we had time to visit the Metropolitan Museum of Art and saw the two new works by Edouard Manet recently purchased by the museum. He rendered the portraits so beautifully. The collection included hundreds of European paintings, Japanese art, and a Roman sarcophagus. I regretted that it had been so long since we had taken time to appreciate art. It was something Wash and I were very interested in during the early years of our marriage, but it had gone by the wayside.

  We visited the Metropolitan Opera for the first time, and I felt lifted into the heavens by the magnificence of the opera house, the glorious costumes, and the wonderful music. We saw 'The Mikado' by Gilbert and Sullivan, and I could not have been more delighted. Wash found it a little silly.

After the opera we visited at Delmonico's, a place we had been fond of so many years ago. We dined on Beef Wellington, their special potato dish, and creamy cheesecake. We took the opportunity to enjoy ourselves— something that had been scarce in recent years. Another wonderful thing about New York City was that Brooklyn, our old home, had officially become part of it.

On the first day of law class, I was nervous and excited, and took an unusually long time getting ready for the day. Wash impatiently urged me out of the bathroom.
"I want to look my best."
"What does how you look have to do with anything?" Wash asked.
"You don't understand anything about women, do you? We are only taken seriously when we are attractive and at our top presentation. That's just the way it is."
I took a carriage to New York University, and a guide led me to the lecture hall. I found a seat near the front of the classroom and took out my journal, pencils, and the new fountain pen Wash had given me.
When Professor Russell arrived, the women whispered and chattered because he was quite handsome. He proved to be as enlightened man as my husband. "I will encourage you toward oral disputation and friendly wrangling without the bitterness of real antagonism," Professor Russell announced. This thrilled me as oral disputation was something I certainly excelled at.
"This is a heterogeneous class," he continued. "The most wifely and motherly women with the most aggressive of those who assert woman's demand for rights still denied. If you look around the room, you will see women like yourselves, but also those of every creed, race,

and social standing. Things are changing in this country for those who are female and those who have been oppressed. Some of you have graduated from college already, and some are the family breadwinners. Some are here as women of fortune, who have nothing else to occupy your time, I am quite sure."

At that, I peered behind me from my front row seat. I discovered many women like myself there, (as Wash had predicted), but overall, we represented a multitude of social standings. Nevertheless, I took issue with his last statement and raised my hand.

"Yes, Mrs. Roebling?"

"I am also quite sure that women of fortune regard their time here and the work presented to be just as crucial to their education as any other student," I said somewhat indignantly. "Are you suggesting that privilege is something that makes one feeble-minded?"

The professor revealed a small smile, paused, and looked about the room before responding. "I see that the oral disputation has begun! Good for you, Mrs. Roebling! That was exactly the response I was hoping for."

"Oh, well, thank you," I sputtered. "Then you agree that all present today are equally valuable to the study of law and worthy of final examination when the semester has concluded?"

"Without question, Mrs. Roebling. Now, shall we continue? I would like to discuss the syllabus in detail so you are all aware of the tremendous amount of work that you will be expected to complete this semester."

I nodded and said nothing further. My mind was twirling, eager to learn. I opened the syllabus and found that the information was in such small print that I could not decipher it, even with my spectacles. Fortunately, the professor covered the expectations aloud, and I was able to understand the expectations by listening closely and committing it to memory.

Classes were invigorating. Professor Russell encouraged discussion and debate among the students, and urged us to entertain the opinions of others, open our minds to more than facts and figures, and consider moral dilemmas and unusual circumstances and situations.

"The mere accumulations of fact-knowledge are thus supplemented by comparison and reflection, and, thereby, enhanced value. An impression is made on the mind of the student that is all the more vivid and permanent for the concrete environment with which it is associated," he said to my delight.

Thinking back on my years of schooling, while excellent, I realized there had been too much memorizing of facts and too little critical thinking and evaluation. I could not wait to debate some of the laws and precedents with the other students.

"Desultory reading, self-imposed tasks, and ill-directed studies cannot exhibit results at all comparable with those produced by an academic regimen that appoints its hours, measures its duties, plans its curriculum, and tests its progress," announced the professor.

His discourse with the students was unfailingly respectful. He never lowered his high standards for our education or our expectations of success. At last: a man who took women seriously!

The curriculum was rigorous, and much of the work was done outside of class. The class discussions gave me the opportunity to hear and understand the ideas and opinions of the other female students. On some days, we divided into smaller groups of five to discuss the assigned reading. The reading could be tedious and dry, even for me. For the first time in my life, I began to enjoy conversing with other women. We occasionally veered off the given topic.

"Would anyone like to join me after class for tea?" I asked one day. "I'm reading the most fascinating book. Have you heard of '*The Awakening*' by Kate Chopin?"

"Yes, I am reading it as well," Mrs. Smythe said. "It's quite titillating, isn't it?"

"I suppose you could call it that," I replied, pulling the book out of my bag.

"You brought it to class?"

"It's not a banned book, for goodness sake," I said. "I would think that women who have found their way into this classroom would be more aware of Miss Chopin's meaning in writing it."

"May I borrow the book when you've completed reading it?" asked Mrs. Carlton.

"Of course, Virginia. May I call you Virginia?"

"Yes, please do, Emily. What is it that you are so enamored of in this particular book?"

"In all of my reading, I have never come across the story of a woman so unhappy with her life as a wife and a mother."

The women were quiet for a moment and looked uncomfortable.

"Oh, come now," I continued. "Are you telling me that you who are here searching for a higher meaning in your existence are not familiar with this feeling? The book is simply conveying something we have all thought."

"And what is that?" Mrs. Carlton asked.

"That there is life outside of being a wife and mother, of course! Isn't that why you are all here?"

"I think we should return to our studies, Mrs. Roebling," Mrs. Bundy urged.

"Yes, of course. But I still hope we can discuss it soon." I looked toward Virginia, and she appeared to be agreeable. I relished the possibility of having a true female friend, a woman unafraid of veracity and liberal discourse, even at this late stage in my life.

When it came time for the exams, my eyes were failing, and in a reversal of roles, I had to ask Wash to read to me on many days. Even his magnifying glass had a dizzying effect on my eyes.

"I assumed you were only auditing this class. I didn't know you intended to take the final exams," Wash commented one evening.

"Why would I do something half-way? Do you even know me anymore?"

We sat quietly for a few moments.

"Truly," I continued, "I thought you were here to encourage my efforts. Or do you think they are frivolous? Do you think I am too old to be pursuing law?"

"I don't understand what you intend to do with this certificate. You cannot spend your whole life presuming that you, one woman, can change the world."

I felt so wounded that I could not speak. What had become of the intellectual equality in our marriage? When did my husband begin to doubt my motives and desire to improve myself?

"You are becoming a disappointment," I said flatly.

"I did not stop needing you after the bridge was completed," he said quietly.

"I am still willing to tend to all of your nervous conditions."

"I'm afraid they still plague me."

"I'm well aware of that, although I believe some of them to be in your mind. You have not been able to let go of the ailments that overcame you many years ago. It's as if they are a part of you."

"Maybe we could avail ourselves of a break," Wash suggested, avoiding further unpleasantries.

"Of course. I'm going to go outside for a breath of air. Please do not join me." I stared at him with a malicious glare.

As I walked down the hallway from our suite, I smelled a wretched stench and was suddenly overcome by a cloud of smoke. Patrons erupted from their rooms, panicked and yelling to each other.

"Fire! Fire!" Someone called out through the blanket of blackness.

I put my hands on the hallway wall and made my way back to our suite.

"Wash! Where are you?" I saw him slowly exit the sitting room, and I grabbed him by the arm.

"Emily! What is wrong? I thought you were going outside."

"There's a fire somewhere in the building. We must leave."

Without thinking to take anything with us, Wash grabbed my hand and we moved down the stairway. By the time we reached the front doorway, the smoke had diminished. Only a few patrons lingered outside, and it seemed as if the panic were for naught.

"Are you all right, dear?" Washington put his arms around me and held me close.

My anger had evaporated in those moments. How much we took our safety and security for granted.

"Yes, I'm all right. I was just worried about you." I began to weep quietly in shame and relief.

"Things are not as bad as you see them, Em."

"Things are not bad at all. It's just that I want so much for you to understand me, not just tolerate me, to know that you are my champion just as I was yours for so many years. Is that so much to expect?"

He did not answer, but looked at me as if he were puzzled, bewildered. Just then, we were told it was safe to go back to our suites. A small electrical fire on the first floor had risen through the heating system, but was now extinguished.

We did not speak of the incident again. Too much had already been said.

Chapter 49

Perhaps it is better to wake up after all, even to suffer, than to remain a dupe to illusions all one's life.

Kate Chopin
The Awakening

In order to graduate, one of our tasks was to research and present a lengthy report on a modern trial and give our own interpretation of it. On the day of my scheduled presentation, I was a bit nervous, unusual for me. On my way to the classroom, I realized that my nervousness was actually anger. My stomach felt clenched and jittery. So much of what I had learned in that semester had ignited a passion in me for justice.

My face burned. I put my cool hands on my cheeks and tried to compose myself. The lecture was to be our final grade, and I intended to give the best speech Professor Russell had ever heard.

When my name was called, I rose calmly, telling myself that public speaking was my forte, that I knew my subject matter thoroughly, that I was Emily Warren Roebling and I belonged in the law class!

"Professor, classmates, I have studied the 1894 case of Madeleine Pollard. At the conclusion, I will present my analysis of the results of this trial." I took a deep breath and nodded to my audience and to Professor Russell. He smiled and nodded back.

"Madeleine Pollard met William Breckinridge when she was 17 years of age and he was 47 years old. Breckinridge was a five-term congressman and was said to be on his way to the White House. That is, until he was sued by Miss Pollard for breach of contract. To be concise, I will only tell you that they entered into an illicit affair and Miss Pollard bore his child at an asylum hospital in Ohio. The child was left there to die. Two years later, she bore another child of his who also did not survive. The reason for the deaths is documented as neglect. Orphan asylums are nothing more than warehouses for unwanted babies." I looked up at my classmates. They appeared as absorbed in this scandalous story as I had been for the past several weeks. Professor Russell waited patiently for me to continue.

"It must be said that Breckinridge was a married man with children and Pollard insisted that he asked her to give up the babies. If she kept them, they would eventually have been traced to him and would have ruined his reputation. She agreed to abandon the children for his sake and to continue as his mistress."

"Breckinridge's wife eventually died, and he promised to marry Miss Pollard, as she was with child for the third time. They set the date for May 31, 1893, but then Breckinridge secretly married his cousin. In her rage and grief, Pollard miscarried the child. I ask you: was Madeleine Pollard duped? What was her recourse at this juncture?" I paused and took another deep breath.

"Miss Pollard sued the congressman for breach of promise. Her life and reputation had been destroyed. She admitted to being a 'fallen woman,' which we all know makes her pariah. There was no possibility of employment for her in the future. She was not respectable enough for any man to want to marry her. She sued him for $50,000."

At that, there were a few gasps in the classroom. I felt my agitation mounting, so I paused before continuing. "The trial lasted 28 days. The judge was a member of Breckinridge's church. Not only are all jurors men, but no women were allowed in the courtroom lest they hear some lurid testimony, was the reason given."

"The judge deemed most of Pollard's testimony as hearsay, and, therefore, inadmissible. I quote, 'too filthy and obscene,' unquote, for the court to hear. As the trial went on, Pollard presented herself as a more sympathetic character. She had excellent representation, which worked in her favor. In the end, she was awarded $15,000. The congressman's reputation was in ruins.

"Of course I believe that justice was served in this case, but it was only due to the courage of Madeline Pollard. When Mr. Breckinridge returned to Kentucky, it was reported that women who had never taken any interest in such matters became active in politics. Thousands of ladies attended protest meetings, asking for the congressman to be ousted. The congressman continued his efforts to be reelected, and he lost, but only by 255 votes, which shows he was still supported by many."

The classroom was silent and attentive. I continued: "You might ask yourself why I chose a case that resulted in justice for this woman. I did so to make four cogent points: One, if Miss Pollard had not had the wherewithal to fight for her rights and to risk being persecuted by the public she would have been banished to a place such as House of Mercy, a home for fallen women, to live out a miserable life. The man, however, would have gone on to pursue whatever he chose, unscathed by her demise. Before Miss Pollard, women were punished for the same indiscretions that men were free to indulge in without fear. Differing standards and expectations for people depending on their gender is inherently unjust and needs to be rectified in this country. Although Pollard was successful, this injustice continues to this day, as you all well know. It matters not what your judgment of their behavior is. That, in my opinion, is left to God. What matters is that there is equality between the sexes in all matters, legal and otherwise.

"My second point: Women do not have the choice to move forward with their lives in a case like this. Madeline would have had no possible way of supporting herself or her children, had they lived. I had a friend in a similar situation, and, were it not for the financial support my husband and I provided, her children might have been relegated to orphanages as well, through no fault of hers!

"Third: Think of the innocent children in this case. They were thrown away as refuse, their lives worthless, to save the reputation and selfish pursuits of their parents. What must we do to save these babies?

"Last, all judges and jurors are men, with an inherent bias toward their own sex. This is something that can no longer be tolerated. Ladies, when you all go out into the world with your law degrees, I implore you to be as brave and courageous as Madeline Pollard."

Spirited applause and congratulations followed.

After class, Virginia Carlton, Carolyn Smythe, and I walked a short distance to a tea room to talk about our studies and *'The Awakening.'*

"Did you complete the book? I know our studies have taken us away from pleasurable reading, but I am delighted to be able to discuss it with you." I said, sipping chamomile tea.

"I did, indeed. I had to hide it from my husband and children. It has such a bad reputation. I heard it might be banned!" Virginia replied.

"To what do you believe the title refers?" Carolyn asked. "Is it a bodily awakening or a spiritual one?"

"I think Edna represents all women, our oppressed passions, our inability to choose for ourselves, the possibility of rejecting societal norms, and being a person of independence," I said.

"But what did you think about her as a mother?"

"Maybe all women are not meant to be mothers."

"Listen to this: 'I would give up the unessential; I would give up my money, I would give my life for my children; but I wouldn't give up myself.'"

"I do not think that means she does not love her children, but that she is a person, too. Why should a woman give up her identity because she has married and borne children?" I asked. The three of us pondered that silently for a few moments, sipping our tea uncomfortably.

"We are enlightened women, are we not? We are in law school. I believe it is the law that limits women's opportunities for individual expression and achievement," Carolyn said.

"I wholeheartedly agree, Carolyn. My husband does not approve of the classes I am taking here, but I insisted that it is my time to do something I want. I have taken care of him and our four children for fifteen years." Virginia added.

"The laws must change in this country. It is the unwritten law of nature, and the expectations of the society in which we live that create these oppressions, surely," I said. "We must not allow our daughters and granddaughters to end up like Edna Pontellier."

Chapter 50

There will never be complete equality until women themselves help to make laws and elect lawmakers.

Susan B. Anthony

On March 30, 1899, I donned my black cap and billowing gown and walked down the aisle of the Concert Hall at Madison Square Garden. The Hall was decorated with flowers that filled the place with a lovely fragrance and a small orchestra played in the background. Wash had accepted an invitation from Professor Russell to sit on the platform with the faculty of the Law School. I was not sure whether I favored the idea at first, but I had shared in his glory and attention for the bridge, so it seemed only fair.

I approached the podium to present my essay, *A Wife's Disabilities*, which had won an award of $50, and considerable attention from the Law School faculty. The eyes of the audience gave me their undivided attention as I read a portion of the essay aloud.

"I believe women wish to avail themselves of the rights given them under the fourteenth amendment to the Constitution in order to have a voice in deciding questions of interest to them in laws made by the legislatures of different states.

"The sacred rite of marriage confers upon wives the honor of ranking in legal responsibility with idiots and slaves. Single women are not encumbered in this way, but the desire of fathers to protect property left to their female offspring from grasping sons-in-law leads to statues that, in effect, prohibit married daughters from obtaining what is rightfully theirs. Compounding the problem is the fact that husbands are not legally bound to leave their wives any of their personal property. To correct this injustice, the statutes should be so changed that the property, real and personal, belongs equally to man and wife and can only be distributed and divided on the death of the surviving party of the marriage contract." There were a few small gasps and heads turned when I called for this elimination of laws discriminating against wives and widows.

"Does the wife not contribute largely to the husband's success or failure in life? Must she not bear with her husband, poverty and reversals of fortune when they come, and shall she not lawfully share in all the profits of his success and prosperity? The law must be changed to protect widows because, despite the generosity of many husbands, there are some who deny their wives what common law has termed their 'paraphernalia,' namely clothing and other personal possessions!" At this point, I paused and looked up at my audience. I saw mostly women smiling and men frowning. I quickly glanced over at Wash and saw a look of horror on his face. I continued making my point by citing the extreme case of conjugal murder.

"If a husband kills his wife in a fit of passion, he would be treated as if he had killed not his wife, but a total stranger. But if the situation were reversed and the wife committed the murder, it would be considered a more atrocious deed. She would be deemed guilty, not only of murder but of treason because of the overriding authority of the husband." I emphasized the word *authority*, and there were more murmurs in the crowd.

"In the past, women have been sentenced to death for larceny, bigamy, and manslaughter, even if it was their first offense. But men are given only a light sentence: a short prison stay for these same offenses. A man is held responsible for his wife's wrongdoing, but he is legally able to keep her in line by hitting her with a stick! A stick as large as his finger, but not larger than his thumb, as many times and with as much force as he can muster. He has the power in his own hands of preventing her from getting him into legal difficulties."

I thought the inequities in the legal system between men and women were quite clear, and I saw no shame in bringing it to everyone's attention. After the ceremony, crowds of women gathered around me with handshakes, kisses and congratulations. Eventually, I moved across the stage to where Wash and Professor Russell were speaking with each other.

"I never heard her essay until tonight, and I do not agree with one word she has said!" My husband practically shouted at the professor.

"Our pupils are allowed to advance any theory they like if their legal reasoning is sound. We leave them the entire responsibility of their essays," Professor Russell said, looking my way sympathetically.

"I did not consult any male advisors in writing my essay, including you, Washington." I said. "I interpreted this topic entirely on my own, and you have nothing to be upset about as far as your own reputation is concerned. I am proud of my achievement, and intend to donate my prize to the Women's Legal Education Society endowment fund."

"That's grand, and it will be greatly appreciated Mrs. Roebling," said the professor. "You have been a wonderful student, and I have enjoyed getting to know you. Good luck in all of your legal endeavors."

As we walked away, Wash said, "I thought you were going to purchase an engraved commemorative pitcher with that money."

"I changed my mind."

We walked silently back to the hotel, the joy I'd felt in receiving my degree dampened by my husband's attitude. Why are men only happy when women are do their bidding?

"Do you remember long ago, before we were married you promised me something?" I asked.

"What was that?"

"You assured me that I would never end up like your own mother, slaving over a stove while her husband was the world traveler and free to do as he pleased."

"And do you think I have not kept that promise?"

"It's not that I've been slaving over a stove, certainly, but I feel as if you have forgotten that I am not a women who enjoys dependence upon anyone or anything."

"That may be so, Em, but you have all the privileges of being a very wealthy woman because you married into my family." He stopped walking and pulled me around to face him. "I do not forget all of your sacrifices when I was afflicted for those many years during the building of the bridge, and I believe you have been given much appreciation for those years. Now you want more and I have not stopped you, have I?"

"You are humiliating me with your statements about my wealth and privilege," I shot back, "Of course, it is due to our marriage and your wealthy family. But that is just my point. What choice does a woman have? If she has no rights of her own, to pursue a career of her own and be considered a full-fledged, legal member of society, she will always be dependent on her husband. Can't you see that?"

"That is the world we live in, isn't it? Are you so unhappy with the life you've been given? Haven't you had more experiences than most women? My God! How much more do you need?"

"This supposed law degree means very little. I did it for my own edification and to satisfy my own curiosity. It will get me nothing because a full two-year degree is open to only a few women."

"Maybe that's the way it should be."

"Oh, Wash, I expected more understanding from you. Why can men never move forward and see new ways of living? It always has to be the way it's always been for you, doesn't it? And you know why? Because as a man, you have never had to fight for any rights. The world is just fine for all of your needs and ambitions. Men do not have constant obstacles to their goals. Stop for a moment and visualize me, Emily Warren Roebling, being chosen as the sole chief engineer of the building of the Brooklyn Bridge for fourteen years. I mean without you, without any man in charge. Can you conceive of that in your wildest imagination? Of course not. Because it has never been done, and why is that?"

Wash didn't say a word, but kept walking steadily ahead.

I continued, "It's because it is not possible. Did you think I had the brains to do it? Did you?"

"Of course I do. You know that."

"Then why couldn't I?"

I received no answer, but we both understood the reality.

"You don't see the need for change; you don't even think about it because the world favors men and always has, and women are supposed to accept that, no matter what their dreams or abilities may be."

We were silent for an uncomfortable time, then Wash spoke up again. "I have never heard you complain about your mansion and servants and travels, have I Emily?"

Crestfallen, I saw my deepest sensibilities were being pushed aside by my own husband. "That is not the point I am trying to make. You will never comprehend this, Washington, and I am done trying to make it so. It profoundly hurts me that you don't even want to understand."

"I was under the impression that I had made you happy all these years."

"It's not that I have been unhappy. It's just…." At that moment a keen vacancy entered my soul, as if all the air had been sucked out of my lungs and blood. The joy of the day had been ruined by this discussion, one we had avoided for so many years. I had kept myself too busy to address the division in our marriage. I had avoided sharing my most passionate beliefs, and now they were out in the open and neither of us knew what to do with this knowledge about each other.

When two people come to terms with disappointment and their true fears, you cannot un-know what you know. You cannot un-say what has been said. After more than thirty years of marriage, we now had to accept the reality of what we had become. It was the growing, the expanding of my mind that had brought all of this on, and I could not turn back. It was the culmination of what had grown in the roots of my spirit. I could not splice myself into the stultified world of men. Everything that had gone unsaid for so long had now been uttered.

"I do love you. I always will, no matter what goals and dreams you have that do not include me," Wash said.

"I love you too. You have put up with more than most husbands ever would. Let's agree that none of this has altered our love and respect for each other."

"On that we can agree, dear." Wash took me in his arms, and for a moment, my heart felt untethered, unguarded again.

We walked dejectedly through the crowded city streets, together and yet alone. I wondered whether we had ever recognized the same revelations at the same time. The only thing we truly shared was our son, yet even the experience of parenting was completely different for each of us. Without John, without the bridge, we seemed split like a butchered piece of meat. Wash began his low humming.

"Wash?"

"Yes?"

"I have been having dreams about the bridge again. It would be such a thrill to see it once more. Do you think we could visit it?"

"Yes, I think that is a splendid idea." He took my hand and held it all the way back to the hotel.

Three days later, we were back at the dining table with our newspapers and breakfasts spread out before us. Wash and I had not spoken again of my speech on graduation night, and the whole event felt like a scar on our relationship.

"It seems you are a star after all," Wash said, looking up from the paper.

"Oh?"

"The *Herald* has made quite a fuss about you and your speech. It lists all the graduates from your class, but shows only a picture of you. You look every bit the scholar, too."

"Let me see that," I reached across the breakfast table and all but ripped the newspaper out of his hands. The photograph was flattering and I appeared younger than my fifty-six years, thanks to fortuitous lighting. I had pulled my hair up tightly into a top knot and wore a high collared, lace-trimmed shirtwaist, with only a delicate pair of earrings for jewelry. My black robe looked regal. I had wanted to appear serious, even a bit masculine, to highlight my abilities, not my feminine wiles. The photograph proved I had succeeded. I did not comment but handed the paper back to Wash calmly, as if it meant nothing. But it meant everything on a day when I felt too weak and in too much pain to go on.

Chapter 51

Pain has an element of blank;
It cannot recollect
When it began, or if there were
A day when it was not.

It has no future but itself,
Its infinite realms contain
Its past, enlightened to perceive
New periods of pain.

Emily Dickinson

Only a few months after my graduation, I was asked to travel to Wellington, Ohio, to speak to the townspeople about my accomplishments. Wash and I tangled over whether I was well enough to go, but in the end, I won as usual.

     Wellington was a small oil town that gave me the feeling of having been dropped into the last century instead of standing on the threshold of a new one. The homes of the community's well-to-do citizens were comfortable enough, heated and lighted by natural gas. Although the townspeople claimed to be educated, they were, in my mind, years behind civilization in their dress and home decor. I was unaccustomed to such unsophistication after a lifetime of living near New York. It was quite a shock, and I was unsure whether my thoughts would be sensible to them.

Nevertheless, the people turned out in great numbers and treated me as if I were a celebrity. I spoke at the City Hall, and following my well-received speech on women's rights and the law, I was entertained at a lovely reception.

"How is it that you garner these invitations?" Wash had asked without any enthusiasm.

"I'm not always sure, but I believe people have read my speeches in the papers or have heard of me from my travels. I received a great deal of attention and accolades at the opening of the bridge, too. You are always welcome to join me anywhere I go, dear."

"My present health will not allow it. You know I have been suffering from bronchitis these past weeks."

"Oh, of course, but I haven't heard you cough for days. Why do you insist that every little ailment is the end of the world? Why do you let it stop you from enjoying the health you now have?"

"It is not the end of the world to you, I suppose, but I must be more cautious."

"That is not what your doctor says. He tells me you are perfectly able to travel now. It occurs to me that you are so accustomed to being ill with the caisson disease of the past that it is a part of your identity."

"That's ridiculous and insulting." Wash got up and left the room which confirmed my assumption.

My interest in the law endured in spite of the awareness that I would never practice it. I wrote to John and asked him to send any books he might have on the sociological view of sovereignty and told him about a recent legal case involving property taxes. The plaintiff was John D. Rockefeller, who contended that his property at Pocantico Hills in Westchester County, New York, should be taxed as it had been before extensive improvements had been made to it. He alleged it was unjust because if he had not undertaken the great amount of work already completed on his property, the rest of the community would not have appreciated in value. The court agreed, and I did, as well. The judge said that the rich as well as the poor, had rights, and they should be respected by the law of the land. I concurred.

John asked me to do some research for him, which delighted me. His road-building and land acquisition work for a railroad company sometimes required him to be involved in legal matters, and I was happy to use some of my new skills on behalf of my son. Professor Russell had recommended *Blackstone's Commentaries*, and *The Encyclopedia*, but I also studied the Magna Carta to improve my understanding of such matters.

My letters were, in part, an attempt to maintain my relationship with my only son, which had diminished after our discussion about dependence. John had moved his family to North Carolina, where he now worked. I knew he was attempting to support his family on more than his allowance, but he seemed bitter about that decision. At first I despaired over their settling so far away but Wash reassured me that I would be able to visit as often as possible. In reality, my health did not always allow such long journeys, and I missed my little grandsons desperately.

In my letter to John I implored him to bring the boys to stay with us for a portion of the summer. The grounds of our Trenton home bloomed with flowering plants and an abundance of wildlife. Siegfried was nine and Paul was six—the optimum ages for learning about the natural world. They also could increase their skills in fishing and hunting. My body continued to fail me in so many ways, and I wanted to spend as much time as possible with the boys. I anxiously awaited a response from John, but my wait was a long one.

Physical pain grinds away at your spirit, scars your soul. It is like a thief stealing the life you built, taking the joy out of work and play, out of living. The worst days reminded me how fragile I was, and that was not something I wished to think about. It frustrated me to the point of anger on many days, and left me in a well of self-pity. At times, I feared life was growing short. The ailments never improved, but multiplied each year. I fought against the idea that I was not long for this world, since I was not, in fact, elderly. I had planned to live a very long life in light of all I still hoped to achieve.

If I could not travel as much as I wished, there was always writing. My body weakened and ached, but my brain was active and alert, in much the same way my husband had lived for so many years. Strangely, I gained more compassion and empathy for what he had been through and focused less on my sacrifices for him. In my mind, there was always a way to make the best of inopportune circumstances, just as Wash and I had after the disease struck him down. There was a need to surrender to circumstances.

At my writing desk, I watched my hand struggle to make the lofty, curly handwriting of my earlier days. I was writing the word *more*, and suddenly remembered the more I had been promised—at least, I believed it a sacred promise. It was in that moment I realized *I* was the more. I had accomplished mostly everything I set out to do in my life. I had never viewed it as enough, but on that day, I made room in my mind for the possibility that perhaps it was, after all. We are given a number of years on this earth; we are given thorns in our sides as the apostle Paul taught us to expect; we are given love along the way to carry us across the troubled times. It had taken much too long for me to understand the message I'd received so long ago, the one I'd taken to heart, whatever its source might have been. It might have been my brain pushing me forward, always forward. I did not know, but I was finally willing to let it be.

Becoming a member of the Daughters of the American Revolution had been a lifelong goal. A great deal of research and work was involved in proving I was a lineal descendent of a soldier of the American Revolution: the key to admission into the organization. It wasn't until this point in my life that I had gathered all the appropriate papers. The DAR's work to promote historic preservation, education, and patriotism aligned perfectly with my own principles and interests. The motto: "God, Home, and Country," summarized all that I had striven for in my own life.

"I suppose this involves more traveling," Wash sighed as he glanced at my notebooks and months of research.

"I assumed we had come to an agreement about that. I have been asked to consider the role of president of the DAR for the coming term. It's a great honor," I said, hopefully.

"Genealogy is a noble calling, and I am prepared to support any efforts you exert on behalf of the DAR, but as always, I am concerned about your health," Wash said. "Even a noble cause is not reason to harm yourself. I still need you as my wife and companion."

My heart melted. In these times, when we seemed frequently at odds with each other, it was satisfying to hear his desire for me. "Thank you, dear. That delights my heart."

"I have other ways of delighting you, if you recall," he smiled mischievously at me.

"Oh my, it's been a long time hasn't it?"

"If you can give of yourself to so many, maybe you can spare some of your attention for your old Wash."

"Of course I can." We moved quietly to our bedroom, where we created a new way to be together. It did not come easily, and I feared our days of intimacy were over, but my dear husband tenderly took me in his arms and my soul soared once again. Secretly I wondered if that would be the last time we would become as one as husband and wife. Our bodies continued to decline, and although we had declared our continuing love, would we ever again be able to enjoy the marriage bed?

In life, we often celebrate the first time for events and accomplishments. We record the first time our child walks or goes to school. We recall our first kiss and our wedding night. But we don't know when the last time for something has arrived. There was a last time John sat on my lap, a last time I read a book to him. The day before my mother died, I was unaware that it would be our last conversation, and I could not recall the last time we had laughed together. I had not seen my friend Mary for years, but when was the last time we spoke? Would we ever meet again? On what day would I give my final speech, kiss my husband, or hold my grandsons for the last time?

While reading his newspapers at breakfast Wash looked up at me with such love in his eyes. Men appear to experience some type of revival from intimacies, and my husband was no exception. "Don't be too busy for me, wife. I know you are preparing to travel to the capital in your bid to become president, but return to me posthaste. I will be waiting."

Diane Vogel Ferri

Chapter 52

I have no life but this,
To lead it here;
Nor any death, but lest
Dispelled from there;

Nor tie to earths to come,
Nor action new,
Except through this extent,
The realm of you.

Emily Dickinson

Traveling was always thrilling and also draining for me in so many ways. I still felt the pull in my spirit to be as involved as possible with the DAR, but my body did not cooperate. I was, however, able to give several speeches on women's equality. Although suffrage was not a focus of the organization, my speeches were intended to promote voting rights through my efforts toward women in general. I spent many nights memorizing my speeches in case the lights in the halls were not bright enough for me to see the written page, although I wrote in very large print. I carried that fear with me everywhere I went.

"As a girl in this great country of the United States, I had the great good privilege of being born into a family that nurtured girls as well as boys in the virtues of education. I did not think of my father as more intelligent or more worthy than my mother. I did not believe my brothers to be more capable than my sisters or myself. The Bible taught us that we were all children of God.

"As I grew to adulthood, I discovered to my tremendous dismay that the laws of this country did not rank my intelligence or views in line with that of men, whether they be geniuses or fools. I asked myself—who gave birth to these males? Who nurtured and taught them from their first days of life? Who sacrificed their bodies and their very lives for them?" There was polite applause, and although pleased with that, I began to feel the familiar discomfort in my abdomen and my eyes began to blur. I silently prayed I would be relieved of it so I could complete my speech. I took a deep breath and continued.

"And then I asked myself—from where did the laws of this land come from? Who gave men the power, the control to deny us our basic human rights? Their ways are self-made and self-approved. Was it divinely conferred on them? No! If they were purely doing God's work they would not be warring and battling each other, killing and destroying the very lives that our mothers labored to give us!" More light clapping.

"Do women work less than men? Do women hold well-thought and informed ideas? Can we read?" I paused here for a reaction, but all I observed was head nodding and smiles.

"Ladies, do we, as American women, believe in ourselves enough to fight for the right to vote, to hold property, to accumulate our own money, and make decisions about our own lives?"

I moved on to the main topic of the day—genealogy.

"Genealogy is not usually an unselfish study. Many investigators, at a cost of time and money, delve into records, public and private, rummage libraries, and decipher tombstone legends, and yet preserve from the tangled web but the one thread that belongs to their kin, leaving valuable information that pertained to neighbors and friends and that ran along with their own family history, to be secured anew at a like expense, or to be lost, possibly forever. Sensible of this, I have tried to preserve and make generally accessible to the descendants of many, information relating to ancestors or connections, which could not have been obtained otherwise."

While the audience appeared to be more reticent to cheer, they did applaud enthusiastically. I was heartened by the many good wishes and compliments I had received, and I was confident that I would be voted in as president of the DAR, a great honor. The position would keep me very busy for years to come.

The biography in their brochure read:

> *It is unusual to find such executive ability so well developed in a woman who has not acquired them in the effort to support herself. She is firm and decided, with opinions on almost every subject, which opinions she expresses with great frankness. Her tact, usefulness and energy are to be admired. Furthermore, her large, beautiful home on the Delaware River, at Trenton, built under her supervision, is well ordered and kept almost with a precision of a military post. Her good nature, her*

skills in organization and socializing has made her popular with the thousands of women who have met her in the many societies with which she is associated.

A messenger arrived at my hotel door to once again relay bad news. President McKinley had died from gunshot wounds he received only days earlier at the hands of an anarchist named Leon Czolgosz. The president had attended the Pan American Exposition in Buffalo and was shaking hands with the public when Czolgosz approached and shot him twice in the abdomen.

I thought about the privilege of attending his first inauguration, how inspired I'd been by his spirited and positive speech. He had served in the Civil War and had brought hope to many in America. Theodore Roosevelt would carry on in his stead. McKinley was the third president to have been assassinated and I wondered why such tragedies occurred in as great a country as America. My determination grew as I knew I must contribute to the growth of the country and bring hope where there was despair.

I was proud of using the knowledge I had gained in law school, and my speeches were well received. But after three days, I became ill with the grippe and took to my bed in the hotel. My throat felt pierced, my muscles sore, my appetite diminished. A doctor was sent to my room.

During the examination, he pressed on my abdomen, and the pain caused me to grasp his hand and pull it away from my body.

"Ahh, stop!" It was like a knife in my stomach.

"Mrs. Roebling, it is my opinion that you must return home to your husband and lead a quiet life in your remaining years. The strain you have put upon your body…." the doctor began.

"Doctor, I have no intention of dying any time soon. Would you have me crawl in a hole and wither away? I am here because I have been nominated for president of the Daughters of the American Revolution, I'll have you know!"

"I highly discourage that, Mrs. Roebling. What does your husband have to say about all this traveling without his companionship?"

"My husband is not capable of further travel, but we have an understanding about my interests and work. I will not be waylaid by your uninformed opinion about what I am capable of, sir."

"I have never heard of such a marriage arrangement, but, very well. I will leave this medicine for you to aid in your recovery. Will you please read the directions written on the bottle for me?"

I took the bottle of tonic from him, but my eyes were unable to focus on the words printed on the label.

"As I suspected." The doctor grabbed the bottle from me. "I could have handed you anything, and you would not have known the difference. It is very dangerous and reckless of you to continue these pursuits, I believe."

"What you believe is of no interest to me. Now, are you going to give me the medicine or not?" I demanded.

He handed the bottle back to me and wished me well.

The doctor was not completely wrong. It was a pity, because I had put up a finer fight than society had ever seen. After a fitful night praying and weeping, I succumbed to the realization that I would have to officially withdraw my nomination and return home to do only the things my body and eyes would allow. I called a messenger to my room and dictated my sincere regrets that I would not be able to assume the responsibilities of President of the DAR after all, although it had been a great honor to have been considered for the position.

Once home, I felt as deflated as a punctured balloon. My dreams had been thwarted, and the rebuke from the doctor stung deeply. As always, writing was my catharsis. I retired to my study each day to keep the dark spells at bay, but I frequently needed Wash to be my eyes, just as I had been his so long ago. He would write as I dictated, and the teamwork soothed our relationship. It was as if we were reliving happier times in the study on Columbia Heights in Brooklyn with the bridge rising triumphantly beyond our bay window.

There were days when I could only work for a short time because my eyes burned and blurred. Other days, the pain in my joints caused me to retire to my bed with hot water bottles on my knees and wrists. At times, the stabbing pain in my stomach was more than I could bear. Often I was unable to eat or hold food in my stomach.

Dr. William Clark had been our family physician, and now, to my dismay, he appeared every other day at my bedroom door. I heard my husband and son in the hall outside of the bedroom—my sickroom—the prison to which I was now confined most of the time.

"She is losing vitality daily," Wash said. "She wants to go to Sharon Springs to the old spa. She thinks the medicinal properties of the waters will revive her, but I do not know how we could possibly move her."

"That will not be a cure for this progressive muscular atrophy she is experiencing, I'm afraid," I heard Dr. Clark say. For once, I kept my mouth shut and listened.

I heard terms I'd not heard before about my own condition. What were they keeping from me? I still held hope that I would overcome this illness and return to my normal life if someone could just identify where all the pain had originated.

"But shouldn't we try?" John asked.

"How do you propose to move her? Wash demanded, clearly annoyed.

"Her heart is failing because of the muscular weakness. She is succumbing from overwork, which has exhausted her vitality. I'm afraid this is widespread among those who display unusual mental or physical activity," Dr. Clark explained.

"Are you saying my wife has worked herself to death? That her brain has worn out her body?"

"My mother has the most indomitable spirit of anyone I've ever known," John said, "If it is a matter of mind over matter, no one will be more capable of healing herself than my mother."

"Mind over matter will not be of help in this case, John. Then there is the matter of the stomach pains and inability to hold food."

I was so overwrought at hearing all of this that I turned on my side, away from the hallway, and covered my head with a pillow. Once again, men were making decisions for me.

Diane Vogel Ferri

Chapter 53

We read that "conscience make cowards of us all" but sometimes it makes other things as well; leads us to efforts that perhaps we would never have made, had it not been for the uneasy stimulus of remorse which incited us to work out our repentance with a visible act of atonement.

Reverend Silas Constant

Years ago, there came into my custody the private papers of an old family. For four generations, perhaps more, these papers had been carefully preserved and handed down from father to son. They were old and musty, and I had not learned to appreciate the value of records of all kinds in genealogical research, and so had them burned to save the care of keeping them, not realizing that, by so doing, I had destroyed links in the chain connecting the past with the present that no amount of thought or search could replace. The burned papers I could never restore, but when an old journal accidentally came into my hands, it afforded me an opportunity to make some amends for my rash deed. It was the journal of the Reverend Silas Constant.

The journal, carefully kept for twenty years, was a mine of names and dates and a record for a part of New York that was deficient in public records of marriages and deaths. To transcribe the crabbed handwriting and place in historical libraries the valuable facts that the journal and its accompanying records contain was my pleasant task. To the simple diary, I added notes on many of the families of whom Mr. Constant wrote.

The weary miles he rode in snow and heat over wretched roads, sometimes so ill he could scarcely sit on his horse, and his gentle summing up of his own shortcomings, at the beginning of each year, brought his goodness and unselfishness so vividly before us that it was difficult to read the journal through without adding after the name Reverend Silas Constant the title, "A soldier of Christ."

He had been such a source of consolation to his parishioners that I felt I must complete the work while I was able. My work was extremely slow because of my infirmities, but I was determined to finish this project. I moved slowly into my study each day that it was possible. Either Wash or one of our servants would take notes for me and substitute as my eyes and hands. I dearly missed the physical activity of the written word, but my choices, my capacity to be self-sufficient, had vanished like the morning star.

After months of effort, the completion of *The Journal of Reverend Silas Constant* brought me a sense of relief I had never before experienced. But it was also one of resignation—an unfamiliar feeling for me. Was it to be my last project? I sought out physicians and tried various treatments but none improved my weakness or my failing eyesight. The nurse rubbed me down each morning with olive oil, which alleviated some of my leg pain. Dr. William Clark visited every other day and tried his best to convince me of my impending recovery, but I was not a fool. I could not subscribe to my father-in-law's beliefs in mind over matter any longer. I could not simply wish away my illnesses with positive thoughts.

My prayer life had been rich enough for me to know that God did not change human circumstances once they had been set in motion. Most situations in life are brought on by our own choices, and I had made many of mine. God brought comfort and emotional strength when needed and provided acceptance when we were ready to receive it. Although God is a loving one, our lives, our free will, are up to us to direct. We blame God for so much in our lives that we create through our own decisions. I could not be ungrateful by pitying myself for poor health after the wonderful life I had been given. It took all of my determination to accept that I would not be healed. My muscles continued to deteriorate, my joints were inflamed and stiff, and the pain in my stomach increased with each passing day, with no explanation from the doctors and no relief available.

Wash hired extra nurses to assist me at home in his brief absences, but they could not repair what was broken already. It seemed that one moment you are utterly immersed in the vitality of life, and the next moment, the life-force drains from you. The only joy left to me was seeing my son and my two beautiful grandsons and holding them close.

I heard Siegfried and Paul racing up the stairs toward my bedroom. I hurriedly donned my lace bed jacket and ran my fingers through my hair in the hope of looking presentable for my dears. They appeared at the door with my beautiful son grinning behind them.

"What a wonderful surprise!"

"Grandmamma! We came to see you!" Paul shouted, now a tall ten year-old. He ran straight into my arms.

"Oh, my, look at both of you, as handsome as your father, and so big!"

"Grandmamma, we brought you these," said Siegfried.

"Oh, some new books! How kind of you. Here, sit on the bed with me and let me look at you." I smiled up at my son and whispered, "Thank you, John."

"Is your Mama here, too?" I asked the boys.

"Yes, she's downstairs making you some tea," said Paul. "Are you sick, Grandmamma?"

"Oh, just worn out, I'm afraid. But nothing will revive me more than being with my grandsons."

"Boys," John said, "why don't you go down and help your mother with the tea and cakes we brought?" The boys scurried out of the room. John pulled a chair to my bedside, sat down, and took my withered hand.

"Mama, how are you feeling?"

"Oh, you know me. Too busy to pay attention to my troubles. Your father has been worried enough for all of us. Those little boys, well, they're not so little are they? They'll enliven me, I'm certain. I just need to recall the feeling of being a grandmother!"

"A well-loved grandmother," John added.

"You and those boys are like a perfect sunbeam in this house. The sight of you does me more good than any medicine. I have been...." Tears began to fill my eyes.

"What, Mama?"

"I have so feared I would not see you again."

"We are here for as long as you want," John looked at me and blinked rapidly several times as he held back his own tears.

"There was so much more I wanted to accomplish, John."

"No woman I know has ever accomplished as much as my own dear mother. You can rest in that knowledge, can you not?" John said.

"Not yet, I'm afraid. I am Emily Warren Roebling. I never give up!" I tried to raise myself off the bed, but the effort was in vain. I still did not want to appear weak to my own son. My muscles felt like sand, shifting and useless.

"Mama, lie back down. Allow yourself some rest."

"That is all I do, rest." I looked into my son's eyes. "Perhaps we could sit outside this afternoon. I miss sitting on the veranda, hearing the birds chirping, seeing the leaves changing colors daily."

"I will arrange that as soon as you are ready."

In late autumn, the multitude of flaming colors surrounding our property brought joy to my soul. One did not need to do anything but be still and and gaze at the beauty. Sitting still had never been my strength, and autumn seemed to be the only time I allowed myself to stop my work and take time to view God's good earth changing seasons before my eyes. I regretted that I had not spent more time in this manner.

My family gathered together on the veranda with me. The boys ran and played in the yard and brought me their discoveries: a piece of granite, two toads in a basket, and a salamander eager to return to its place under a rock. I looked at the faces around me and felt a rare and unexpected peace.

"This is a perfect day, is it not?"
"It certainly is, my dear Em."

Chapter 54

After this I looked, and behold, a door was opened in heaven and the first voice which I heard was as it were of a trumpet talking with me; which said, come up hither, and I will show thee things which must be hereafter.

Revelations 4:1

The next morning, I could hear Reta and John attempting to quiet the boys.

"Shhh, your Grandmother is sleeping," Reta said in the hallway.

"Oh please, let them come in." My voice was a whisper, and they couldn't hear me. I had never felt so helpless in my life. When the nurse came in, I demanded that she dress me and take me to my grandsons.

"Oh, Mrs. Roebling, you are supposed to stay in bed today."

"I'm in bed every day! I am tired of these four walls. Now, please help me up and bring me my clothing." The nurse did as she was told. She left the room briefly and Wash appeared at the door.

"Did the nurse tattle on me?"

"Yes, she did. Em, I don't think it's wise."

"I don't care what you think at this moment. I intend to spend time with my grandsons. I don't want them remembering me this way. I don't want them to be quiet while they're here. They are children!" I attempted to stand up, but pain sliced through my stomach. I inhaled deeply and closed my eyes until it released its grip on me.

"I know what you're going to say, but please don't."

"Very well. Let me find someone to help move you to the dining room. John and his family are having breakfast there."

Wash held my right arm, the nurse held my left, and we slowly moved into the dining room.

"Grandmamma!" Siegfried called out, "Are you better now?"

"Just seeing you makes me feel better." My heart quickened at the sight of my family.

"Can you eat something, Mother?" Reta asked.

"Oh, no, I will be happy to sit here with all of you. I might have some tea to settle my stomach, though."

"Can I read to you?" Paul asked.

"Well, of course!"

Paul looked up at me with such adoration that tears filled my eyes.

"This is my new book. It's called *'The Wonderful Wizard of Oz!'* It's very magical just like the book you read to Papa, *'Alice in Wonderland!'*"

"Dorothy lived in the midst of the great Kansas prairies with Uncle Henry, who was a farmer, and Aunt Em, who was the farmer's wife." Paul stopped and looked up at me.

"That's like your name, isn't it? Have you ever been to Kansas? I've never been to Kansas."

"Yes, I have. It's very flat and full of farms and animals."

He continued, "Their house was small, for the lumber to build it had to be carried by wagon many miles. There were four walls, a floor and a roof, which made one room; and this room contained a rusty-looking cooking stove, a cupboard for the dishes, a table and three or four chairs, and the beds. Uncle Henry and Aunt Em had a big bed in one corner and Dorothy had a little bed in another corner...."

I felt as if I, Emily Warren Roebling, were falling into Alice's rabbit-hole. I could hear Paul's sweet voice, but I could not comprehend what he was reading. It took all of my strength to appear lucid. I did not want him to know that I was struggling to stay upright and attentive. Suddenly, Siegfried was by my side, although I had not seen him move from his chair.

"Are you all right, Grandmamma?"

"Oh, Siegfried, you are so tall, so handsome." I put my arm around his waist. "Please don't forget me."

There is more, there is more. My own voice awakened me.

"Emily, dear, what is it? You were talking in your sleep." Wash was sitting on the edge of the bed, holding my hand. "Was it a dream?"

"No, no, I heard myself and I was remembering something...something I never told you about."

"What is it?"

"Years ago, I heard a voice." I saw my husband's face fall in concern, as if he pitied me. "It was in my head, but audible all the same. It happened only a few times. I know you must think me mad, but I'm not, really, I'm not."

"Of course you're not, but I don't understand."

"I don't either. I could only believe that it was God speaking to me, that He had to be so bold and so loud that I would stop and listen. All of my life, I have been trying so hard, working, striving, and for what? Did I ever stop to listen, or did I always do all the talking? Did I enjoy all I've been given, appreciate it, and give thanks for you, for John...." I put my hands to my face.

"Emily, dear, I don't know what you need to hear, but you have been the most wonderful wife and mother anyone could have. Your striving brought you many accolades and admiration. Isn't that what you wanted?"

"After all this time, I'm not sure what I wanted, why I worked so hard. I thought I should use what God gave me."

"And you did, certainly you did."

"There is more than this, Wash."

"More than what?"

"More than this life. Maybe this is just the beginning. That's what He was telling me...."

When I opened my eyes, Wash was sitting next to me. It was dark, although I had been talking to him in the brilliance of the morning light. I smiled at my husband and he smiled back, squeezed my hand, and tucked the covers closer around me.

"We know each other now, don't we Wash? I mean truly...all these years, now we know..."

Wash gazed at me tenderly, as he had at our first meeting at the Officer Ball.

"I remember love," I whispered.

I heard my son John saying, *I love you Mama* in the distance. My eyes were open, but I could not see him. I heard the music of my grandson's laughter.

Then I was standing on the Brooklyn Bridge. Crowds of New Yorkers were waving at me. I wore my royal blue dress and hat with the peacock feathers. Wash was standing next to me, healthy and strong, and John was but a lad. I smiled at them and waved at the people below.

Oh! We have come to see the bridge one more time, just as I dreamed we would. My eyes are healed, and I can see everything! The cities, the beautiful river, the sky. I knew I would return to health. Emily Warren Roebling never surrenders.

"That's my Emily," I heard Washington say one last time.

Diane Vogel Ferri

Afterword and Acknowledgements

In the fall of 2018 I began reading about the Brooklyn Bridge in anticipation of walking across it with my husband and dear friends, Susan and Fred Backer. It was something I'd dreamed of since I first viewed the magnificent structure many years before. I came across the story of Emily Warren Roebling and found it fascinating, but when I attempted to read more about her, all I could find was a short biography written in the 1980s, a couple of children's books, and a chapter in *The Great Bridge* by David McCullough.

I did not intend to ever write another novel but this story was too good to pass up. In an era of the "me, too" movement, and the continuing fight for girls to enter STEM careers and possess equity in all things, I believed it was time to bring this remarkable woman's story to light. To me, her life accomplishments in the latter part of the 19th century would have been unbelievable if they were not true!

No Life But This is a work of fiction, but the many well-known historical figures that appear in the book are largely in a realistic context of Emily's story. The only characters completely from my imagination are the O'Connells.

Information about the building of the Brooklyn Bridge is based on fact. The speeches, newspaper reports and quotes that appear in italics are true and are taken from the tour de force, *The Great Bridge* by David McCullough. I took great effort, after months of research, to detail the building of the bridge and the events surrounding it as close to reality as possible.

Emily Warren Roebling's accomplishments are based on fact, as well. These include, but are not limited to: her travels to Europe and encounters with Tsar Nicholas II and Queen Victoria, attending law school and her winning essay, "A Wife's Disability," her involvement in women's organizations such as Sorosis and the DAR, her efforts at the 1893 World's Columbian Exhibition, and her volunteer work in the Spanish-American War at Camp Wikoff.

Emily Warren Roebling's inspiring life and accomplishments have gone unrecognized for far too long, and this is why I wrote her story as realistically as possible. There is a corner named for Emily at Columbia Heights and Orange Street in Brooklyn and a plaque with her name on Brooklyn Tower. She is buried in Cold Spring, New York, and The Roebling Museum is located is in Trenton, New Jersey.

My deepest thanks go to my first readers, Gail Bellamy, Peggy Chevako, and Patricia Fernberg, and to my supportive friends and family who ask about and read what I write.

Special appreciation to Susan and Fred Backer, and my husband, Lou, for walking across the Brooklyn Bridge with me.

Bibliography

McCullough, David. *The Great Bridge.* New York: Simon and Schuster, 1972.

Weigold, Marilyn. *Silent Builder: Emily Warren Roebling and the Brooklyn Bridge.* Associated Faculty Press, 1984.

Wagner, Erica. *Chief Engineer, Washington Roebling: The Man Who Built the Brooklyn Bridge.* Bloomsbury Publishing, 2017.

Roebling, Emily Warren. *Richard Warren of the Mayflower and some of his descendants, 1901*

Roebling, Emily Warren. *The Journal of Silas Constant, Pastor of the Presbyterian Church of Yorktown,* New York, 1903

Diane Vogel Ferri

About the Author

Diane Vogel Ferri is a teacher, poet, and writer living in Solon, Ohio. Her essays have been published in *Scene Magazine, Cleveland Stories, Cleveland Christmas Memories,* and *Good Works Review* among others. Her poems can be found in numerous journals such as *Plainsongs, Rubbertop Review,* and *Poet Lore*. Her previous publications include *Liquid Rubies*, (poetry), *The Volume of Our Incongruity* (poetry), and *The Desire Path* (novel), which can be found on amazon.com. A former special education teacher, she holds an M.Ed from Cleveland State University and is a founding member of Literary Cleveland.